Cheerfully Yours

Laura W. Chance

Copyright © 2016 by Laura W. Chance.

All rights reserved. This book or any portion thereof may not be reproduced or used in any manner whatsoever without the express written permission of the author.

This book is a work of fiction. Names, characters, places, events and incidents are either the products of the author's imagination or used in a fictitious manner. Any resemblance to actual persons, living or dead, or actual events is entirely coincidental.

Scripture taken from the HOLY BIBLE, NEW INTERNATIONAL VERSION ®. Copyright © 1973, 1978, 1984 by International Bible Society. Used by permission of Zondervan. All rights reserved.

Photo and cover art by Greg Tackett.

Rejoice with those who rejoice;

mourn with those who mourn.

Romans 12:15

Prologue

June

Julie's cove one year after her death

The waves are my constant in this place that so reminds me of Julie. I sit on the topmost rock before sunset looking out at the sea in front of me, the wind howling in my ears, and my scarf and hair whipping in the breeze. I hold my knees to my chest as if I can protect myself by what I am still afraid to feel.

Loss. Grief. Sadness. Pain. These have been my companions the last year.

Just when I think I am turning a corner, it feels like a betrayal to Julie, and I am undone. I woke up this morning, and felt her presence in my bed more strongly than I have felt in months. It was as if she knew I needed to feel her today of all days. I could not speak. I could only curl into a ball and weep.

Even now, I look at the rocks around me, the very ones that I spread her ashes on almost a year ago, and I realize my face is wet and my nose is running from tears I have not even felt fall. After all this time, I still find myself feeling numb.

There are good days of course, and the last few months, I have figured out how to manage living. I run the business on my own now with the help of a local girl for a few hours three mornings a week. Gus checks on me every time he comes to see Tabitha. I have become like an aunt to him I think. He brings me for a walk down here, or we sit in the garden and have a drink. He is heartsick himself, but at least he has hope. Grace calls me regularly and with technology, we can see each other's faces, as she demands to do. She would not believe otherwise that I am eating enough or taking care of myself.

Then, there is Alice. We are friends now. But throughout the last year, she has made her intentions clear. She wants more. I thought she was joking at first, but now a year later, I know she is not. Every time it has come up, I have always said that it had not even been a year yet. It was too soon. She would let it go.

But today is a year.

I begin to talk to Julie as I have from this rock for the past twelve months. It no longer feels weird or insane, but quite the contrary. I think it is what has kept me stable.

"Darling...I don't know what to do. I know that you wanted me to be happy again with someone. I don't feel ready yet. But Alice has been patient thus far, and I do not know if it is fair to expect her to wait much longer. I do like her, and I even feel attracted to her, although I did not realize it at first. Is that wrong to say to you?"

I gaze out at the sea, and far off down the coast, I can see a couple walking a dog, enjoying the end of the day.

"I miss you, Julie. You were the love of my life, and nothing will ever change that fact. Nothing. But I am so tired of being lonely. I stay busy during the day with work and with friends checking on me. I know that I am cared for, but it is not the same. I go to bed every night in our room, where we made love so many times, and I feel lost. As if I no longer belong. Or as if I lost a piece of myself on this rock a year ago."

I force myself to lower my knees and take a deep breath in. I need the oxygen to get out this next part.

"Julie, I have to let you go. I have to try to see if I can be happy with Alice. Because otherwise, I am going to become a bitter old woman. And I am too young for that to happen. I hope you don't think I am selfish."

I start to sob again, but this time, I am fully aware of my tears as they are racking my body. I feel as if I am wrenching part of my heart out of my chest.

But then I feel something shift. Through my tears, I suddenly feel peace. I look up and the wind calms down ever so slightly. I can feel her here. I know in this moment that she understands, and will love me still. Even if I begin to love someone else.

July

Chapter 1

Alice has made me a lovely dinner this evening in her flat above her store in Penzance. It is a Monday, and I do not have any guests in the B&B. We both work many hours during the weekends, and so we have taken to getting together early in the week, usually in a pub, or at each other's flat. Our relationship is uncertain, but I know Alice is trying to be patient with me.

After my declaration to Julie in the cove on the year anniversary of her death, nothing has happened with Alice. I know I need to give her a chance, but I also knew then that I needed to get past all of the anniversaries of Julie's death and memorial before I could shift to think of anyone else. However, tonight feels different. I am not sure why, perhaps it is in my head, but I can feel the tension between us. It is palpable as I pour wine in our glasses, and help bring the food over to the table.

Alice and I have become friends this past year, yet to say it has been odd is an understatement. I have grieved for Julie every day, and I have made no effort to hide it, while Alice has quietly shown me attention and hinted at her feelings for me. It is unsettling, but humbling. I do not think I would have been so patient if the roles were reversed.

She turns from the stove where she has prepared our plates of grilled fish with fresh vegetables, and brings them to the table. We both sit down, and clink glasses briefly, before beginning to eat.

Why do I feel incapable of speech? This is not like me at all. With Julie, I was the one who led in the relationship. I was the experienced lesbian, and even though Julie was older than me, she was so laid-back that she was happy to let me get my way most of the time. I was rather selfish in many ways with her. I regret that now. Just as I feel my throat start to close with emotion, I force myself to stop this train of thought, and finally look up to meet Alice's eyes. She is watching me, and if nothing else has happened in this past year, she has learned to read me and know when I am thinking of Julie.

"Everything alright, Hilary?" she asks me, as I take a sip of wine. Her voice is soothing, a bit lyrical even. She is almost half a foot taller than me, but seated across from one another, I can meet her at eye level. Her red hair and freckles on her thin frame make her appear youthful and rather sporty. She is not a great beauty, yet I find her striking. More importantly, she has a good heart.

"Yes, I am. The fish is good, Alice. Thank you for cooking."

She nods, silently assenting to my unwillingness to share my grief tonight.

Thankfully, she changes the subject. "I got a new shipment of clothes in tonight for autumn. I am going to close the shop early the next couple of nights to do inventory. I wondered if you might be willing to help me tomorrow. Charlotte cannot stay late, something about her boyfriend performing with his band somewhere."

"Of course I can. What time?"

"About five would be fine. Perhaps we can get a bite in the pub afterwards? I doubt I will feel like cooking."

"That will be fine."

Once again, she nods, and I look down at my food. I have no appetite. I have eaten about half, but I know if I eat anymore, I will lose it all. For all of Grace's worrying, she does have some reason. I have lost about a stone this year, and I am down one clothes size. I could count my ribs this morning in the bathroom mirror. Perhaps I should pick up a few items in the shop tomorrow night when I help with the inventory.

Even though I made the decision to attempt a relationship with Alice a few weeks ago, I never told her. I keep putting it off. Maybe that is the tension I feel; it is within me knowing that I have told her I needed a year, and yet, here we are several weeks past and I continue to circumvent the topic. As I sit here, looking at my dinner, knowing that I cannot eat another bite, I realize we need to talk about it. I have to now or I never will. I want to claim I have a headache, and go home, but she has been here for me this year. I need to try. I need to at least try.

I look back up at her. She has been eating the entire time, as I know she has learned to be comfortable in my dark moments.

"Alice?"

"Hmm?"

"I have been thinking…do you still…fancy me?"

She almost chokes as that is the last thing she thought would come out of my mouth tonight, I am sure. "You know I do, Hilary. Why?"

"I don't feel ready. I doubt I will ever feel ready. But it's been over a year now. I am not through grieving, so if you want to continue to wait, I understand. But if you want to try and can continue to be patient with me, I think I could try." This pitiful speech has taken a lot of effort, and I look back down at the table and reach for my wineglass. She puts her knife and fork down, and reaches for her own. She pauses before speaking.

"I do want more with you, but I do not want to push you if it is too soon."

I feel agitated as I ask, "What does that even mean though? What is too soon? It's been almost thirteen months. Will fourteen months be perfect? Will fifteen months be magic? I don't know. All I know is that I still feel a giant hole in my heart, and I am lonely. I know this probably doesn't make me sound like a great potential girlfriend, but I am attracted to you. I have been touched that you have been so caring and thoughtful this past year. You have not tried to fix me, but instead you have listened to me, and cared for me. I…do not think I have thanked you for that. For your friendship and kindness and patience." I find myself staring into her bright green eyes, and they captivate me. Julie's eyes were green as well, but so pale they almost looked blue at times.

She reaches her hand across the table, and places it on top of mine. It is warm and smooth, but her touch sends a cold shock down my spine. She looks at me, and her eyes become sad. "I want to be with you. But not until you are ready."

This woman is infuriating! I finally have the nerve to tell her I want to be with her, and she turns me down. In the back of my mind, I am aware that what she is saying is for my benefit, but in my present state, I cannot get past the fact that on the surface, it feels like rejection.

With her hand still covering mine, she looks down at them both, and whispers, "You are still wearing your wedding ring, Hilary." She lightly rubs it with her fingers; the touch feels like an indictment against my soul.

I can bear it no longer and stand up to say goodbye.

"Hilary, please don't leave yet."

"I need to get back. It's late."

"It's only half past seven. You haven't even finished your fish."

"I'm not hungry. Thank you for a lovely dinner, Alice. See you tomorrow."

I am out of the door before she can say another word, and as I drive back to St. Just, I can barely see through my tears.

***

The next day, I compartmentalize what happened the night before, as I have learned to do this last year, and get all of my work done by late in the afternoon. I received an email from Grace this morning wanting to video chat today, but I have put her off until tomorrow, as I know she will ask about Alice, and I do not want to talk about what happened last night.

By half past four, I am headed back to Penzance, although I am dreading it every minute of the way. When I walk into the shop, Alice is behind the counter counting the till, and she smiles at me in greeting. I do not say anything as I do not want her to lose track.

I walk around the shop for a few minutes looking at some of the summer clothes on sale. I find a baby blue button up shirt and a pair of grey trousers on clearance a size smaller than I usually wear. I hold them up in front of the mirror, and I have no doubt they will fit my smaller form. I walk up to the counter, and ask Alice as she is closing the till if it is too late to purchase them.

"Yes, it is, because they are a gift."

"Rubbish. I can pay for them."

"I know you can. I don't want you to. Besides they are on clearance. End of the summer line. The blue will look good on you. Please take them. As a thank you for working tonight if that helps."

I nod assent. I have barely made eye contact with her since walking in earlier. I am not sure how to respond. I already feel off balance after last night, and now with her gifting me clothes, I feel absurdly close to tears. I think she knows this, and takes the garments from me, and turns around to the counter where she boxes everything up for customers. She takes out one of the boxes with some yellow string, and begins to fold and wrap both items. I do not bother to tell her I do not need a box. I know she takes pride in the safe handling of her merchandise, and would be put out if I suggested carrying them unwrapped to my car. I notice that she checks the tags. Like a tailor, Alice can look at someone and instantly know their size. As I have shopped here for a number of years, I have no doubt she has noticed the change in size, but chosen to not say anything. I watch her move meticulously, and I feel a stirring inside. Her long slender hands move efficiently and with precision as she ties the string, and turns to face me.

"All ready for you later."

"Thank you, Alice. That is very kind," I struggle to make eye contact again, but when I do, she smiles and I relax a little bit.

She moves to the door, and locks it now that I am here, and checks to make sure the sign has been turned to say, *Closed.*

"Now, if you don't mind, we need to pull everything out of the boxes and see what we have first."

I follow her lead, and we work together for a couple of hours before I hear Alice's stomach start to grumble. She looks up at the clock, and says, "Perhaps we better stop for the night. Charlotte said she can stay late tomorrow and help me finish."

"Alright, where should we move the clothes that have not been sorted yet?"

We begin to move things out of the way for business tomorrow, and as we put the last few supplies behind the counter by the till, I turn towards the wrapping counter, just as she turns away from it. In that tight space our bodies press against each other for an instant, and I hear us both take a sharp breath. During the past year, she has shown me brief gestures of affection as I have cried beside her, but it was always in the context of giving comfort. Our bodies have never touched in this way in such close quarters. I meet her eyes, and suddenly, I want her. The need is so great, that I ignore the warning bells in the back of my head, and I feel my arms reaching for her and pulling her to me, as I lean in to kiss her full lips. I feel heady with the sensation of head to toe awareness. The kiss is soft, sweet, and reciprocated, but almost immediately I feel a crashing wave of guilt so strong that I forcefully push her back, and turn away. Tears do not adequately express my reaction as I begin to sob. I feel her arms wrap around me, and I realize that she is helping me sit down on the floor for fear I may collapse. She keeps her arms around me as I lose control.

The tears are ugly, my nose begins to run, and my chest starts to heave as I struggle for air. She is whispering soothing sounds as though I am a child, and I try to get out a few words, "I'm so…sorry…Alice…so sorry."

"Shhh. It is okay, Hilary. I know."

She reaches into the shelf under the counter and grabs a box of tissue. I take several, and try to pull myself together.

"I am so tired…of crying…"

She does not say anything, but she reaches for my hand, and holds it.

"I was angry and hurt last night when I left. But you are right…I am not ready."

"I know."

"But when will I be? I cannot ask you to wait forever."

"Whyever not?"

"That would not be fair to you."

"That is for me to determine. I don't want you to feel pressure, but I love you, Hilary. And if that means waiting on you for an undefined length of time…as long as I know you are interested, I am willing to wait."

"Oh." Where has my confident personality disappeared to over the last year? I fear even Julie would no longer recognize me.

"How are you feeling?"

I grimace. "Not good." I cannot make eye contact again. I feel as though I have cheated on Julie somehow. I know that is foolish, but emotions are inexplicable, or at least mine are these days.

She sighs gently, and squeezes my hand. "I know you will always love Julie, and there will be a piece of your heart that will always be hers. I understand, and I am not asking for that to change. But whenever you have another part of it free, I will be waiting." I sit up on my own, and lean my head against the wall next to the counter and close my eyes.

She looks at me appraisingly. "You don't want to go to the pub, do you?"

"No, I don't."

"Alright, on one condition."

I do not like the sound of this, but I look up at her, and she continues, "That you eat two eggs and a piece of toast before you leave here. Let's go upstairs and I can at least make you that. I do not trust you to remember to eat when you get home, and you are at the brink of becoming unhealthy."

I look down at my body, and I recall seeing my ribs in the mirror yesterday morning, and I know she is right. I follow her upstairs and allow her to care for me once again.

***

Grace sees right through my thinly disguised smile in the morning to the distress lurking inside.

We speak through video chat, after I have finished work and she has arrived at her office for the work day. I make a pot of tea and bring my teacup over to the dining table as I ring her. She answers right away.

"Good morning Grace."

"Hilary! How are you?"

"I am good. And you?" I struggle to make eye contact as I answer her.

"You're lying. What's wrong?"

Damn it, she knows me too well. Julie was right, she has seen through the walls and fortresses I build around myself, and I let her inside long ago. I need to be thankful she loves me, and not be resentful that I cannot get away with anything, but in my present state of mind, that is difficult.

"Grace…I know you are planning on coming for your summer holiday next weekend. Do you think there is any way you could come earlier?"

"Are you asking me to come now?"

"Yes, I think I am. I need you here," I answer as I fight emotion.

To her credit, Grace never asks why. I see her pull her calendar towards her on her desk, and before she minimizes the video screen, she tells me to hold on. A few moments go by, and she comes back into view.

"It looks like I can get a flight tomorrow night from Atlanta into Heathrow. Will that be early enough? That means I would be in St. Just in about forty-eight hours."

I nod through my tears. "Do you want me to pick you up in London?"

"No, let me get the train. Don't tell Gus yet. I will let him know when I arrive."

"I will pick you up at the train station in Penzance on Friday."

"Alright. Will you be okay until then? Should I get Gus or Alice to look in on you?"

"No, I will be fine."

"I regret I didn't come three weeks ago on the anniversary. I am sorry."

"Grace, don't be silly. I could have asked you to come then, but I know you were busy with studying for licensure. I hope it is not going to mess up your work schedule by coming early."

"I don't give a damn about that. Just you. Do you hear me, Hilary? I wish I could hug you right now and hear what is going on, but I know this is a poor substitute. But I will be there soon. Promise me that you will remember to eat and sleep and take care of yourself for the next two days or I will call Alice."

Before I can say anything, she adds, "Forget that. I know whatever is going on has to do with her." I startle at her perceptibility. "Well, I do," she continues looking at me as if she can see into my soul, "So, go right now while I wait and grab something to eat. A piece of fruit, some cheese, or something. I will watch you eat. I have ten minutes before my first client, and I want to make sure that you eat at least one meal today."

I grumble, but I know she is right. I go into the kitchen, and find an apple and a block of cheddar cheese. I get a knife and a plate, and I return to the table where Grace can see me on the laptop.

Conversationally, as if this is not bizarre for her to be watching me eat, she asks, "What did you get?"

I hold up the wedge of cheese and apple, and ask, "Does this meet your demands?"

"Yes, thank you." She sits back and watches me eat the entire time, as if I might sneak a piece on the floor. "Do you want to talk about anything now?"

I look down at my hands, and I see new wrinkles now that I am thinner. "No, I don't think I can."

"I can't wait to see you, Hilary."

"I will have your room ready. Although, I do wish you would let me give you a bigger room. I am sure Gus would appreciate it."

She sighs. "We have been through this. If you persist in not charging me, then I insist on having the least expensive room, and as it was Gus' and my room last year, it has a lot of happy memories."

"Those single beds though, Grace. He is six feet tall."

"I have never heard him complain, Hil." She laughs, and I join her. She is good for my heart, even if she is a bloody nuisance sometimes about eating.

***

That night, I dream about Julie.

She is huddled in a ball on our bed, and I am trying to comfort her. But she keeps pushing me away. I ask her over and over what is wrong, but she will not respond. Finally, when I can feel my anxiety peak, she rises up in the bed, and says through bitter tears, 'You kissed her, Hil. You kissed her.'

I wake up at that moment to find myself drenched in sweat and my heart racing. It is my turn to curl in a ball and weep.

Chapter 2

I manage to make it through all day Thursday and Friday morning while feeling like I have a horrid hangover that will not leave. Come to think of it, perhaps I am nursing a hangover, as drinking wine is the only thing I remember having last night. I frown as I realize that is often the case these days.

I drive into Penzance to meet the train from London. I am looking forward to seeing Grace. I know she is who I need at the moment, yet I am also a bit apprehensive, as she has wisdom and will speak the truth that I often do not want to hear.

This will be Grace's third trip back since last summer when Julie passed away. She came for almost a fortnight at Christmas and a long weekend in the spring. Gus has been to Nashville a couple of times, and she is trying to talk me into visiting her this coming autumn. I know that had she come as arranged next week, it was to be for ten days. I hope by asking her to arrive early, she will not have to shorten her stay.

As I walk into the station, the train is pulling in, and I anxiously scan the crowds for a young woman who will invariably be wearing a long skirt with chin length light brown hair. I do not have to search for long, as I hear my name above all of the crowd noise, and as I turn in her direction, I am attacked by her energy and enthusiasm as she barrels into me, and knocks me off balance. I am able to smile and laugh for the first time in days, as I breathe in her presence, and feel her warm arms around me.

She pulls away, while maintaining her hold on me. She is smiling so wide, that her mouth is open, and it extends to her bright blue eyes.

"Hilary, I am so happy to see you."

"Darling, the feeling is mutual. You look glowing. Like a woman in love."

She nods in agreement, but then her face falters as she looks me over slowly. It has been about four months since I saw her last in person, and I know I have lost half a stone since then. Strangely enough, I ate fairly well the first few months after Julie passed. It has been the last six months as the daily reality of being alone has sunk in that I cannot seem to force myself to eat anymore.

She meets my eyes again, but now hers are sad. "I wish I could say the same for you." She reaches up to touch the side of my face, which with anyone else would be considered a romantic gesture. For Grace, I know it is a sign of affection and concern, but more importantly, it conveys to me how worried she is for me.

I feel uncomfortable and do not respond, but instead we gather her luggage and go out to the car. I turn down the street towards St. Just, but Grace stops me.

Firmly, she says, "No, we need to eat lunch first."

I had not even thought about food yet, but glancing at my watch and seeing it says half past one, I know she is right.

I find a small bistro that is quiet and not too crowded with tourists, and we sit down. Thankfully, she does not say anything further about me eating, but she watches me closely.

I manage to eat part of a sandwich and some fruit, before we head back to St. Just.

I help her get settled in her room with the single beds and the window seat. As soon as she has her hands free, she opens the windows wide, and leans out.

"I'm back, Cornwall! Grace is back!"

She has done that every time she has visited, but it still brings a smile to my face.

She turns back around into the room, and becomes serious again.

"Alright, where do you want to talk? Do you want to go downstairs or Julie's cove?"

"Let's go downstairs. I know I will cry, and I don't want to see anyone else right now."

"Fair enough."

She follows me down to the flat, and without speaking, I decant a bottle of wine, and find the glasses. A year ago that would have been enough for both of us, but now, I notice Grace rummaging around the kitchen gathering snacks. I may have lost a stone in the last year, but I have a feeling that she is going to try and force me to gain it back in a matter of days. She does not say anything about the food, but places it on the dining table for easy access, and then we both sit down across from each other on the love seat with our glasses of wine in tow.

She is quiet as she waits for me to begin. I appreciate that even though she knows the subject matter will be deep, she has a relaxed posture that gives me peace from the turmoil that I feel inside. I know she probably has guessed at what I need to say, and while she may pressure me to eat, she will be patient with me to speak.

I take a long fortifying drink of my wine first.

I look down at my right hand holding the wineglass, and it is shaking. I hold it still with my other hand, and I look up into her kind face.

"I kissed Alice the other night."

"I take it that it didn't go well."

"It was a disaster." I force myself not to cry yet, as I continue to confess the depressing state of my life.

"Why is that?" she asks quietly.

"A host of reasons. The first is that I had told Julie on the anniversary of her death that I needed to try with Alice, because I am attracted to her, and I have made her wait a year already. Then, I finally got the nerve to talk to her on Monday about trying to have a relationship, and she turned me down. Said she wants more of me, but not until I am ready. But then on Tuesday, I was helping her do inventory, and we bumped into each other behind the till, and I suddenly realized how much I wanted her in that moment, and I lost all reason, and kissed her."

"What happened then?"

"I immediately pushed her away because I felt such a crushing wave of guilt, and I sobbed on the floor in her arms for about ten minutes afterwards."

I am crying now, but thankfully not enough to hinder speaking. It is more due to embarrassment than anything else. I cannot believe that I have become this person who cries all the time and lives under a cloud of sadness and loneliness.

This was not supposed to be me.

I realize by Grace's face that I said the last thought aloud.

She says, "No, it shouldn't have been you. Or Julie. But you are going to come out from under this cloud. I believe it." She continues in a matter-of-fact tone, "Did you enjoy the kiss?"

I am starting to feel like she is in professional mode, and I am a client. She is too cool and too reserved. I need to know that is a façade and she is struggling with emotion inside like I am. I know this is not the same situation as last year when I teased her about Gus. There is nothing here that bears a resemblance to that time, yet I dislike feeling lopsided in our relationship. Perhaps she felt this way last year, but I am not handling it well from this side. While I might need a levelheaded perspective, I do not want that with Grace. I want her to be my friend.

"What?"

I can still be confrontational when it is not about Julie or Alice.

"I need you to be my friend right now."

"Of course I am your friend."

"But right now, you are sounding like a therapist. I know that is what you do every day, especially with people in grief, but don't treat me like a client."

"Okay, I am not sure how to reply. I understand what you are saying, but you are sharing deeply personal things right now. What would you have me do besides listen and ask you to tell me more?"

"I don't know, Grace! I just…I don't bloody well know anymore. I made it through the first year thinking that things would be better after the anniversary. I told myself that I just needed to get through each milestone, birthday, Christmas, wedding anniversary, death anniversary. That somehow, living through the first of each of those without her would make the second better. I even fooled myself thinking that by the second year, I would not be alone anymore. Alice would be my reward for making it. That I would be able to function somehow and enter a new relationship."

Grace's face is beginning to change as she hears the emotion in my voice. My eyes and throat feel raw from the emotion that is beginning to unleash.

"But nothing could be further from the truth! Three weeks into the second year and the second year has become harder than the first! Because now, I can no longer hope with every fiber of my being that the last year has been a nightmare that I can ever hope to wake up from! Instead, with every day that passes, I know my reality is that I will never see her face again. I will never see her smile or hear her voice. I will never kiss her lips. I will never hold her hand. I will never wake up beside her in the morning. Again. It's over. I go to bed every night alone and broken. And I am afraid that I am becoming bitter. Alice has been my friend and a great comfort, but now I have let it become awkward. I am clearly not ready, yet I believe…No, I *know* I have to attempt a relationship with her now, or I will lose myself in this depression that is trying its damnedest to overpower me."

I swallow, and realize that my voice is becoming scratchy. Grace has started to cry, and it helps me to continue, as I know she is fully present with me now, "You asked if I enjoyed the kiss? For those first two seconds, all my sadness melted away. I felt alive for the first time since Julie died. As if maybe there was hope. Then, when I felt the bone-crushing guilt, all the pain I had felt was magnified as now; I felt I had been unfaithful to Julie. In the back of my mind, I was even aware of how I hurt Alice by my reaction, yet I am unable to even process that enough to get outside of myself to comfort her."

I look down at my hands, and I tell her about my nightmare, and the pain and emotion floods back to grip me in its grim grasp, "The night I asked you to come, I dreamt about Julie. But instead of it being bittersweet, it was a nightmare. I dreamt that she was sobbing on our bed, and after begging her to tell me why she was crying, she said it was because I kissed her. She knew I had kissed Alice. I know I have not cheated on her, but I cannot seem to convince my heart of that. Why, Grace? Why is she gone?"

Grace pulls me to her, and as the sun lowers in the sky, she holds me for a long time as the shadows lengthen across the room. We cry together that evening, and I know she is crying for Julie as much as she is crying for me. I am doing the same, but at least tonight I am not alone.

***

Grace finishes crying well before I do. But she continues to hold me, and I gradually become aware of the clock ticking on the wall, the breeze turning slightly cooler from the open window, and Grace's heartbeat as I continue to rest my head on her shoulder. Grace is a beautiful young woman, and I love her dearly, but I have never felt any attraction towards her. Perhaps it is because I always knew from the beginning that Gus is her one and only, as I always believed Julie was mine. It is hard to say how I view Grace, because I have never had close female friends who I was not romantically involved with before, unless I count my mum. It would be a stretch to say she is like a sister as she is fifteen years younger than me, but as I am an only child, I imagine she represents the closest I will have to that relationship. Regardless, it feels natural to rest my head on her shoulder, and be comforted by someone who I know is not hoping for something from me that I cannot give right now.

The tears have stopped and I feel ready to sit up and regain my own personal space. I find some more tissues for both of us, and I go to the loo to try to repair the ravages of the tears. It is hopeless, but after blowing my nose and splashing some water on my face, I feel a bit better and return to the living room.

Grace has moved to the dining table and is eating some of the food she had set out several hours ago.

I join her at the table even though food is the furthest thing from my mind.

When I do not pick anything up at first, she asks, "Would you like me to fix you something else? Does anything sound appetizing?"

"No."

"You know you are too thin, don't you? You have lost at least ten pounds since I saw you in March, and when I met you a year ago, you were already thin. If I had to guess, you have lost at least fifteen pounds since she died. Am I right?"

"I am not sure. I have not weighed in a while."

"Do you own a scale?"

Damn her. I do not want to do this right now. "I do, but Grace, not now. I know that I am too thin. I know, alright? If I eat tonight, will you back off a bit?"

"Yes." She continues eating her apple slice, and I pick one up, as she continues quietly, "I'm worried about you, Hil."

I make eye contact, and I am gentler as I say, "I know."

"So, what do you think you can stomach?"

"Why do you ask like that?"

"If you had an appetite, you would want to eat something. Since you have been skipping meals, my guess is that when you do eat something, it makes you nauseous."

"Yes, it does."

"Something with low acid would be good. I could make an egg white omelet maybe."

"Alright."

She stands up, and begins cooking in the kitchen as she did all last summer and every visit in between. She does fit in well here.

"Have you told Gus that you are here yet?"

She looks over her shoulder. "No, not yet. I wanted to get settled and spend time with you first."

"You better call him after we eat. He will never forgive me if he misses a night with you." I cannot help myself by making an innuendo.

She turns back around and smirks at me, before saying, "He will survive. But I must admit I am anxious to call him."

As she brings the meal over to the table, we begin to eat, and I focus on getting the omelet down. I chew more times than necessary, and I swallow carefully. Grace finishes before me, and busies herself with cleaning up the kitchen. I know this is to give me the opportunity to focus on eating. I have to stop several times, but I manage to finish at last. With the omelet tonight and the sandwich and fruit at the bistro in

Penzance, this is easily the most food I have eaten in one day for weeks.

She refills our wineglasses, and we move back over to the love seat. Once again, she becomes professional, as she asks me, "How are you feeling now?"

I shrug my shoulder as I no longer know how to answer that question.

She nods, and asks, "I know that we both got emotional earlier. I wanted to make sure before I called Gus that you had the opportunity to finish if there was anything else you wanted to talk about tonight."

I begin, "About Alice…"

"Yes?"

I struggle to know how to frame my thoughts, "I don't know what to do. She seems content to wait, and I understand maybe that is the safest thing for her, but I do not think that is the best for me. I am sure it is selfish on my part, but I have been focused inward these last months. Something has to change. I know myself well enough that I have to begin to attempt change even if I fall flat on my face."

"Are you sure? Falling on your face right now could be catastrophic."

I do not pause. "Yes, I am sure. I either risk falling on my face and dying, or dying a slow emotional death due to atrophy."

"I think you are right." Her eyes are sad again, but she becomes thoughtful as she tries to find words. "Do I take this to mean that you want my advice?"

I nod anxiously.

"I think you need to start slow, as though you are young again in school. Did you ever have a crush on someone when you were a child or teenager?"

I think back, "When I was about seven at my local primary school, I had a crush on a girl in the year above me. She had long blonde hair that was always plaited. I only ever saw her on the grounds. I doubt she even knew I existed, but I thought she was beautiful."

"Alright, if you could have done something to let her know how you felt, what would that have been?"

"I haven't a clue. Hold her hand or kiss her cheek perhaps?"

"Exactly. A show of affection that is not threatening yet shows interest. That is what you need with Alice."

"What on earth do you mean? We are not schoolgirls with plaits in our hair. We are both in our forties!"

"You need to take all the pressure out of this to have sex or even to be officially partners, and simply begin to show one another affection in non-threatening ways. I know that you both rarely go out together. You go to each other's flat or the pub for dinner, and that is the extent of it. I think you need to ask her out on a real date. Nothing fancy, but nothing you normally do either. Pick a few tourist things in the area that you have never done before or take a new coastal walk, and do them together. Then, when you are together and the mood strikes; hold hands. This is important though, Hilary. You need to start off small, and until it feels natural and comfortable to hold hands, do not progress further. If it makes you feel guilty, back off for a date or two, but no longer than that. You don't want to get stuck in the guilt. Keep pressing forward, but slowly. Then, when you can go for a week or more with holding hands comfortably, add kissing on the cheek, then on the mouth, and so on and so on. The longer you can prolong each step forward; I think you will have the most chance at success."

As I process her strategy, I realize what she is saying. "If we do as you suggest, this means that it will take months before we make love."

She looks me in the eyes, and says, "That is my whole point. Think in small steps…even when you get close to that stage; figure out how you can slow it down like sleeping together in the same bed first before you actually make love." She reaches for my hand, "You are in a precarious position. You know you need to push the issue by trying and Alice wants to wait. I think your only hope of convincing her to try now is to talk about this idea, and attempt to stretch the boundaries of what most couples do these days. Honestly, Hil, I think if you try this, it will give you both comfort. It will help your anxiety and guilt as you navigate this new territory, and it will help Alice know that you are taking care of yourself so she can learn to trust you. Don't be offended when I say this…Alice may love you, but I do not think she trusts you."

"I have done nothing but focus on myself this year. I would be shocked if she did trust me. I enjoy her company, and I am attracted to her, but I know very little about her."

"So, change that."

"Perhaps I will. Let me think about it."

She stands up and walks towards the door, "I am going to call Gus. Do you want me to come back while I wait on him, or do you need some time on your own?"

"I will be fine. You go and ring him. I will see you in the morning."

She nods, but before she gets to the door, she turns back around, "And Hilary?"

Why do I have the feeling that what she is about to say is something she has been debating for the entire evening, and whatever it is will cut me to the core? I hold my breath in anticipation.

She meets my eyes and says, "Hilary, before you date Alice…you need to take off your wedding ring."

I do not trust myself to speak, as she rushes over to kiss me on the forehead where I am still sitting on the love seat, and then leaves before I can say anything.

I look down at my left hand with the plain white gold wedding band that has never left my finger for one second since my wedding day, and I cover it protectively with my right hand. In my heart, I know she is right.

***

Grace knocks on my door an hour later to tell me that Gus is on his way to collect her and then they will head out to the pub. She confirms that they will both be down early in the morning for breakfast, and she will help with the guests as usual. She is bursting with excitement at seeing Gus, and she gives me a quick hug before going out the front door to wait for him to arrive.

I shut the door, and go back to the love seat. My emotions are at war with each other, because I am thrilled to have Grace back for a visit and I am happy for her and Gus.

They get so little time together, and at least I had every day with Julie once we were together. But I must admit that I am jealous as well. To be at the beginning of a relationship instead of the end of one, would be the better place to be. However, if things work out with Alice, perhaps I will be at the same place soon.

With that somewhat positive thought, I go out to reception to get my laptop and bring it back into the flat. I decide if I am going to ask Alice out on a date, I need to research some possible locations. The magnitude of this plan causes me to hold off, as I spend half an hour replying to reservation requests, and updating the available booking dates on the website. Finally, I can put it off no longer, and begin to search for things to do in Penzance.

I agree with Grace that we need to do things we have never done before, but I also cannot see myself doing anything grandiose. To begin, I decide we need to be able to successfully have a nice dinner out somewhere, and see what happens. I read a few reviews and decide on a new Italian restaurant with some attractive coastal views if their website photos are to be believed. I ring them and book a private table for Monday night at half past seven. If Alice turns me down, I will tell Gus to take Grace.

Again, I become agitated and do not immediately ring Alice. I pour another glass of wine, and I widen the windows to get a better cross breeze. I take off my heels, and find my glasses. I sit back down on the love seat and look over at the picture on the side table of Julie, Grace, and me last summer.

I pick it up, and look at Julie. "I am going to ask Alice on a date. I have to, or I am going to go barmy out here alone. I know you understand, but I need to tell you all the same." I stop talking and slowly set the picture frame back on the table. I pick the phone back up and ring Alice. She answers after a brief pause.

"Hello?"

"Hello Alice. It's Hilary."

"Oh, hello Hilary. I have been wondering how you have been the last few days."

"Things have been busy. Grace arrived today."

"I thought she was not planning to arrive until next week."

"She was, but I asked her to come early."

"Oh. Everything alright?"

"Yes, but I needed to see her. It's been a hard week."

"Yes, I know. Is there anything I can do?"

"Actually, I was calling to ask you something."

"Alright."

My throat feels dry as I have the sudden urge to hang up on her. "Alice, I wondered if you would like to go on a date. There is a new Italian restaurant on the waterfront. I made a reservation for Monday at half past seven…if you do not want to, I can always tell Gus and Grace to take it…"

Slightest of pauses as I wait for her reply. "Hilary, I would love to go on a date with you."

"Oh. Good."

She laughs softly. "Were you expecting a different reply?"

"To be honest, I am not sure what I was expecting."

"I look forward to it."

"Brilliant. I will come to your flat a few minutes after seven. Then, we can walk to the restaurant if you would like."

"Sounds lovely."

"See you later then."

"Goodnight Hilary."

I hang up the phone, and take a deep breath. Feeling flushed, I go to stand at the window, and I lean out to take another breath of fresh air. For another hour, I flip back and forth between a few BBC programmes, before deciding it is late enough that I can attempt sleep.

I change, and read for a while propped up in bed. It is peaceful even if it is a bit lonely. The window is wide open, and there is moonlight tonight as I can make out the fields beside the B&B.

After a while, I hear the front door open and close and footsteps on the stairs. I look at the bedside clock, and see that it is ten. It is probably Gus and Grace coming back. I lean back on my pillow, take my glasses off, and close my eyes.

I wish I could simply be happy for them. I know they are probably already in the throes of passion from spending months a part, and instead of smirking and going back to my book, I look at the bed beside me and wish someone was smirking right now about Julie and I making love.

I have read articles in the past that suggest lesbians do not have much sex, but that was never the case with Julie and me. We were very active in the bedroom, and it is another part of my life that is missing and vacant. I think making love is how I felt attractive and it was also how I dealt with stress much to Julie's chagrin a few times. But more than anything, to me, it was making love, not simply sex. It was a way of showing Julie how much I cared for and loved her more than anyone else in the world.

This idea of Grace's about taking things slow focused mainly on the physical side of the relationship. It has a great deal of merit. Without ever needing to ask, Grace knows this is the piece I struggle with right now. It is why I feel so much guilt. I want a relationship with Alice, but I will not be content if it does not include sex. I want to have it all, not just friendship or platonic affection. But like any woman in life, straight or lesbian, so much of the physical is in my head, and

I have to get out of my head right now. I trust Grace, so for now I will listen to her.

Which means...which means that if I am going to listen to her counsel, the counsel I requested she give, I need to do one more thing.

I look down at my left hand. I use my right hand to move the ring around my finger. It is such a perfect fit that I never even think about having it on. It became a part of me the last eleven years. I bathed in it, slept in it, gardened in it. But Grace is right. I cannot possibly expect Alice to date me, when I am wearing a wedding ring to someone else. Especially when that someone has been dead for almost thirteen months.

I get out of bed, and go to the wardrobe, where I find a small lockbox at the back. After opening it, I take a moment to look at the documents on top. I read the wedding certificate, both of our birth certificates, passports, and the last is Julie's death certificate. I run my fingers lightly across her name, and then move it to the side.

At the bottom is a small jewelry box. Inside are my mother's and grandmother's wedding rings, and my grandmother's cameo brooch. Nestled beside them is Julie's wedding ring, an exact match to my own. I pick it up and run a finger along the edge. Tilting it towards the light, I can make out the engraving inside. *Forever*, it reads, as does mine. I set it back down next to the other rings and brooch, and I look down at my left hand. I reach to take my ring off, and it is a struggle both mentally and physically. When I wrench it off, I am left with a stark white tan line on my finger, as if I have a permanent tattoo to show my illicit behavior. I glance at the engraving inside to confirm its existence, and then I gently and reverently place it beside Julie's ring. The action feels like the death of our marriage more than anything else has these last thirteen months.

Chapter 3

The alarm wakes me at seven as usual on Saturday morning. I dress in the new baby blue blouse and grey trousers that Alice gifted me this week, and I put on the kettle for the massive amounts of tea and coffee that I will begin serving my guests shortly. The B&B is full this weekend as it is peak season in July.

Grace knocks a few minutes later.

"Good morning!" She says as I open the door. I have my hands full chopping fruit, and I motion her inside with a kiss on the cheek.

"Good morning, Grace. It is lovely of you to help me. I usually use Heather only two or three mornings a week, but with the week I had, she came every morning."

"Of course. I would have helped regardless. What can I do?"

"Go and gather some eggs first from the coop."

She walks out with the basket. I watch her cross the yard and my heart feels lighter this morning. When she returns, I feel ready to ask her about Gus.

"Oh, he's wonderful," she says rather dreamily. "He will be down soon. He has to be on the boat by nine."

"I hope he was not put out by me asking you to come early or with you for not telling him you were coming."

She looks up from the eggs she is breaking into a bowl. "No, he understood. He confided in me last night about how worried he has been for you, especially with your weight loss and how he was not sure if he should tell me."

"Oh bugger."

"Hilary, don't feel bad. He cares for you, and more importantly, he knows how much I care for you. He told me the last few times he has visited here or taken you to the pub, you barely touched any food. But he is English like you, and his levelheadedness prevailed, especially since he knew I was set to come next week anyway."

"I am not really put out. I could have guessed he was concerned last week when he visited. I had rather a lot to drink, and scarcely ate as you said, but I am glad he did not tell you all the same."

There is a knock on the door.

"Speak of the devil." I open the door, and there is the tall, dark-haired man who has Grace's heart in the palm of his hand. "Hello Gus, come on in."

"Good morning, Hilary," he stoops to give me a kiss on the cheek, and then turns to wrap his arms around Grace's waist, as he says, "Good morning again."

"Get a room, you two."

"We just left it," Grace smirks at me.

This time though, I am happy for them.

***

After breakfast and cleaning the rooms, Grace and I take a picnic lunch down to the cove so she can talk to Julie for a few minutes and give a proper hello to Cornwall. Or at least that is how she terms it. I enjoy every moment that I get to spend with her. Because she was here when Julie passed, Grace is my last link to that time. She has helped me share the memories, but more importantly the burden of what that time took out of me. When she is here, I feel her shoulder some of the sadness, and I feel lighter and even hopeful as a result.

We arrive at the bottom of the coastal path out of breath, but in good spirits.

"Shall we go to Julie's cove of rocks first? Or do you want to eat first?" I ask.

"Let's leave everything here, and go to the cove. Then, we can eat when we walk back."

We place our basket away from the path on top of a high rock, and we walk towards the rock where I spread Julie's ashes almost thirteen months ago. I find myself telling Grace about the night I came to watch the sunset on the one year anniversary. I had told Grace when she rang me that week that I had gone, but never shared the details. Today, I confide in her what I told Julie about Alice, and how peaceful I felt at the end, as though I felt Julie's presence here once again.

Grace listens, and when I reach the end, she reaches for my left hand to hold. She has a jolt of realization as she raises my hand up and confirms what she already knows.

"You took it off?"

"Yes, it was time."

She looks as though she may cry, and I cannot handle it if she does. I shake our hands and say before letting go, "Do not start crying. Please."

She blinks while looking back towards the rock, and returns to our previous conversation, "I am glad that you can visit her so easily. I could not think of a more perfect place to have her ashes spread, and I think it allows you some comfort in the midst of the pain."

"At first, I thought it was worse, because I cannot escape those memories now in this place. But now…now, I do think it has become sacred for me. A safe place even for me to feel my grief. I think Julie was very intentional in that regard when she demanded I spread her ashes here. I did not want to at first. I wanted to keep them in the church columbarium, or even at home. But she pushed me, and I think she was right."

After we sit and talk to Julie for a bit, we walk back to our picnic. The first thing I do as usual is pour the wine. But when Grace hands me a sandwich, and I begin eating, albeit slowly, I feel proud of myself. Perhaps I am crossing a hurdle. We enjoy the sea breeze and lay back and watch the clouds float by for a long time, before I hear Grace snoring softly beside me. Gus must have kept her up last night. I let her sleep while I think over the last twenty-four hours.

It has been emotional. I have wept again more tears than I will ever know, yet once again, I feel cleansed and ready for change. I have regained my close connection with Grace, and we have picked up as if we have never left off. Gus had confided in me a few weeks ago that he wants to ask her to marry him, but he is trying to plan the right moment. I wonder if he will propose while she is here this time. I hope so.

As far as Alice goes, I have a knot of nerves in my belly regarding Monday night, but I recognize them as being due not only to the unknown but the excitement of being with someone again who loves me, and who perhaps I can learn to love. I want and need that again, even if it will be challenging.

At forty-one, I can no longer lie on these rocks for hours on end without feeling my body grow stiff. After about half an hour of introspection, I gently wake up Grace and we head back to the B&B.

As we walk back into the flat, I ask what her plans are for the rest of the day.

She tells me that Gus will not be back until late, but she is going to visit Tabitha and little Stephen for tea.

Before she leaves, she asks, "Do you want to have dinner tonight?"

"Of course. What time will you be back?"

"I am not sure. I will pop by if that is alright?"

"You know it is."

"Great. Actually, I have a request if it is not too much to ask."

I wait for her to tell me.

"Would you be willing to show me your photo albums tonight? I would love to see some pictures of Julie and you early on. That is, if it would not be upsetting to you."

"Perhaps, but I would love to show you."

She smiles at me and waves goodbye.

***

Later that night after dinner, I pull out several albums to show Grace at the dining table. I begin with our wedding album from eleven years before in London, including a few pictures towards the end of our legal ceremony in the cove a couple of years ago. She makes flattering comments about our dresses and how happy we looked.

We were very happy on those special days, as well as our entire relationship. We rarely fought, and even when we did, we always apologized and worked it out later. I share with her our travel album which includes pictures of our holidays in Paris and various parts of Great Britain. There are also a number of pictures of our flat in London, and friends who we knew from our life there.

"Do you miss London?"

"Sometimes. Not enough to go back. Cornwall is home now."

She nods, and looks back at the pictures. "Julie was gorgeous, wasn't she? How did you describe her to me once? Like an angel?"

"Yes, I have never known anyone to have such long hair that would seem to float like hers did. It was soft and often looked like a cloud or halo."

"I love this picture of you in the park. What are you laughing at?"

I do not have to look. I know the picture well. I am sitting on a park bench by a fountain and my mouth is wide open as I laugh with abandon. I am looking off to the right; completely unaware that Julie had taken the picture. A young boy had run away from his nanny and climbed into the fountain and was splashing around with such delight that I could not help myself. The nanny was put out with the boy as well as with me for laughing, but it was her own fault. She had not been paying attention to him and it was a scorching day.

I tell her the story, and she looks back at it once more. "You are beautiful, too, you know. Your beauty is more within you though. When you let it out like this, it becomes almost blinding."

"What a kind thing to say."

I show Grace one more album. It is small and battered. I almost left this one in the wardrobe, but I think she will appreciate seeing it.

She opens it and takes a sharp breath.

I feel vulnerable as I explain, "I do not have many childhood pictures. But I thought you might like seeing the ones I do have."

She flips slowly through the album, making comments and asking questions. She pauses for a long time to look at the few pictures I have of my father, and she smiles at ones of my mum and me. When she reaches the last two pages, I startle as I had completely forgotten about them. They are pictures of me in university. With Margaret.

"Who's this?" she asks.

I feel my mouth go dry. I have not thought of Margaret in years.

"Her name is Margaret. She was my first girlfriend at university my last year. We were flatmates at first, but then we started dating."

"How long were you together?"

"About a year."

"What happened?"

I debate briefly how much to tell her. I know Grace loves me, but I wonder how she will feel if she knows the truth.

"We were young, but also in love. I thought she was my soul mate. We started as best friends, and then realized we were attracted to each other."

"She was your first, wasn't she?"

I smile at the memory, "Yes, she was. I had thought I was a lesbian for years at that point, but it was still rather taboo in my family, and so I kept hoping that I would find a man, any man who would make me change my mind. I never did, and by the time I met Margaret, I was old enough that I decided to be true to myself. It was exciting, but we were both children of divorce and we were damaged. We had long-term plans and I thought that would include a future together."

"What happened then?"

"She broke up with me."

"Why?"

It is not until this moment that I decide to tell her. Up until now, I thought I could deflect the conversation, but I admit defeat.

"I cheated on her."

"You didn't!" She says not with condemnation, but disbelief.

"I did. I am not a saint, Grace."

"Will you tell me the story?"

I allow myself to think back and say, "I was nearing graduation, and I was doing an internship at an architectural firm. There was a woman who was a few years older than me who was my supervisor. I reported to her on a daily basis. I was naïve at first to her advances, but I figured it out. She led me to believe that she could employ me after graduation if I slept with her."

"But she was your supervisor! That was not ethical!"

"Perhaps not, but Grace, I was twenty-two. I knew exactly what I was doing when I went to her flat one night. At that point, my mum had died and I had not talked to my father in a long time. I needed to find work after university to survive, and so I fooled myself into thinking that it would be alright to sleep with her one time if she would employ me."

"But it only happened once?"

"You do not need to defend me. I cheated. It does not matter if it was once or for many years. I hurt someone whom I claimed to love."

"How did Margaret find out?"

"As soon as the deed was done, I was shattered by it. I could no longer lie to myself that what I had done was anything other than wrong. I confessed to Margaret. Although she eventually forgave me, after a couple of months of trying to make our relationship work, she admitted that she could never trust me again."

"I see."

"Hurting Margaret, the first woman who loved me and then losing her as a result was the reality check I needed. The night we broke up, I saw myself for whom I had behaved like…my father. I knew the pain that my mum had lived with, and that I had lived with when he left us. I had betrayed Margaret in the same way, and I wanted to cease existing. The guilt I lived with during that time was horrid. But that first night was a turning point. I vowed that never again would I cheat for any reason. I had to remove myself a few times from temptation, but I have been faithful to every woman I have been with since."

"Did Julie know?"

"Of course. We told each other everything. In fact, I told every woman I was with afterwards. There were only two more before Julie, but I told each of them early on, because I wanted to earn their trust."

"How did Julie take it?"

"She was by far the hardest to tell, because I had more to lose. I knew I was in love with her almost immediately, and I also found out early on that she had divorced her husband for cheating on her. She told me that she would trust me until I gave her reason not to. I do not think I was ever even tempted when I was with her. I knew how devastating it would be to lose her."

"What ever happened to Margaret?"

"I heard from her about five years ago. She was living abroad with her partner. She seemed happy. We were never able to maintain a friendship, but she was always kind to me, even when I did not deserve it."

She appears thoughtful, "Will you tell Alice? Or does she know already?"

The thought had not occurred to me. Possibly because it has been almost twenty years ago and an event of the distant past for me. But Grace is right. I should afford her the same courtesy.

"I will tell her."

But not Monday.

"Thank you for telling me."

I feel unsettled, as though I should say something. Somehow I need her approval.

As if she can read my mind, Grace closes the album and looks up to meet my eyes.

"We all do things we regret. You learned from your mistake, and have not repeated it. That is all any of us can do."

I accept the grace she gives me, and I put dear, sweet Margaret out of my head once again.

Chapter 4

I am staring at the wardrobe early Monday evening trying to decide what to wear for my first date with someone other than Julie in well over a decade. Yesterday was a blur as I was forced against my will to join Sunday lunch with Gus and Grace at Tabitha's house. I did enjoy myself, but the activity exhausted me. After lunch, Gus, Grace, and I spent time in the garden. Without anyone saying anything I was offered food steadily throughout the day, and I did my best to eat as much as I could. It is a bother having people worry, but I know the only way to make them stop is to take better care of myself.

All day today, I have felt as though I have had a hangover. This is not far from the truth, as the two empty wine bottles by the flat door are evidence of last night's behavior. I know that Gus and Grace drank with me, but I also know that I am still drinking too much. I need to cut back.

I sigh as I look through my clothes once again. I need to think about shopping for some new things. Everything I own has some connection to Julie. I look at one dress, and remember our anniversary a few years ago. Another dress was a gift for my birthday from her. The only items I have gotten since her death are the dress I bought for her memorial and the blouse and trousers Alice gave me last week.

Just when I decide to wear the blouse and trousers, I hear a knock on the door.

It is Grace. She looks excited as she holds up a package.

"Where have you been today?"

"St. Ives with Gus. But I hurried back, because I found you the most unbelievable dress and I thought you could wear it tonight for your date!"

I am speechless. I open the door wide, and she hurries through straight for my bedroom, where she places the package on the bed, and begins to open it.

Out comes a sleeveless cobalt blue dress of textured silk, with a V-neck, and pleats around the full skirt. It is knee length, and as she holds it up for inspection, she leans side to side to show me the skirt's movement.

She chatters on, "I thought it would look lovely on you with your dark hair. And you could wear those killer black heels with them. You know the ones I am talking about?"

I nod, but I cannot say anything, and she realizes this suddenly as she stills, and asks anxiously, "Hilary, don't you like it?"

I find my voice. "Grace, it's lovely. I am speechless. I cannot imagine what possessed you to buy me a dress."

"I did not plan to, but Gus and I were sharing a pasty for a snack this afternoon, and we passed this shop by the pasty vender, and the dress was in the window. It occurred to me that I did not think you had purchased many clothes in the last year and you might not know what to wear tonight."

I feel tears prick my eyes, as yet again, Grace has ministered to a need that I did not know I had.

My voice is thick with emotion, as I take it from her hands and tell her thank you.

"I got a new dramatic eye liner and eye shadow a few weeks ago. Would you like to try them?"

I do not wear a great deal of makeup, but this dress calls for something special. I tell her yes, and she races upstairs while I change. I shut the bedroom door in case she returns before I am dressed. I gave Grace a key to the flat long ago, and she rarely knocks these days.

I slip my robe off, and lay it across the bed. I look down at my black bra and knickers and decide they will be fine under the dress. I glance at myself in the mirror before picking it up. I can still see all of my ribs clearly defined, but I look healthier today. There is color to my skin, and the dark circles that have been under my eyes for the last year look less pronounced. There is no need to look further as I am the only person who currently sees what I look like unclothed.

I lift the dress up, and with the soft folds of the skirt, it appears to have life of its own. I unzip the back and step inside. As I pull it up, I tug gently on the zipper. Of course, like all dress zippers, they are chauvinistic and require help to secure all the way to the top. Absurdly, I want to cry as I wish

Julie could help me zip up. It is such a little thing, yet another indication of how lonely living on my own has been. I can already hear Grace in the other room, and know that I can ask her for help, so I take a fortifying breath to quell the tears, and open the door.

She is anxiously waiting in the living room. She hears the door open and turns to face me. Her face lights up as she says, "Oh Hilary, you are gorgeous! Maybe I shouldn't have bought you this dress. Alice won't be able to keep her hands off of you!"

I stand taller for a moment. Then, I remember the zipper. "Grace, be a dear, and help me with the zip."

She zips it to the top and secures it with the eyehook, and steps back. "Where are your black heels?" she asks.

"Oh yes, I meant to get them." I walk back into the bedroom and snatch them off the floor. I sit on the side of the bed, and put them on. They are three-inch heels, with numerous straps all the way across and around the ankles.

When I return to the living room, Grace is sitting at the dining table with a makeup bag. She looks up. "You look wonderful. Those shoes are exactly what that dress needed. Come, sit down, and I will show you what I have."

She tries to tell me how to use the liner to create a cat eye effect, but before I know it, I have submitted to having her do it for me. I sit patiently while Grace works her magic and she continues talking excitedly, which keeps me rather calm since there is no reason for us both to be jittery.

"I never used much makeup until starting work last year, but one of the ladies I work with does this amazing cat eye technique and it inspired me to try. For the last few months, I have enjoyed playing around with it, although I still go days at a time with not wearing any makeup."

I close my eyes and listen, while she pokes and prods me until she declares her work finished a few minutes later.

"All done, and not a moment too soon. Looks like you have just enough time to drive to Penzance."

I glance up at the clock by the door, and feel my chest tighten as I realize she is right. It is time to leave for my first date since Julie's death.

Grace sees the panic in my eyes, and reaches for my hand.

"It's going to be alright. Try to have fun. You deserve it. Don't worry about anything here. I will hold the fort."

I grab my bag and walk out to the car park with her. Before I get to my car door, I turn back around and go into the kitchen for a pair of secateurs.

Grace calls, "Where are you going?"

Without answering, I walk back outside and around the edge of the house where my roses are blooming. I select a beautiful yellow rose, and snip it carefully to have a long enough stem for a vase. I say nothing as I hand the secateurs back to Grace, and I get into the car with the yellow rose beside me. I do not trust myself to speak, as I gather Grace understands, because she leans down and kisses my cheek through the open window before standing back up and walking inside.

Chapter 5

I arrive at Alice's flat with a few minutes to spare. Before knocking, I look at myself in the reflection of the shop window. My dark hair is long and loose. I have not cut it this year, and it now extends a couple of inches past my shoulders. The makeup that Grace put on looks nice, but as it is more than I usually wear, it makes me feel like I am trying too hard. But what I really see in the window reflection is a sad, depressed, middle-aged woman who is playing dress up, holding a pathetic yellow rose for a date who said that I was not ready to date her only last week. I stand still as I continue staring at myself, and I feel a lump form in my throat. I make the unconscious decision to leave due to the sudden panic gripping me. When I have turned around and taken no more than two steps, I hear the door next to the shop leading up to Alice's flat open, and her concerned voice behind me.

"Hilary? Everything alright?"

I turn slowly to face her, feeling as though she can read my thoughts as they race in my mind.

She is standing beside the open door in the most breathtaking jade green dress I have ever seen. It is knee length like mine, but there the similarities end. Her dress is form fitting with a scoop neck that shows off her décolletage with a spattering of freckles across her chest. I have never realized before that Alice has such lovely curves. The dress matches her eyes, and makes her hair color pop. As my eyes gaze down, her legs never seem to end. She is wearing heels as well, but hers are only about an inch and a half. I wonder if she wore them on purpose so as not to tower over me.

We are standing facing each other for what seems forever. Finally, I speak.

"Yes. Yes, Alice. Everything is alright." I take a step towards her. "You are beautiful." I realize that this is true. I have always seen her as attractive, striking even, but not beautiful before. Even though we are both dressed up far more than normal, I feel as though I am seeing her for the first time.

I see her eyes light up as she smiles at me, and I watch her look slowly from my head to my toes, and I feel myself straighten. "I could say the same for you."

I realize that the yellow rose is hanging by my side, and I lift it towards her.

"I brought you a rose from my garden."

"It's lovely, Hilary. Come inside for a moment, so I can put it in water."

I follow her up the stairs, as she takes the rose from me, and puts it and some water in a short vase before placing it on her dining table by the window.

"It's beautiful. The room will smell good when I return tonight."

I feel an absurd amount of pleasure at her happiness due to my afterthought.

"Yellow roses are supposed to be cheerful and a symbol of friendship or a new beginning. Some even say it can be touched with sorrow. Either way I felt as though it was fitting for us."

She walks back to the top of the stairs where I have remained standing, and says, "What a beautiful sentiment. Thank you. Shall we go?" The tightness in my chest begins to dissipate as I nod and follow her back down the stairs.

We arrive at the restaurant in time for our reservation, and as requested, we are taken to a private table towards the back of the restaurant. There are windows all along the side of the building, with coastal views from every table. The linens on the table are crisp white, and the serving staff is attentive without hovering. We order a bottle of wine and some bruschetta, before perusing the menu. We are silent as we read.

During the last year, Alice and I have been together on many occasions, yet often without speaking. This is not unusual. As I sank deeper into this depression or grief or whatever the hell it is, she has been there, but she has often remained silent. I actually prefer this to someone saying things one knows nothing about, or worse trying to fix the situation in some way. Alice has let me be.

The month after Grace went home was the worst period of time. By that point, the shock of Julie's death was starting to wear off, and the reality was setting in. I had to adjust to running the business completely on my own, and even though Grace begged me to hire someone to help, I refused at first. I knew that the busier I was, the less I would have time to think about how alone I am now. Those first couple of months consisted of an endless cycle of work all morning for the B&B, grocery shopping for the guests' breakfasts and the off license for my wine after lunch which I rarely ate, a bit of gardening in the afternoon, and then when I could no longer do anything else outside of the flat, sitting in the living room with a bottle of wine and the television on for company, before somehow managing to get a few hours of sleep, often on the love seat because the bed was too vacant. It was a miserable existence. I remember little of it, other than the fact that Alice made the drive to see me once or twice every week to check on me, and usually bring me food. We rarely spoke, but she was there. Gus checked on me weekly as well, and somehow I survived day after day. I know I am not better yet. I am far from it in fact, but if tonight is any indication, perhaps I am on the mend. I am here in body at least, even if my mind is struggling.

I shake my head to clear my thoughts as I realize that Alice has said something that I have not paid attention to; hopefully she has not said it more than once.

"Hilary, do you know what you are going to order? The waiter has been by more than once, but I could tell you were not ready."

"Oh, I am sorry. I can order if you are ready."

"What are you going to order?"

"Oh, um. I think I will have the risotto." I look hurriedly back down at the menu to confirm that they serve risotto.

Alice catches the eye of the waiter, and we order. The sommelier returns with our wine, and we taste it before he leaves the table. I lift my glass for a toast. "To tonight," I say, and Alice clinks her glass to mine. I drink half of it before I realize it, but it helps to calm my nerves.

Alice says, "It was lovely of you to invite me here tonight."

"You were not shocked?"

"I did not say that."

I smile as I recognize that I am teasing her, even if she does not realize it yet. I lean forward though to convey the importance of what I want to say. I look into her green eyes, and I attempt to formulate the right words, but how the hell do I even know what the right words are? She looks at me expectantly, and I try again.

"I know that we discussed beginning a real relationship last week, and it was determined that I was not ready, and that you were willing to wait." She tilts her head at me, willing me to continue, but she remains silent.

"As you know, I asked Grace to come for her holiday early as I was struggling last week with all that happened between us. I hope that does not bother you."

"Not at all, if it means that this evening is a result of her visit."

"Yes, well, Grace has wisdom for her age due to her career, and of course she was there when Julie passed, so we have an unusual connection."

"I understand."

"I know you do."

"You were saying about Grace?"

"Oh, yes. Grace suggested that perhaps if we took things exceptionally slow, we could begin to date now; but that we should do so by doing things together that we have never done before such as having a nice meal out instead of eating in our flats or in the pub." I feel awkward at this next part, but I think Grace is right, and it needs to be out in the open. "We have been platonic friends for so long. Yet for us to be in a real relationship, I would want to have romance and affection again. Desire even, but I am skittish. I think it might help me if we begin by holding hands, and taking our time before we kiss, and progress further, so that I can get used to being in a relationship again. I need to get out of my downward spiral, but I am sure it must be unsettling to you to have me say I want to date you and then have such a terrible reaction such as what happened the other night."

She looks down at the table and will not meet my eyes.

I look at her and will her to look back up at me. She does and her eyes are bright with unshed tears. Before I lose the nerve, I say, "I am sorry I pushed you away, Alice. I know that I have pushed you away the last thirteen months both metaphorically and now physically as well. But I feel as though I have reached the bottom, and now I need to claw my way back up. I need to have hope again, and learn to laugh and share life with someone. I have to come up for air now. I remember telling Grace when she was afraid about leaving Gus to return to the States the first time that when you love someone you jump in with both feet and if things do not work out, you hope the tide will take you back to shore. I feel as though I have made it back to the coastline and only one brief moment before I would have drowned. Now I need to figure out how to love someone again. I know that I am not a safe bet, and I know that it is probably terrifying to think about dating me, but will you take a chance?"

Her voice is emotional when she speaks, and I lean toward her to hear, "Of course I will, Hilary. I have been waiting to hear you say something like this for a long time."

At that moment, our food arrives, and the mood shifts. We begin to eat, and as I use my knife and fork, she glances over at me and then does a double take. I know why. Slowly, I lower my knife and fork to rest on the plate, and place my left hand flat beside my bowl of prawn risotto.

Alice does not say anything, as she timidly reaches her hand to cover my bare one. The warmth of her touch begins to thaw my cold broken heart.

***

I drive home late that evening in a contemplative state. I realize as I leave Alice's flat and get in the car to drive away that I had an enjoyable evening. Perhaps the first one since before Julie died. After the initial deep discussion that I felt needed to be out in the open, it became more casual. Alice may have been a staple in my life for the last thirteen months, but I do not know her. Or perhaps she has told me about herself, but I have not listened.

Tonight I found myself interested and engaged, beginning to remember what it was like again to be attracted to someone and feel that rush of connection and excitement. It has been a long time. I check myself and realize that I do not feel guilt. Or at least not in this moment. I would not go so far as to say that I feel happy, but perhaps I am content. Even hopeful.

I smile to myself as I consider one detail I learned tonight. I did not like Alice at first, because I always thought she had fancied Julie several years ago when we began patronizing her shop on occasion. I remember that Julie had come home from shopping in Alice's store one day, laughing that Alice had asked all kinds of questions about me. I think we both assumed Alice was verifying that Julie was taken. I was always watchful of Alice when I would shop with Julie, and behaved rather stiff and formal towards her. After Julie died, and Alice started coming around, I did not trust her, but as I was lonely, I never questioned her about it.

Tonight, Alice told me when I walked her back to the flat that it was me that she always was attracted to; but that she had too much respect for Julie to ever let me know. She clearly remembered the day when she asked Julie about me. Julie was in the store looking for a dress for my birthday, and she apparently chatted to Alice for a long time telling her about meeting me in London and why we moved to Cornwall. She admitted asking a lot of questions to keep Julie talking and telling her more details. Before putting her key in the door, Alice looked at me and said, "Hilary, Julie and you had been married at that point for years, and she still sounded like a bride in the first flush of wedded bliss when she spoke about you. She said to me at one point, 'How lucky I am to have Hilary.' No matter how much I was attracted to you, there was no way in hell that I would have ever disturbed your relationship. What you had was special, and I genuinely liked Julie. She was a kind soul."

I wanted to cry when she spoke about Julie, but I maintained my composure. Before turning to walk to my car, she whispered, "I hope I can be the lucky one now."

Even though I feel as though I should cry after this revelation as I ruminate over it on the way home, instead I force myself to focus on the positive. And the overwhelming positive that I can see is somewhat egotistical. I always assumed that Alice had wanted Julie, and now to find out I had the wrong idea; it makes me feel desired in an entirely new way. It also makes me have a higher level of respect for Alice. Not only did she not interfere with Julie and me, but she has been patiently watching me grieve another woman, hoping for me to want a relationship with her. It is humbling and strangely uplifting all at the same time.

August

Chapter 6

Grace's holiday is all too short, and before I know it, I am saying goodbye the following Thursday morning outside in the car park. Gus is driving her into Penzance to take the train to London.

She hugs my neck in almost a stranglehold, and with tears in both of our eyes, we tell each other goodbye.

Gus got up the courage to propose last weekend on the boat at dusk, and she cannot stop smiling. Apparently, he has connected with an old mate's brother in the immigration office, and they think it may be possible to fast-track the paperwork to get Grace her visa. They still have a long road ahead of them, but for now, it appears as though they can start making tentative wedding plans.

"You will ask Alice to find you a dress for the wedding, won't you?"

"Of course. Does it need to be a particular color?"

"Just something suitable for summer on the coast next year. Beyond that, it is up to you. I know you will look beautiful as you always do."

"I will do my best."

"I must say that I feel better about leaving you. You look like you have gained a pound or two these last two weeks. You have more color in your face."

"I feel better."

"You won't relapse?"

"I am not an addict. But I cannot promise that I will not still have low points. You know that, Grace. But I will try to do better, and I believe I am."

Gus walks up after stowing her luggage, and clears his throat. "Time to go, love."

Grace gives me another bone-crushing hug, kisses my cheek, and says, "I love you, Hilary. Keep me posted about Alice."

"Love you, too, darling." But I make no promises about Alice.

***

It is the height of tourist season, but Alice and I are trying to have a real date once or twice a week. As a result, we had two other dates when Grace was in town. Nothing near as fancy as our first evening out, but she came to St. Just one afternoon when Charlotte could run the shop, and we took a long coastal walk up to the Cape. Another day, we were both pressed for time with work, but we met in Penzance for an afternoon coffee in a local café. It has remained casual, with only minimal hand holding, but the intention of our relationship has shifted and I can feel the difference. I cannot speak for Alice, but I know I am making better eye contact, and I am asking questions and listening as I learn more about her. I am smiling at her often, as well as to myself throughout the day.

Even though I am full tonight with guests, I have asked Alice to come for afternoon tea. It is not realistic with work to assume that we will be able to always date outside of our flats, so instead I sought to suggest something we have never done together. I love tea and drink it every morning as most English people still do. However, I have never been an afternoon tea person. I have always felt that if it is late enough for tea, it is late enough for wine. But in keeping with the goal of putting some weight back on, I decided to invite Alice for afternoon tea, and I have made some light sandwiches and a few scones.

After making tea in my mum's old teapot with gardenias on it that I remember from childhood, I am moving it and the tea tray over to the dining table when I hear a knock on the door.

"Come in!" I call.

Alice opens the door, and walks into the kitchen behind me, holding a small nosegay of multi-colored flowers.

"I got them from the stall by my shop. Shall I put them in water?"

"They are lovely. Please do," I tell her as I pour our tea. I remember that Alice takes milk and no sugar, and I am proud of myself that I am beginning to remember details about other people again. Apparently, it makes an impression on her as well, because when she joins me at the table with the nosegay in a small vase, she looks at her teacup in delight.

"You remembered. Thank you."

"I am sorry that it took so long."

"I would have waited longer."

I change the subject, because I refuse to become emotional right now.

"How was your day?"

"Good. Business is thriving right now. Of course, the majority of it is tourists just looking for a hat or beach attire, but I will take it. Good to get away for a bit though today and let Charlotte run things."

She smiles at me, and before reaching for a scone and sandwich, she reaches to squeeze my hand. I return the touch, and she continues talking to gloss over any need to call attention to the gesture.

"Did Grace get off to the station all right?"

"Yes, Gus took her this morning."

"Was it hard to say goodbye?"

"Yes, it always is, but now that she and Gus are engaged, I think we all hope that they will live close by soon. It does not seem as sad as it was the first time she came to visit for Christmas and the New Year. That was the worst having her leave, when it was so dreary here, and not knowing when she would come back."

"I can imagine. When you rang to invite me today, you did not mention when they are to be married. Have they set a date yet?"

"No, there are a lot of details to work out with immigration and a visa, but their hope is next summer. In fact, Grace asked me to find a dress. I am to be her maid of honour, as she calls it. She wanted me to talk to you. Do you think you could find something suitable for me? She says that it can be any color. It simply needs to be something that can be worn on the coast for an outdoor wedding."

She looks pleased as she says, "I would be delighted. I would love to dress you for the wedding."

I feel the air heat up at her words that I know have nothing to do with sex and everything to do with owning a smart dress shop where she excels in selecting clothes for women to wear just as a tailor would for a man. But everything about that comment oozes innuendo, intentional or not. I am at a loss as to what to say.

She pauses a second too long before realizing how it sounds and gives a shrug. "It goes without saying that I did not mean that the way it sounded. Yet, if you took it to mean that, I would not be opposed."

I sip my tea to cover my discomfort as well as my interest. I decide not to comment further.

I remember to ask her, "Would you like to go to St. Ives with me next week? There is a new exhibit at the Tate that I thought we could peruse and perhaps have dinner together if you could have Charlotte mind the shop? I plan on asking Heather to stick around late that afternoon in case any of my guests need anything."

"Yes, when?"

"Monday or Tuesday would be good for me. Would either work for you?"

"I think Monday."

I nod agreement, and focus on chewing for a few minutes. To anyone on the outside looking in, this conversation might seem boring or routine. But for me, it is anything but those things. I am starting to be considerate and a decent human being again, considering someone else's needs besides only my own. I feel a strange sort of pride, and in a bizarre way, I believe Julie is cheering me on.

"Would you care to sit in the garden for a bit?"

She looks at her watch, "Yes, I think I could for a few minutes, before I need to head back and help Charlotte close the shop."

I tell her that I will clean up later, and we walk outside and sit on the bench overlooking the sea straight ahead and the farm fields on the left. So much of life has happened here on this bench. So many memories with Julie and even Grace and Gus. But I know I need to build memories with Alice here as well.

Alice sits next to me; close enough to hold hands, but not so close to be touching otherwise. The breeze is blowing the flowers and plants every direction and it is spreading beautiful floral scents all around us.

"Have you always enjoyed gardening?" she asks.

"Yes, my mum gardened all the time. She taught me everything I know. I do not have time to do near as much as I would like, but it feels peaceful to get outside and help plants grow and thrive."

"I gave up on keeping things alive long ago. Every window box I ever had on my first floor flat never made it long. I never remember to water them. I am rather forgetful in that way I fear."

Finally, something that Alice is not competent at. I try not to smile at her confession, but it is difficult.

As the silence lengthens, I realize that Alice has turned to face me. She lifts her hand to my face in a caress. I am gripped with fear as I think she may kiss me, and I whisper desperately, "Please. Not here. Not yet."

There are far too many memories of Julie here on this bench. Embraces. Kisses. Laughter and tears. Maybe one day I can kiss Alice here, but not today. I need the *next first time* to be in a neutral location.

She must understand, because she drops her hand, but leaves it within easy reach, almost tantalizing me with its nearness.

I change the subject instead.

"I know you have told me before, but remind me please. How long have you lived in Penzance? Did you open the shop straight away?"

She leans back on the bench, and begins telling a story I know I have heard before at least three times, but for the life of me, I can never remember it in its entirety. Mainly due to the fact that on the rare occasion when she would chat to try and get my mind off my grief, talking about living in Penzance was an easy story to tell. I am determined to listen and retain it today.

As she begins speaking, I casually reach for her hand. She smiles at me and says, "Well, I have been in Penzance for about fifteen years now. And yes, I opened the shop straight away. I have always worked in the retail side of business. If you recall, I am from Winchester, and when I was young, my friend's mum owned her own dress shop. Her mum was so chic. She always looked like a cross between Jackie Kennedy and Audrey Hepburn. My friend and I would go and visit her after school every day, and she would let us help her restock the shelves, and if we were well-behaved and had clean hands, she would even let us try on a few things. I knew that I wanted to grow up and do the same thing. It seemed so glamorous to be able to sell such pretty things for attractive women to wear. I went to university and studied business, and after living in London for a few years working as an assistant in various shops, I moved here to Cornwall, and the rest is history."

  Something does not add up, but I am not sure what it is.

  I ask, "But why Cornwall? I don't remember you ever saying why." I take a breath and lift her hand to place in my lap, where I begin to trace her fingers with my other hand. Neither of us talks for a moment as we adjust to the sensation and our breathing normalizes. But nothing bad happens. No lightning bolt from the sky. No ghost of Julie hovering over us.

She looks away from me out to the sea, and says, "Cornwall was about as far away from home as I felt comfortable moving while staying in this country. That was good enough for me."

"What was so bad about being close to home?"

She abruptly pulls her hand away and stands to leave. "I need to get back, Hilary. Charlotte will be wondering where I am."

It is my turn to feel off balance as though I have been rejected in some way. Even though I experience a jolt of discomfort, I believe that I deserve to know how it feels as I have behaved similarly to Alice for months.

All I do though is follow her to the car to send her off, as she drives away without waving goodbye.

Chapter 7

Monday morning, I wake up at my normal time, and get the breakfast things ready. I only have one couple who stayed over from the weekend this morning, but I have three rooms checking in after lunch. That is a little unusual for a Monday even at this time of year, but I am grateful for the business.

After over a year of running the B&B on my own, I have gathered a variety of easy breakfast recipes, many of them written in Julie's own hand. This morning, I pull out the vegetable quiche recipe, and measure out the ingredients for the crust. Even after making it many times, I always check to make sure I use the right amounts. I learned early on not to trust my memory in its present state, as in my grief I switched the sugar and salt measurements a few times.

I get out the tea and coffee things and move everything into the guest dining room. After walking back into the kitchen, I stir up the egg mixture and add it to the cooked crust, and put it back into the oven. After cutting up the fruit, I am ready for whenever the guests arrive downstairs.

    I fix a small plate for myself and a cup of tea and sit down at the dining room table. I have opened the windows already this morning. The sun is bright and the air warm as it blows softly through the room. I turn my face towards the sunlight and close my eyes.

    Heather will be here later this afternoon to stay while I am on my date with Alice in St. Ives. She is young and fresh out of school, and cannot decide what she wants to do with her life. I am trying to encourage her to go to university, but she says she has no money. I think it has more to do with the fact that she fancies one of the local fishermen, and does not want to leave him. She lives with her parents and younger siblings and for now, works a lot of odd jobs around St. Just, including helping me two or three mornings a week. I do not think I really need it, but I am grateful for it. It helps me to not get exhausted or feel too tied down, especially on a day like today. I would not normally feel I need to have someone here, especially on a Monday. However, with multiple guests arriving who are new to the area, I did not want to feel as though I needed to be in a rush to return home or even worse, be on call if one of them needs help.

I am finishing my small slice of quiche, when I hear voices in the hallway. I move to put my dishes in the sink, and I open the door to greet them.

"Good morning, Mr. and Mrs. Curry. Did you sleep well?"

The couple is in their late fifties on a short holiday down from London, and they turn towards me as I come into the room. Mr. Curry replies, "Yes, Ms. Mead-Harrow, we did. It has been a lovely holiday."

I motion them towards their table and ask them if they prefer tea or coffee. They both take tea, and I serve it to them, before going back into the kitchen to get the quiche and fruit.

I give them some time to eat privately, before checking on them later. They have finished eating, but are lounging over their tea while reading the local paper. I check the water in their teapot, and am just going back to the kitchen to get more hot water, when Mr. Curry becomes talkative.

"Have you lived here long, Ms. Mead-Harrow? Forgive me, but you do not have the local accent."

"You are correct, Mr. Curry. I am from London. Born and bred. I moved here eleven years ago, and I love it. It's beautiful and the people are kind."

"I do not mean to be intrusive, I am simply curious, but do you run the business on your own?"

"I do now. My wife of ten years used to run it with me, but she passed away last year."

His wife glances up at that, and they both appear shell-shocked. Whatever they were expecting me to say was not that. I feel much the same way, as I think up until this point, I have not told another guest such personal information since she passed. I have sidestepped or avoided previous questions and curious glances, especially when I was still wearing my wedding ring.

To his credit, he recovers after a few moments, and says, "I am sorry for your loss."

The conversation has become awkward, and with them both watching me, I nod at them and carry their teapot into the kitchen for more hot water. Nothing further is said.

***

Several hours later, I have checked Mr. and Mrs. Curry out, cleaned their room, and welcomed my new guests. Heather arrived earlier, and I asked her to dust the lounge and guest dining room for me. She will do a little cleaning for me tonight, but otherwise, her main job is to remain available for the guests if and when they need assistance.

I am sitting out in the garden waiting for Alice to arrive. We had agreed that as soon as Charlotte could come to relieve her at the shop, she would drive here to leave her car, and I would drive us both to St. Ives.

The heat is cloying today. I have dressed in linen trousers, a sleeveless loose blouse that will hopefully keep me cool, and flat sandals that are comfortable for walking short distances. I am nervous for our date, but as that has become a normal feeling, it does not bother me as it did several weeks ago. The difference now is that I know some of the nervousness and anxiety is connected to excitement in seeing Alice. Yes, there are many fears and a great deal of sadness connected to Julie. I doubt at this point that it will ever truly go away. But I remember clearly one of our last conversations. It was the Saturday before she passed away, and I was making notes as to her requests for her memorial.

Julie was laid-back in many respects. But when she had conviction about something, there was no more stubborn person than she was. It was that way when it came to being cremated and spreading her ashes in the cove, and it was that way when she told me to date again.

She had already made several comments to that effect before that day, but I had waved her off. After she had gone over all of her final wishes and I put away the notepad and was starting to stand, she said, 'Hilary, there is just one more thing.' I looked back down at her, and I knew what she was going to say before she said it. After living with her for five years and then married for ten, I could often look at her, and know what was going through her head. I think she knew the same about me. I remember saying, 'No, darling, don't say it.'

But she just looked at me, shook her head, and held her hand out towards me. I sat on the edge of the bed and held her hand. It was so fragile and pale at that point. The bones felt brittle. She said, 'Hilary, I will always love you, and I know you will always love me. But you have to love again. You have so much to give in this life and someone else needs to be as blessed to have you as their partner the way I have been blessed all these years to have you as mine.' I shook my head no, rather violently, and started weeping. She grabbed my hand much more forcibly than I would have thought she could, and as firmly as I have ever heard her speak, she said, 'Yes, Hilary. I *demand* as my final and most lasting wish that you do your best to fall in love again. You will show me how much you love me by not letting yourself withdraw from life and be alone. You are too special and too precious to me for that to happen. Promise me that you will try. One day.' She waited ages, but I finally got my sobs under control enough to whisper, 'One day,' before we both wept in the other's arms for long into the night.

At that moment, I see Alice's car turn into the driveway, and I wipe my eyes, and put that memory out of my mind, as I stand to greet her. My remembered promise though gives me peace, and soothes my nerves. For now.

***

The Tate is as beautiful as always. It hosts a wealth of modern art, and every time the exhibit changes, I always make a point to visit. I prefer more ancient and classical art that is on display in London, but I do appreciate modern art and the boundaries it crosses. As Alice and I walk through the whitewashed building in St. Ives, we do not speak much, but we spend time walking side by side and stopping to peruse the pieces on display.

I reach for her hand at one point, and although she allows me to hold it, something is not right. Her hand is ice cold, and it is shaking slightly. She has appeared on edge all afternoon, but I have not pried. I look up at her face, yet she will not make eye contact.

When we walk outside, I ask her if she wants to walk through the sculpture garden. She nods, and we continue walking hand in hand towards it. There is not a soul about, and by unspoken consent, we sit down on a bench in the shade.

I know that it is my turn to show care and comfort, but I am at a loss for what to say. It has been too long since I have played this role. While I gather my thoughts, I focus on stroking her hand. She does not pull away, but neither does she respond. I look at her face in profile, and she is pale, with the spattering of freckles on her face and neck in sharp contrast. Her eyes look sad and lost, and there are dark circles under them. She continues staring straight ahead, and I realize that she is not avoiding me, as much as she is trying to rein in her emotions.

Finally, I find words. "Alice, what's wrong? Will you tell me?"

At my words, I break the dam, and the tears silently flow down her face in droves. She keeps her body rigid, but I feel the most compassion towards her that I have ever felt before, as without thinking, I reach up with one hand and push her hair behind her ear, and stroke her neck and back. I make shushing noises and with the other hand that I am holding hers with, I stroke it methodically. I try not to overthink what I am doing, even though I am aware that it is the most physical contact we have ever had.

She finds a tissue in her bag, and tries to speak. "I have been having nightmares again. Since the night we had tea together last week."

I process this, but am confused why nightmares would induce crying during the day hours after having them.

She looks at me to gauge my reaction, and then looks down at her hands. "I know that sounds odd. But when I have nightmares, they are specific to something that actually happened to me. I have not had any in years, but something triggered them last week, and they have occurred every night since. Last night, it must have happened as soon as I fell asleep, because I woke up at around midnight, and I never went back to sleep."

"Do you want to tell me about them?"

"I think I need to tell you about what happened to me first."

I nod, and wait for her to begin.

She looks straight ahead as she begins speaking, "My realization that I was a lesbian did not occur until I was at university. I had been rather naïve early on, and although I had never been attracted to men before, I had not put two and two together to understand why. Going away to university, I started seeing everyone around me shagging, and I started to wonder why I was not interested. There was a girl who lived in the same quad who had a few mutual friends. She had gone through a breakup before coming to university, and was a bit depressed at first, but it was months before I ever understood that it was a breakup with another girl. The friend who finally told me looked at me as if I was daft for not knowing. From that moment on, I started wondering. I realized that I found her attractive, and it was not long after that we started spending more time together."

She pauses for breath, and I stay still beside her.

"We eventually fell in love, and the next term, we managed to become flatmates. All of our friends knew, and they were very accepting. However, I knew that my family would not be. I asked Ruth not to tell anyone outside of our circle of friends. She was from a wealthy family and had a trust fund. She had been out already for a couple of years, and even though they were a bit posh, she was an only child and could do no wrong."

"What happened then?"

"For two years we kept our relationship a secret from the outside world. I never even mentioned her name in the context of friendship to my family when I would go home on holiday, although she did eventually tell her own family about me."

She looks down at her hands, one still within my own, and I realize that she is trembling. I have never seen Alice out of control, and it is scaring me. I clasp her hand harder, as if that can somehow fix the pain she is experiencing.

"My third year at university, I left Ruth for the Christmas holiday to see my family in Winchester. She went home to London as usual. She was increasingly frustrated at me for not wanting to tell my family. By that point, I had visited her home numerous times and everyone was kind and welcoming. I think Ruth thought my family would be the same way. But I knew better. So, I kept pushing her away and telling her that I needed more time."

She looks over at me and stops talking for a few moments. Her green eyes are staring at mine, and all I see is pain and sadness. The starkness is unsettling, and I know that I am seeing in her eyes what she has been seeing in my own for many months now.

"That Christmas, my grandfather was very ill and dying in hospital. It was Boxing Day, and my parents had gone to visit him, and I had opted to stay home to take a phone call from Ruth. Unbeknownst to me, my brother came home while I was speaking to her and overheard me say a lot of incriminating things. She and I were having a row, which I am sure is what got his attention, because she had wanted to come to Winchester for the last few days of the holiday, and I told her that I still was not ready for her to meet them. We had been separated at that point for a week, and we were missing each other, so we made up and promised to speak further when we both returned to university. It was not a long conversation, yet by the end of it we were saying words of passion and lust and love. And my brother heard me say her name, so there was no doubt I was speaking to a woman."

"You speak as though it was a crime."

"To my family it was...my brother is not a kind person. He is only two years older than me, but he was the favored child. When I rang off, he made his presence known, and he accused me of being a dyke. I tried to defend myself, but it was hopeless. He repeated word-for-word several things he had heard me say. I screamed at him to leave me be, and went to my room and slammed the door. I knew he would be thrilled to tell our parents as soon as they came home, so I decided to pack up and leave. It was too soon to head back to university, but I was fairly confident that Ruth and her family would let me stay with them."

At this point in the story, Alice begins crying again, and I pull her towards me. She leans her head on my shoulder, and I look over her head on the lookout for other visitors to the garden. Thankfully, it is quiet today, and we have privacy, but I know it is only a matter of time before someone walks this way.

I am at a loss as to what is going on. Obviously, Alice is upset, yet nothing she has said thus far warrants this kind of reaction twenty years later. I am feeling increasingly agitated as I know something horrid must have happened for her to still be this emotional. Alice has always been levelheaded and calm, showing little emotion the entire time I have known her. When she settles down enough for her to hear me speak, I ask, "Do you want to keep talking here or should we go somewhere a little more private? I am concerned other patrons could walk up without warning."

"Perhaps we better go. Let's walk down to the coast. There are enough areas away from the crowds where we can be assured of seeing someone walk up before they get within hearing."

I stand and offer her my hand, and less than half an hour later, we are sitting on some flat rocks far down from the sunbathing tourists. The sun is out and some birds are swooping down into the water looking for a lazy fish to snatch. Alice has had time to compose herself, and seems ready to talk again.

"Are you ready to continue?" I ask her, afraid of her reply either way.

She nods, and she clasps both of her hands together around her knees that she has raised to her chest. I recognize this gesture well. It is a sign that she is trying to protect herself from something she knows is painful to feel. I sense my body tense in anticipation, but I attempt to hide it from her, by smiling and keeping my posture relaxed.

"While I was in my room packing, my brother's friend came over. I could hear them in the kitchen talking, and I caught a few words here or there that made it obvious he was telling him about me. This friend of his was training as a boxer. He lived in our neighborhood, and he and my brother had grown up together. I had never liked him. He was a cruel bully even when we were young. I had turned down his advances a few years prior, and he hated me ever since."

I feel my heart constrict, as I have a horrible feeling where this is going. Please God, let me be wrong. So wrong.

"I was zipping up my suitcase on the bedroom floor; when he threw my door open. I could see my brother behind him glaring at me. He said, 'Your brother and I are in a bit of disagreement. He thinks you are a dyke, and I don't. He suggested that we prove it to him.' I stood up to face him, and I told him with more bravado than I felt that they could both go to hell. He slapped my face so hard I thought he loosened a few teeth. I fell hard, halfway on the bed, and before I knew it, he was on top of me. I fought back, but it was useless. He was almost eighteen stone and even taller than me. Within seconds, he had ripped off my shirt, pulled my trousers and knickers down past my knees, and forced my legs apart. I knew there was no sense in screaming. I struggled and tried to get away, but no one was going to help me. When he…when he penetrated me, I screamed from the pain. I can still remember hearing my brother laugh in the next room. His friend was so heavy that I could barely breathe, let alone get away, but I desperately wanted to hit him hard at least once. I waited until he closed his eyes and I swung with everything I could while lying on my back. I barely fazed him, but in reply, he hit the side of my head with such force that he split it open and I blacked out."

We are both crying at this point, and I feel numb with disbelief at her words. I cannot fathom what she has lived through. I say nothing, as I want her to be free to continue with whatever she needs to say.

She reaches up absentmindedly, and touches a thin silver scar on the left side of her face that I had never noticed before, starting at her temple, and disappearing into her hairline. I follow her touch with my own fingertips, and I ask quietly, "This is where he hit you?"

She nods and continues, "After I came to, they were both gone. There was blood everywhere from multiple areas of my body. I tried to stand up, but I almost blacked out again, so I managed to crawl into the kitchen and used the phone to ring Ruth. I was afraid they would come back before she could come all the way to Winchester, so she arranged for a cab to pick me up and take me to the train station, and I somehow managed to get myself dressed in clean clothes and drag my suitcase onto the front steps to wait for the cab. I have never seen any of my family since then."

I am outraged. "What do you mean? You didn't press charges? Wouldn't your parents have done anything?"

She looks at me, and speaks kindly, but as though I could not possibly understand, which is probably the case, "Hilary, my father had abused my mother my entire life. She always had cuts and bruises and even a couple of broken bones. I am fairly confident that he forced himself on her as well, if some of the noises I heard at night are any indication. She would say she tripped or fell, but eventually, she knew that I knew the truth, and she began saying it was her fault. As if that somehow made it better. My father focused his wrath on my mother, but that is not to say that my brother and I did not receive some of it from time to time. My brother learned how to abuse from an abuser, and he had already beaten up his girlfriend at least one time that I knew of when the rape happened."

I am horrified, and I have no idea how to respond. It is not that I did not know things like this happened all over the world, but never before had something like this happened to someone I am involved with romantically.

"They never tried to contact you?"

"No, I lived in the same quad the rest of university, and I never heard from any of them ever again. Ruth was exceedingly kind, and although we stayed together until the end of our studies, it was not the same. I was broken for a long time after that, and Ruth did her best to love me through it, but we were both too young to navigate that storm. Without Ruth though, I have no idea what would have happened to me. My parents had been abusive and neglectful, but they had paid for university up until that point. Ruth started filtering a little extra money from her trust fund, to cover both of our expenses, and I got a part-time job. Somehow, I made it work, but those were hard years."

She is slowing down, but I realize there is one piece of this story that she has not finished yet.

"Alice, are your nightmares about the rape?"

"Yes, it happens as though in slow motion. I can feel the pressure and the weight of him on my body with his hands groping and clawing, and sometimes I even feel the pain in my dream. I wake up after he hits me just as I think I am about to black out. Without fail when I awaken, I am drenched in sweat, my heart is pounding, and I am close to hyperventilating."

At this point, the sun is starting to set. No one is around us, and I feel such compassion for Alice, that I take her in my arms and hold her as we continue talking. I push back her hair, and kiss the scar, yet she is so far away in her mind, I do not think she notices.

"What do you think caused the nightmares to start again?"

"I really do not know. The last time I had them was ten years ago."

"What was going on in your life ten years ago that is similar to now? Anything you can think of?"

I watch her as she processes this question, and then she swallows before speaking. "Yes, actually, ten years ago was the last time I became involved with someone."

I try not to show shock that it has been ten years since her last relationship.

"I was interested in a woman that I met with periodically to buy merchandise from for the shop. We were just beginning to see each other, and the nightmares started."

"Do you remember how long they lasted? Or what you did to stop them?"

"They only happened periodically. Not every night like these last few days. But they eventually went away on their own. I think the relationship progressed from friendship to lovers around the time when most of the nightmares occurred. The relationship did not last long; only about a year. It was more a fling really. We only saw each other once or twice a month, so it was never serious."

"It sounds as though becoming intimate is what stressed you out."

"You are probably right."

"So perhaps we are good for each other, because I am stressed about taking that step, only for different reasons."

She smiles weakly.

I cannot help myself, "There has been no one since in nine years?"

"No. No one. I would rather be alone than be with someone simply to be with someone."

"I guess I know now why you are so patient with me."

She seems to focus again, as she looks down at our hands, "Yes, Hilary, you do. I will never pressure or force you to do anything that you are not ready to do. You have my word."

As I meet her green eyes, my only thought is that I need to kiss her. I need to feel her lips, and I need to do it now before I lose my nerve. I lift my hand to touch her face, and I lean towards her and give her the softest, most tender kiss I can manage. She yields to me, and without thinking, I search her mouth with my tongue. As the heat is beginning to build, I pull gently away, as I want this kiss to end far better than our first. She opens her eyes, and smiles at me.

I say softly, "We did it. We kissed without any theatrics."

She chuckles softly.

But I become serious again when I say, "I am so sorry, Alice. I cannot imagine…I don't know what to say. I…thank you for trusting me enough to share this with me. I know it was not easy to tell."

She says, "It's strange. It's been so many years ago now. I did go through psychotherapy a few years after it happened. At this point, I am able to go long periods of time without even thinking about it. Overall, I feel like it is in the past, and I do not live in fear. I have lived a somewhat monastic life for many years, but every time I begin to feel sorry for myself, I remind myself of my mother staying in an abusive relationship, and never having the courage to get out of it. If nothing else happened that day, I learned that I needed to break away from my toxic family, and it has made life far less chaotic. For that, I am thankful. I only wish that I knew how to break this cycle of nightmares."

I say with more conviction than I feel, "I know. We will figure something out."

Although I know it will break the spell, I am conscious that we need a recess from this heavy subject matter so I add, "Let's go find some dinner. I am hungry."

Hand in hand, we walk along the coast back into St. Ives.

***

As I pull into my garage later that night, I put my hand on Alice's arm to stop her from getting out of the car. I have been contemplating what to do the entire way back to St. Just, and I am still unsure what to suggest, but I know I have to do something. I cannot let her go home right now, knowing these nightmares are plaguing her.

"Alice, I don't want you to go home tonight. I am worried about you. You need a good night's sleep…I…I am not ready to share my bed, but I have a room available tonight or you could even have my bed, and I could sleep on the love seat in my flat. Do you think a different environment would help stop the nightmares?"

She appears thoughtful as she answers, "I don't know. I have never considered it."

"Please. Let me care for you tonight."

"Alright. If I won't be any trouble."

I find myself smiling and we go into the B&B together. I relieve Heather and thank her for coming, and although she appears inquisitive at Alice coming into the flat with me, she knows better than to say anything.

After debating briefly, Alice expresses concern that if she sleeps in one of the rooms upstairs, she may cry out in the middle of the night and disturb the other guests. She does not think she screams in her nightmares, but she has no way of knowing for certain. Much to her chagrin, I end up demanding that she take my bed, and I sleep on the love seat.

"Hilary, I cannot force you out of your bed."

"You are not forcing me. I have invited you to stay, and I want you to have a good night's sleep. As I am not ready to sleep with you, I will sleep on the love seat. I will be fine."

"I should be the one sleeping on the love seat."

"Stop that now. You are much taller than me. And you are my guest." I point towards my room, and she meekly goes inside, where I follow her to turn down the bed, and gather my pajamas and glasses to take back into the living room. I rummage around for the longest pair of pajamas I can find, and she takes them into the bathroom, along with a spare toothbrush I give her to use.

Within ten minutes, we are both changed, and lying down. Alice has left my bedroom door open, and I can see the light from the bedside clock illuminating the wall. I shift on the love seat to try and get a little more comfortable. I know that it would be easier on my body to go and lie down in the bed beside her, but it would be far harder on my mind. So, I stay put.

However, as I lie back looking at the ceiling and trying to calm my mind, I realize that the most interesting aspect to this evening is how I responded tonight. I started to take charge, and it felt good. I was decisive. I figured out what I needed to do, and I did it. I got outside of myself long enough to think of someone else. It felt good, as though I am becoming my old self again.

Now, if only Alice can sleep through the night.

***

Miraculously, Alice does manage to sleep all night. At one point, she woke me up moaning while tossing and turning, and I went to sit by the bedside for a few minutes ready to wake her up if her distress escalated. But it subsided soon after, and she slept the rest of the night. I did not sleep well of course. I am too old to think I can sleep comfortably on the love seat, but it is Tuesday morning, and in a few hours after I finish my work, I can have a lie down if need be.

I dress in the bathroom, and start getting the breakfast things ready for Alice and my other guests. She emerges from the bedroom soon thereafter with a glorious case of bedhead. I smirk, and she knows immediately what is adrift, and races off to the loo. Soon after, she is dressed in her clothes from the night before with her hair put back into place and ready to leave. She still looks tired, but not as drained, and I tell her as much.

"Yes, I slept much better."

"Did you dream at all?"

She says, "No, I don't think so. Why do you ask? Did I call out?"

"No, you did moan a bit. I was concerned that the nightmare might be starting, but I was ready to wake you if it got worse."

She smiles at me, and comes over to the counter where I am standing, and gives me a hug and a kiss on the cheek. "Thank you," she whispers in my ear. She walks over to the door, and starts to say goodbye, when I interrupt.

"Aren't you staying for breakfast?"

"That is very kind of you, but I need to get back. The shop opens in a couple of hours, and I need to count the till from last night. Charlotte is honest, but not always the best at maths. I like to double-check when she closes for me."

I nod, feeling rather disappointed. "Do you want to come back tonight?"

"Let me try tonight at home. See if I broke the spell last night. Perhaps we can see each tomorrow? Would you like to come to Penzance for coffee?"

"Alright."

She smiles, and walks out the door. I watch her from the window walk across the gravel car park to her car, and drive away.

Why do I feel as though I had a one-night stand?

***

I struggle through the morning on a few hours of sleep, and a stiff back from my night curled on the love seat. Sometime after lunch, I can take it no longer, and I go into the bedroom for a lie down. I open the window wide, and I take my shoes off. I lie back on the right side of the bed, which has always been mine nearest the window. As the breeze wafts through the room, I can still smell Alice's scent from the night before. It is a cross between something citrusy and vanilla. I doubt the two scents are from the same perfume, but rather a combination of lotion or hair products that she uses and it has become her own personal scent that I have learned to recognize.

I shift to get more comfortable on the bed, but I begin to think about our day yesterday, and my mind will not shut down. Alice's story of her rape and the nightmares that still torture her from time to time left me feeling incompetent, as though I can never hope to understand or love her as she deserves to be loved. The details that she shared about the rape horrified me. I cannot get certain images out of my head. I feel self-centered and foolish, as I remember thinking several times over the last year that Alice is always too in control and could not possibly understand what it is like to grieve or be damaged in some way. Bloody hell. What a fool I am.

As I start to feel my body relax, and I know that sleep is imminent, my mind shifts to something unexpected. I begin to think about the kiss that we shared yesterday after she shared her story, and how lovely it felt. Her lips were soft and warm as we sat on the coastal rocks in the sunlight.

As sleep overtakes me, I begin to mentally undress her. We are in her flat, and I am kissing her and unbuttoning her blouse while we are standing in her living room. My hands move to her hair, her neck, and down to her breasts, and…

***

Suddenly, I am dreaming, as I am in bed with Julie in London our last night before coming home mere days before her death. It is dark in the hotel room, but there is a small shaft of light from a chink in the curtains which allows me to see her profile in shadow, and I can hear the noise of the London traffic.

I shift the duvet, and roll my naked body gently on top of hers. She is so frail and small, and I am terrified of hurting her. I kiss her mouth with a hunger I cannot sate, and although she keeps her hands still with one wrapped around my neck and the other around my back; I know her body is receptive to mine. I find myself needing to touch, caress, and kiss every square inch of her, and I move to the top of her head, and begin making my way slowly down. Sometime much later, I come back to her mouth, and our tears have mingled together and become one.

'I love you, darling. With all my being, I love you.'

I feel her smile against my mouth as I continue kissing her, 'Oh Hil, I have loved you more than I ever thought it possible to love someone. I always will. Forever.'

I know deep in my being that this is the last time we will ever make love, and somehow I need to show her how much I love her with everything I have. I know she does not have much energy; the cancer has taken it away. But I determine one last time to give her pleasure with my mouth, and I am rewarded with hearing her breath shorten and her cries of ecstasy as she says my name. I curl up beside her to hold her as she falls asleep, but she surprises me by moving within easy reach. Although I protest, she puts one finger across my lips to shush me, and her other hand much lower. I know she will not stop until I finish, so I focus on relaxing against her touch. I, too, find my release, and minutes later she falls asleep on my shoulder.

    I jolt awake, and my body is wet from sweat, my heart is pounding, and my breathing labored. I push off the duvet that I had pulled across my feet before falling asleep, and I fling my shirt off to get some relief from the fire that my dream stoked to a full flame in my body. I lie back, and try to get my breathing under control. I look down at my chest, and it is glistening from beads of sweat, and my bra feels soaked through. The window is still open to any passerby, but I could care less. I am a mixed bag of emotions, as I remember the last night Julie and I made love well, and the dream was an accurate representation of it. It makes me feel both joy and sadness. I also find myself feeling guilt that I fell asleep thinking of Alice and then dreamt of Julie. As if Julie is reproaching me for beginning to think of Alice in a sexual way. I can acknowledge the feeling, but I also must force myself to recognize how false it is. I know Julie would be pleased, as much as I do not want to think about it. I know she would be. The guilt is simply a carryover from this morning when Alice left so suddenly without breakfast. I have never had a one-night stand before; I cannot think why I felt as though I did. I also realize how long it has been since I have made love, and I am feeling the desire kindle again, and it both scares and delights me.

    I glance over at the clock and I realize that it has only been an hour since I decided to lie down. I need to get up and change. Perhaps take a walk. Anything to get my mind off its current trajectory.

I find a clean shirt, and put my shoes back on. I decide that a walk is a good idea when I hear the video chat ring on my laptop. I wonder how Grace always knows when to ring.

I hurry over to the dining table and lift the screen.

"Hi Hilary!" she says as soon as the chat screen pops up. She is seated in her office, wearing a sleeveless blouse and trousers. She looks smart and professional. I glance at the clock and confirm that it is early morning there.

"Hello, darling. You are looking smart. How are you today?"

"I am well. And you? You look a bit different. Everything alright?"

"Yes, I think so. A bit tired is all."

I begin to tell Grace about the last twenty-four hours, minus Alice's personal account. When I reach that point, I explain that Alice shared with me about a traumatic event, and it caused me to feel a great deal of compassion and concern for her. I know Grace would understand far better than the average person about the trauma of rape, and probably be able to give me suggestions on how to help her, but I would need

Alice's permission. It is not my story to tell. Thankfully, Grace takes it in stride, and I think whatever she images happened to Alice, the reality is far worse.

"Well, whatever she shared, it is obvious to me that you feel closer to her," she replies.

I tell her about having Alice stay the night and how I slept on the love seat, as well as how I felt after she left this morning. I even tell her about what happened just now during my lie down.

"Ah, you are lusting after her now!"

"Oh, piss off."

She starts laughing at me, and I cannot help but join in, because she is right.

After a few moments, she stops laughing, and says, "In all seriousness though, are you getting close to sleeping with her?"

I stop laughing as well. I do not know. I know that I want to at this point, but I also know how tumultuous that could be for both of us in our present states of mind.

"I don't think so. I want to, but I think based on what she shared and how she is struggling right now, as well as my own grief, I think it is too soon. Besides, yesterday was the first time we successfully kissed. We probably need to do that a bit more first."

"I agree…I was thinking though…it is just a suggestion. But I know that whenever you get to that point, it will probably be her staying over with you than the other way around with having the B&B."

"I haven't given it much thought. But you are right of course. I cannot make a habit of staying away at night even when I do not have guests in case anyone calls for a last minute reservation."

"Exactly. So, my suggestion is that when you do get close to that point…redecorate. Paint your bedroom; buy new linens and a new duvet. Make it feel different."

I nod my head. It is a brilliant suggestion, and one that I would never have thought of straight away. It will be hard to do away with traces of Julie in my bedroom, yet I know that it is time for change. It will help me, but also Alice, if and when we go to bed together.

Grace and I spend time talking about Gus and their wedding plans. There is nothing much for her to tell, but she remains hopeful details will fall into place. I do as well. We say goodbye with a promise to speak again soon.

After closing my laptop, I stand up to take a walk.

September

Chapter 8

It has been a month now, since Alice shared with me about the trauma she endured. She is sleeping better, and tells me that the nightmare has occurred only twice since staying the night in my flat. When I question her about it, she admits that both nights were after we were together, one night only a week ago when we ended up snogging for a bit. While I understand why physical contact would be a trigger for her, it is not good for my ego to know that I am contributing to her problem. However, because we are both struggling, we are taking things slower than the average couple would. Since it seems to be a mutual need, it makes it a little easier to manage.

Once again, I have taken Grace's suggestion to heart, and I am redecorating my bedroom. I have chosen a sea green emulsion to replace the purple on the walls, along with a white duvet, and accent pillows and new window treatments that have a mother-of-pearl tone. I have also found new linens in complementary colors, and several art prints of the sea from a local artist for the walls that will go on either side of the window.

    While I had planned on working on everything in stages, Grace recruited Gus and Tabitha to help me behind my back. I think she believes that I will be distraught once my room is changed and should not be alone, but I think she is overreacting. Yes, I am sad at the thought of one more change in my life, but I am resolved to do it. I know it is time. Now, one Monday afternoon, I am waiting on Gus and Tabitha to arrive. Between the three of us, we will have the painting done in no time; although I am fairly confident it will need two coats. I am prepared to sleep in a guest room for the next couple of nights if the fumes are too strong. I have moved all of my furniture into the middle of the room, and covered everything with older linens and towels in case any of the emulsion splatters.

    I hear a knock on the door, signaling the arrival of Gus and Tabitha.

"Hello, you two! I hate that you both felt you needed to come. I could have managed."

Tabitha says, "Are you kidding? Painting seems fun compared with a young toddler running around the room. Stephen will be fine for a few hours. I never get a break."

She says this without rancor, but I know from talking to Grace, that she does not get many breaks from her young toddler. I find it a bit sad that painting could appear as an enjoyable activity for this lonely woman. I look at her smiling face with her darker coloring so different than her brother. Although she looks tired, she seems happy to be here. I resolve to be thankful and try to make the evening as pleasant as possible for her.

Gus walks in behind her, and quietly leans down to kiss my cheek. It is the first time I have seen him in several weeks, and I realize I have missed him. He places his hands gently on my shoulders, and searches my eyes, while looking me over. He has done this since Julie died, and I understand it is his way of showing care. There is nothing sexual in his actions. Often, he says nothing, but his gaze conveys his concern as he tries to discern if I am alright. Ah, this man is a dear. Grace is a lucky girl.

He gives me his verdict after a bit, "You look good, Hilary." Still holding me by the shoulders, he says, "Don't take this the wrong way, but I think you have put on a little bit of weight since I saw you last."

I consider giving him a hard time, but I realize that I have already given him a hard time over the last few months when I was barely eating, and he was not sure if he should tell Grace. The fact is, I have gained weight over the last few weeks, my appetite has returned, and I feel healthier.

Instead, I look him in the eyes, and say, "Thank you, Gus. I have put on weight, and I am feeling much better."

He nods and gives me a bone-crushing hug. My throat constricts as the full extent of his concern hits me. I really did have them all worried.

I lead them both into the bedroom, and we commence getting the emulsion poured out into trays and decide what brushes and rollers to use first. I hold a paintbrush loosely in my hand, and I look one more time around my purple bedroom. This has been my sanctuary for eleven years. It was my happy place with Julie, and over the last fourteen months it has been a safe place to grieve.

I have to take a deep breath before I put the paintbrush against the wall for the first time. I know Gus and Tabitha notice my hesitancy, as they stand quietly for a moment and let me make the first mark. As I spread the sea green color along the corner edge of the room, I release the breath I had been holding. As soon as I do, they get to work beside me, and within two hours, the first coat is complete.

I gather the brushes and rollers to wash them out, and I look up at Tabitha. She is looking green, and altogether unwell.

"Tabitha, are you alright?"

"I think the fumes are starting to get to me, Hilary."

"Go stick your head out the window and get some fresh air."

I hand the brushes to Gus, and I follow her to the open window, where she takes a few breaths.

"Feeling better?"

"Not really, no."

"Perhaps you need something to eat? I will treat you both to dinner at the pub if you like."

She makes a face, and says, "No, food has been part of the problem."

"What do you mean?"

She looks behind her to make sure that Gus has taken the brushes to clean, and looks back at me. "I cannot seem to keep much down the last couple of days. I thought I had food poisoning a couple of days ago from some fish that I cooked, but Stephen ate it with no problems."

I look at her face, and she suddenly looks so tired. The previous energy she had when she first came in the door has vanished, and been replaced with a tired woman who looks as though she can hardly stand. Yet, there is something indiscernible about her as well. Something humming below the surface.

"You're pregnant." I say without thinking. But the moment I say it, I know I am right.

"Shhh. I don't want Gus to know before I tell Stephen."

"So, you are?"

"Well, I can't be sure. I have not taken a test yet. But yes, the signs point to it."

"Congratulations!" I whisper as I give her a hug.

"Thank you."

She does not sound pleased. I pull away, and look at her. "Is it not happy news?"

"Yes, of course, it is. Just not planned either. I need to get my mind in the right place."

"It's difficult, isn't it? With one little one already?"

She is fighting emotion as she nods and says, "Yes, yes, it is."

I look around the room and realize she should not have been inhaling emulsion fumes if she is pregnant. She knows what I am thinking, because she whispers right before Gus comes back into the room, "Don't worry, I was careful. If you noticed, I painted this wall by the window the entire time."

I feel doubtful at her reasoning, but I accept it. When Gus suggests dinner, he and I walk to the pub. We try to convince Tabitha to join us, but she declines, although I do make her promise to eat something at home.

Gus and I sit down away from the bar, and I lean back in my chair to stretch my back and neck.

"You're tired, aren't you?"

I nod, and stifle a yawn. The simple act of sitting down has made me realize just how tired I am.

"You really do look better, Hilary. I was starting to worry over the summer."

I smile at him. "I know. I gave everyone a scare, but I think I had to scare myself first before anything could change. The summer was hard. Far harder than I anticipated. There was the year anniversary of Julie's death, and then a few issues got stirred up between Alice and me. I was not eating much, nor was I functioning well. When Grace came for her holiday, I think I saw myself through her eyes and something shifted."

Gus' beer and my wine arrive, and shortly thereafter the server brings our fish and chips.

Gus is thoughtful as he eats and says, "I remember when my mum died. The second year was just as difficult as the first. In some ways, it was more so. The reality finally sets in, and there is no denying it any longer."

"I said much the same thing to Alice and Grace this summer."

"It's true. But I am glad that you seem to have crossed a bridge. I did not know Julie well, but from what you and Grace have shared, she would not want you to be unhappy."

"I know. Sometimes that knowledge makes it worse though. As if there is some pressure to find love again. And yet, how the hell do I find love without comparing everyone and everything to Julie? I know that I cannot; it is not fair to Alice. But it is almost inescapable."

"You will figure it out. You are a good woman, Hilary, with a lot to still give."

"How kind you are to say that."

We continue to eat and he spends time telling me about Grace and their wedding plans. He will be flying to the States in a few weeks to see her, and she is planning to come back to Cornwall for Christmas. They had invited me to go with him to visit her, but I decided that they needed the time alone, and I could not afford to be away from the B&B for so long.

After dinner, we walk to the bus stop, where he waits for the last bus, and I walk back alone to the B&B. When we say goodbye, he promises to come back tomorrow night to finish painting with Tabitha. I thank him, and walk back home.

Inside, the fumes are strong, so I gather a few things, and go upstairs to what I now affectionately think of as Grace's room. I feel as though I am trespassing on her personal space as I prepare for bed, and lie down on the twin bed that I know she and Gus use closest to the window seat. From my position, I can see the moon from the open window. It is a clear night, and there are stars. As I am nodding off, I feel grateful that I live in the most beautiful place on earth.

Chapter 9

As promised, Gus and Tabitha help me finish painting the next night, and over the course of the following week, I slowly work on putting the finishing touches on the bedding and changing over some of the pictures on the walls, as well as a few trinkets on top of the bedside tables.

I refuse to put away all of my pictures of Julie, but after careful consideration, I know that I need to put away the majority of them, especially the ones of our wedding. Alice could not possibly feel comfortable staying here with wedding photos in the bedroom. I pack them carefully away in a small box and store them in the back of the closet.

As I look around the room a week later, I barely recognize it. It is so light and bright, more in keeping with a beach cottage in many ways. I am drawn to more bold colors, but when I considered redecorating, I knew that I needed a more calm and peaceful color scheme. I am pleased with the results.

I have invited Alice to dinner here in my flat the following Monday night after painting. I had mentioned to her that I wanted to redecorate a few weeks ago, but I have not told her that I have already done so. While I hope this change does lead us to sleeping together soon, I know that we have time. Taking it slow is helping both of us. By showing her the room tonight, I hope she will not feel pressured to stay, but that maybe we can begin sleeping side by side on occasion, before planning to make love. There are times I curse Grace for her suggestion of taking things slow, because I enjoy sex. I want to have it. But I also know that like an immature teenager, my heart is still not ready. Thankfully, it is on the mend though.

  I change into a fresh pair of trousers and a new red silk shirt that Alice found for me in her shop a few weeks ago. It is beautiful, and feels cool against my skin. I go into the kitchen, and open a bottle of wine before preparing dinner.

  Tonight, I am making some lemon pepper chicken with some grilled vegetables from my garden. It is not grand, but I have at least learned to cook some basic meals over the last year. I am preparing a salad when I hear Alice's car pull up. I wave at her through the kitchen window, and she walks into the flat without knocking. She holds up another offering of flowers, and I smile my thanks, as she comes over to kiss me lightly on the mouth.

"Hello, Hilary. You are looking well. The red is beautiful on you. I should find you a dress for Grace's wedding in that color."

I feel pleasure at her attention, and I take a moment to look at her from head to toe. She is wearing a daffodil yellow sundress that would wash anyone else out who tried to wear it, but with her red hair, it is striking.

"Daffodil yellow is your favorite color, isn't it?" I ask with sudden understanding.

"Yes, just as daffodils are my favorite flowers. It's such a happy color, and the flower always brings the promise of spring."

I smile at her as I finish the salad and we move all of the food to the table. I pour her a glass of wine, and we sit down across from each other.

"How have you been, Alice?"

"I am well. Business has slowed down in the last week, but the summer was very profitable and busy this year, so I am ready for a small reprieve. Has business slowed down here?"

"Yes, thankfully. A real shift in the last week here as well. I told Heather just this morning that I would only need her twice a week until spring. I still have a number of bookings over the next few months, but for several weeks there in the summer, I was full almost every night."

She nods her understanding as she eats. "It is interesting how both of our careers depend on tourism, yet in different ways."

"Yes, it is…Alice?"

"Hmm?"

"I have been thinking. I have not had a holiday in ages, and I think I would like one. Would you like to go away together somewhere? Perhaps before winter? Just for a few days. When we feel ready to stay together?"

Her entire face lights up. "I would love to!"

I grin back at her. "Alright, well, let me look at a few places online. See where we can find the best deal. I think I could get away sometime in the next month or two if that would be alright with you."

"Sounds lovely. I hardly ever take a holiday."

"Nor I. It is always ironic to me that my work surrounds me with other holidaymakers, and yet I rarely go on holiday myself."

"True. But we do live in such a beautiful place, that I often do not feel I am missing out."

"Did you like growing up in Winchester? Apart from your family I mean?"

"Winchester is a charming city. I grew up appreciating the historical connection to Jane Austen, and I loved living close to London, although I did not often get to go. I did have an older cousin who would take me on occasion when I was a bit older. I have not been back to Winchester since…everything happened. A place can change a lot in twenty years. It could be completely different from what I remember."

"So, not only have you not been back, but you have never had any contact with anyone since?"

"No, and I don't plan to, Hilary. For many years they knew how to reach me, and they did not. Even now, if they wanted to badly, they could track me through old friends, but they choose not to, and I choose to leave them be. I am not bitter. But I am very matter-of-fact about them. They are my past, but I will not have them part of my present."

Something is confusing me, and I try to reach back in my subconscious to retrieve whatever buried memory lies dormant.

"Don't you have a nephew here?"

Now it is her turn to look confused.

"The band we saw in St. Ives when Grace was here last summer. Didn't you say you were there seeing your nephew play?"

Sudden recognition dawns on her face. "No! The keyboardist is my neighbor Martha's nephew. She had invited me and a few other locals in Penzance to go with her that night. I do not even know if I have a nephew. Frankly, I rather hope my brother did not procreate."

Ah, it makes sense that I would not have paid close attention to that detail when my grief was so fresh. I feel myself sigh. "Well, I can understand the feeling. It sounds healthy to me that you don't want a relationship with your family with what you have experienced. I just cannot imagine. I had such a wonderful relationship with my mum. She has been dead for many years now, but she was delightful. She loved me for who I was without trying to change me."

"She knew you are a lesbian?"

"Yes, she was the first person I told when I knew for sure. Although I am quite sure she knew already. She was dying from cancer at that point, but she looked at me, and asked, 'Are you happy?' I told her that I thought so, and she said that was all she needed to hear."

"That is lovely."

"I did not tell my father until a year or so later. He was not so accepting, but we were already estranged, and my mum had passed by then, so…"

"It did not carry the same weight, did it?"

"No, it did not. He had failed and disappointed me years before, so I guess it was my turn to do the same to him."

"His loss."

I smile at her, as I stand to move our plates to the kitchen counter. "Would you like some strawberries and cream for dessert?" I ask over my shoulder.

"Sounds delicious. I am going to the loo, and then I will help."

I hear her cross the room and close the door to the loo. I begin putting the leftovers away, and stacking dishes in the sink to be done later in the evening. I get the strawberries and cream out of the refrigerator, and begin assembling everything in bowls. I hear the water turn on and the door open afterwards. I anticipate Alice walking up behind me any moment, and when she does not, I turn around. I see her standing with her back to me in my bedroom doorway, motionless. Instead, I walk towards her slowly, and I put my hand tentatively on her shoulder to not startle her.

She turns around, and says, "I know you mentioned redecorating, but I had no idea you already had."

"Gus and Tabitha helped me paint last week, and I worked over the last few days on everything else. Do you like it?"

"Like it? Hilary, it is beautiful. But it is so different. Are you alright with the changes?"

"Yes, I am. It was hard, but I needed a fresh start." The implication that I need a fresh start with her seems to be hanging in the air. I know that I feel it, even if she does not.

"May I go in?"

I wave her inside, and watch her as she looks around at the new artwork from local galleries that I have selected, as well as the duvet and curtains. She reaches out to touch the pillows on the bed and a blanket slung across my reading chair by the window. After a few moments, she appears confused as she looks around the room and at the bedside tables.

"Where are your wedding pictures?"

"I put them away."

"But…"

"I do have two small pictures of Julie and me on my bedside table, and there are a few in the living room, but I put away the rest."

She glances at the bedside table to confirm this and then asks, "But why, Hilary?"

I take a step closer to her, as I say, "Because I cannot imagine asking you to stay the night with me at some point, whenever that is, and having my bedroom filled with wedding pictures of my deceased wife. It does not seem fair to you."

"You want me to stay with you?"

"Yes, I do. Hopefully, in the near future."

I see her swallow as I continue walking towards her. When I reach her standing by my bedside table, I put my hand up to her face. It is shaking, but I do not pull away. Instead, I move my hand lightly across the spattering of freckles on the side of her face, as I lean forward to kiss her. The day in St. Ives, she was receptive, but it was more one-sided. This evening though, she answers back. I feel her hands move to embrace me, as I move my tongue in a brand new dance with hers. It is exhilarating. I reach with my other hand around her back, and the one that has been touching her face, I move to her hair and neck. It feels heavenly, and my entire body begins to heat up.

We stumble over to the bed, and without thought, we lie down together on the duvet, and continue kissing. I become bolder, as I reach my hands under her shirt, and I hear her moan. I caress her breasts still trapped in her bra, and they are round and firm, with her nipples hardening at my touch through the fabric.

As I continue touching her, I turn her on her back, and gently roll on top of her. When I straddle her, I feel her body stiffen, at the same moment that I am reminded of my dream of Julie only a few weeks ago where I rolled on top of her.

We both stop and look each other in the eyes.

"What's wrong?" We both ask at the same time.

"You first," I say.

"Um…I am sorry, but I don't like to have anyone on top of me. Bad memories…"

"Oh god!" I immediately roll off. "How foolish I am. I should have realized. Alice, I am so sorry."

She touches my wrist, "Hilary, it is alright. You didn't know."

"Well, I knew about the other. I should have guessed."

"No. It is not for you to guess. It is for me to tell. And I have. The end."

"I won't do it again."

"Please do not panic about it. It is not that you cannot ever be on top. I will probably need warning though."

I nod. We are both still lying on the bed, facing each other.

She asks me quietly, "Why did you stiffen?"

I stammer, "I had a dream recently…about the last time with Julie. It started out with me rolling on top of her, and I remembered it all of a sudden."

"I see. Was the dream based on reality?"

"Yes."

She smiles as she shifts on the bed. "We have sufficiently broken the mood. I think perhaps I should go home."

I feel sad even though I know she is right.

I follow her to the flat door, but before she leaves, I grab her hand and turn her towards me as I kiss her more passionately than I ever have before.

When we pull away, she opens her eyes, and I say, "We will make this work one day. I believe it."

She whispers, "One day," as she walks out the door and I wave goodbye.

She has no way of knowing her words mirrored my own promise to Julie right before her death.

Chapter 10

At the end of the following week, the phone rings after lunch, and I answer to hear Alice on the other end.

"Hilary! It's me. Do you think you could come for coffee this afternoon in Penzance? I have something I want to talk to you about in person."

She sounds excited, which makes me curious. I agree, and we set the time and agree to meet in our usual place.

After ringing off, I have an hour or so before I need to leave, so I go out to reception to work on the laptop while I wait.

Shortly thereafter, I hear a car pull up in the car park and a few minutes later, a man in his forties walks in through the open front door. He is tall, muscular, and has a nose that has obviously been broken before, likely multiple times. He has short blonde hair, and brown eyes, and is carrying a small overnight bag.

"Hello, may I help you?" I ask.

"Yes, I was hoping you have a room for the night."

"Yes, just for yourself?"

He nods, and I consult my book to make sure that I remember which rooms are already full, before offering him one. I have two rooms available, Grace's and another one at the opposite end of the hall with a double bed. For some inexplicable reason, I do not want him staying in Grace's room.

"I have a double room with en suite. Is that suitable?"

"Lovely."

I have him fill out the guest form, and he gives me his credit card to swipe. I look down to read his name. *Eddie Smith*. A rather forgettable, innocuous name. Normally, I escort all of my guests upstairs for the first time, but I hesitate. I do not know why, but I do not like this man. I trust my instinct. I fold his receipt, and get his key from under my desk, and I hand them both to him.

"The room is at the top of the stairs, and to the left."

He pauses, and looks at me one second too long for comfort while his gaze lingers at my chest, before saying, "I was rather hoping you would show me to the room."

"I am busy at the moment." I refuse to look away. Nor do I smile at him either. I have had the rather unpleasant task of dealing with aggressive men over the years in this business, but I have learned not to show fear or discomfort.

He waits another moment, but I do not budge, and he reluctantly climbs the stairs. As soon as I hear the door close behind him, I lock up my desk and bring my laptop back into the flat. Within five minutes, I am in my car headed to Penzance.

I did not need to leave quite so early, but I realize as I drive how tense I am. After arriving at the café in Penzance ten minutes before Alice is to meet me, I get out of the car, and walk for a few minutes. I end up on an adjacent street overlooking the water, and I stand still facing it. I roll my shoulders a few times and move my neck from side to side.

I may be a lesbian, but I am apparently attractive to the opposite sex, as evidenced by the many times over the years I have received unwelcome attention from male guests. I have always been able to deflect it, but it was easier when Julie was alive and we would laugh it off together. Normally the men would back off when they realized I was not interested.

However, there have been a handful of times when I have been physically backed into a corner usually while they were intoxicated. I have been kissed and groped, but the men were all decent human beings. The moment that I pushed each of them away, and in one case actually slapped the man, they backed off, apologized, and stumbled to their rooms. I still have a feeling about this new guest I cannot shake. This is the first time I have received unwanted attention since Julie died, and it makes me feel more alone than I anticipate. I make a mental note to get an old cricket bat out of the garage to bring into my flat, as I attempt to let it go.

I head to the café determined to do so. When I enter, I order a coffee for Alice and a pot of tea for me. I look at my watch to discover that I am still a few minutes early.

I sit back and try to relax. The café is quiet today. There is only one other table across the room with customers. The waiter brings me our drinks, and I hope Alice arrives before her coffee grows cold.

I add milk and a touch of sugar in my teacup, and begin to sip it. It is restorative. I close my eyes and breathe in the bergamot and lavender from the Earl Grey, and I feel soothed.

I open my eyes to find Alice standing in front of me, staring.

I smile at her, and stand up. "Hello Alice."

She greets me and we kiss briefly on the cheek. I can smell her scent of vanilla and citrus, and I feel much better.

She sits down next to me, and says, "I hope I am not late."

"I was here early. I needed to get out of the B&B."

"Why was that?"

I wave my hand in an irritated gesture. "Oh, I had an annoying guest."

"In what way?"

"He was just an arse. He wanted me to show him to his room. Made me uncomfortable, so I refused."

She looks troubled. "Are you alright?"

"Oh yes, of course. Nothing to worry about."

She seems unconvinced, but does not question further.

"What is it you wanted to tell me?" I ask.

She becomes excited and leans forward before saying, "I know that you mentioned last week that you would like to take a holiday together. Were you serious?"

"Yes, of course. Although I have not had time to look online yet."

"I have an old mate of mine from university. He and I speak a few times a year. He owns a small business as well, and we have stayed in contact as colleagues. Anyway, he and his wife have a flat in the south of Spain. They let it out on occasion, and he has offered it to me in the past. He rang me last night and during our conversation, he said we could have it for a few days at the end of October."

She looks at me expectantly, and I am touched she is so excited at the prospect of going away together to Spain. I have never been before, but I am sure it is beautiful. Having sun every day would be magical, as by that time of year, we will likely have a lot of cold wind and rain in Cornwall.

But I stay frozen for a moment as I realize the magnitude of what we are discussing. If we go away together in a few weeks, the expectation will be that we will make love and sleep together as a real couple. Even if she does not expect it, I will. I acknowledge the feeling, and quickly try to let it go.

I reach for her hand, and say, "Yes, Alice. That would be brilliant. I have always wanted to go to Spain."

She kisses me impulsively again on the cheek, and sits back with her coffee appearing as though she is a giddy school girl. I find myself feeling rather protective of her, and wanting to reassure her of how I feel.

We speak about the details for a few minutes, and I write down the dates, so that I can discuss them with Heather as soon as I return to St. Just.

Prior to saying goodbye, I ask, "Before we go on holiday…do you think you could stay over a few times? Just so we could get used to it?"

She smiles at me, and says, "I have been thinking about that. I think it's wonderful that you redecorated your bedroom. But I think our first time needs to be in a neutral location, which is why I am suggesting we go to Spain. Perhaps it does not matter to you, but it matters to me. All I can think about when we are in your flat is that I am intruding on Julie's personal space."

I start to interrupt. She says, "I know that is not true, but that is how I feel."

"I know. I am sorry. And I agree with needing a neutral location, but I actually meant perhaps we could sleep in the same bed a few times first. Not make love though until we go on holiday."

"I see." She pauses as she appears thoughtful. I hold my breath, as I await her verdict.

Finally, she says, "Let me think about it." She stands up, kisses me goodbye, and before I know it, she is gone.

***

I am more shaken by my new guest than I let on to Alice, because I spend the next couple of hours meandering around the streets of Penzance. I do not want to go home yet, and although I think it is likely nothing would happen, I trust my instinct, and continue to delay returning to St. Just. Now that I run the B&B on my own, I carry a mobile with me whenever I leave. I rarely use it, but all of the guests are given my number upon arrival in case they need anything when I am not there. I never go out until after all the guests check out each day, and I am careful to be there to greet expected ones, but I learned soon after Julie's death that I cannot be home every minute of the day. I do not leave for more than a couple of hours at a time without having Heather there, but I also have to be able to go out without feeling guilty. This afternoon though, I purposely did not give the new guest my mobile number. I feel a moment of remorse at my irresponsibility, but I shrug it off.

I do a little bit of shopping. I go to the off-licence for wine, and I call in at a few boutiques. Alice's birthday is at the beginning of October and I need to find her a present. I have never bought her a gift before. Last year, I do not think I knew when her birthday was, being so deep in my grief. But in one of our conversations recently, it came up, and I wrote it down after she left. As I search for something for her, I realize what a difficult task this is. With Julie, we often bought each other clothes for our birthdays, but with Alice owning a clothing store, it does not seem proper. I continue shopping, and enter a jewelry shop, where I find a beautiful pair of vintage earrings in a geometric starburst design with citrine green and vivid orange stones. These will look brilliant with her hair and eyes, and I do not even glance at the price before deciding to buy them. No matter how dear they are, Alice deserves them, if for no other reason than that she has put up with me the last fourteen months.

  When I walk out of the store, I breathe a sigh of relief I found something suitable, and I walk towards my car to stow my purchases. On an impulse, I decide to walk into Alice's shop, *Daffodil Yellow*, to see if she has anything new for autumn or for our holiday in Spain. There are a few customers when I walk in, but Alice waves to me from behind the counter where she is helping a customer. I wonder around the shop. I have put about half a stone back on since this summer, but I still need to buy new clothes. Things that do not remind me of Julie. I find a couple of pairs of trousers, and a new jumper for the winter. Before going to the changing room, I meander through the back of the store to see what is still lingering from summer. There is not much, but I do find a cotton summer dress in a muted pink with a scoop neck that I pick up. On impulse, I snatch a black bikini off the back wall as well. It has a halter top and a basic bikini bottom. I know the weather in Spain will likely be cooler by the end of October, but I can hope that it is warm enough to sunbathe while we are there.

    I let myself into a changing room, and I first try on the trousers and jumper. Nothing exciting, but everything fits well, and I move them all to the side. Next, I try on the pink dress. It is flattering, but simple. The fit is slightly loose, but I think it will work well, especially as I still plan to gain a few more pounds. At least I can no longer see every rib so clearly in the bathroom mirror. I am about to take it off and try on the bikini, when I hear Alice's voice on the other side of the door.

"Hilary? Is that you?"

"Yes, it's me. I hope you don't mind that I let myself in the changing room."

"Of course not. What are you trying on?"

"The pink dress on clearance."

"May I see?"

I open the door, feeling a bit shy. I know the dress is becoming, but it is encouraging to see the look of appreciation on Alice's face when I step out.

"It is lovely," she says.

"I thought I would get it for our holiday."

"Oh, I am glad. What else are you trying on?" she asks as she peers over my shoulder into the changing room. "Is that a bikini? Do I get to see that as well?"

"No, you do not. I cannot believe I even grabbed it." I tell her, as I try to push her out of the changing room, so I can shut the door.

She protests, but stays outside the door and continues to talk. "I spoke to my friend and confirmed we would take the flat. We need to look at airfare soon."

I murmur agreement, as I pull the dress off over my head.

I struggle to get the bikini on. It has been years since I have worn one, but I need one if I am going to Spain. I do not want to be considered past it and I do not intend on sitting in the sun all covered up with a big hat. I stand looking at myself in the mirror, and turning to the side and looking from the back, I think it looks alright. Not great or even sexy, but presentable. I hear Alice tell me that she is going to lock up, as it is gone five and closing time. I hear her walk away from the changing room, and I breathe a sigh of relief for the moment.

I am going to Spain with Alice. I am jittery, but I feel energized, yet I cannot name why. As I stand looking at myself in the mirror, wearing my first bikini since Julie and I travelled to Brighton a number of years ago, I understand. I feel excited. The very emotion is foreign to me after months of grief and depression that I continue to examine my head and my heart. But yes, I am excited. That must be it.

I startle when I hear Alice's voice again as she walks back to the changing room.

"Everything alright, Hilary?"

Instead of answering, I open the door, so she can see me wearing the bikini.

She is clearly about to speak again as her mouth is open, but no sound comes out. Rather, she walks forward and gently pushes me back into the room and against the wall, as I am engulfed by her mouth on my own and her hands begin to search my body. I gladly let her explore. Only seconds go by though before she stops and pulls away.

"I'm sorry. I got carried away. You are so beautiful, Hil." She says, as she tucks a piece of hair behind my ear.

"I am not complaining," I say, and begin to reach for her again.

But she grabs my hands and kisses them before saying, "Spain. I want to wait for Spain. We have waited so long; let's make it special. It is only a few more weeks."

I want to groan in frustration, but she is right of course. Nothing says low-class like sex in a changing room.

She suddenly cocks her head, and places a hand on her hip, "I just realized…were you not supposed to head home after we met this afternoon? Why are you still in town?"

"I decided to do a bit of shopping." This may be part of the truth, but it is not the whole truth and she knows it.

She stares at me, before guessing correctly, "It's that guest, isn't it? You don't want to be there alone when he is there."

I decide to be honest. She has figured it out anyway. "No, I don't."

"Is he only staying for the night?"

I nod.

"Alright. That settles it."

"Settles what?"

"You change, and I will go upstairs and pack an overnight bag." Before I close the changing room door, she looks back and says, "I guess we will see if we can sleep together before making love after all."

***

An hour later, we are back at the B&B. Alice followed me home in her own car, as she will have to leave early in the morning to get back to the shop. This late in the month of September, it is getting dark earlier in the evening. Now, it is twilight, and the air is crisp. I gather my yellow box of clothes from the backseat, and walk to the back door, where Alice is already waiting on me holding a small overnight bag.

When I reach the door, I remember something, and without speaking, I hand her my box, and walk back towards the garage. I rummage around and find an old cricket bat. Julie used to play with her father and brother with this one when she was young. It is weathered and aged and has her initials, *JH*, carved into the handle. I pick it up, and as nonchalantly as possible carry it with me to the back door where Alice is waiting. She raises her eyebrow at me, but says nothing, as I open the door.

She follows me inside. No one is about, even though four of my five rooms are full tonight. However, it is the end of the week, and in all likelihood, everyone is out having a good time.

I let Alice into my flat, and I lock the door behind us. We walk to the bedroom, and she sits her bag on the floor by the left side of the bed, and I walk around to my chair by the window to put my box of new clothes down. I take the cricket bat, and put it under my side of the bed.

"Is the cricket bat necessary?"

I look into her eyes and I realize she is not teasing me. She looks serious, and I understand that I am scaring her by my actions.

I walk around the bed to embrace her, "I am sorry, Alice, for bringing you home with me tonight. You don't need this stress. Perhaps I am overreacting."

"Hilary, sweetheart, I have never known you to overreact about anything. Be depressed or sad? Yes. Grieving so hard that you forget to eat or are in another world? Yes. But at your core, you are the most levelheaded person I know. If you are nervous, I am taking your apprehension seriously, and I want to be with you."

I feel touched, but I cannot speak without risking tears. I nod, but resolve to change the subject. After all, we are safe here in the flat.

"What would you like for dinner? I have some steaks, and a few vegetables. Does that suit?"

She smiles and agrees.

We go into the kitchen where I tie an apron around my waist, and get all of the food set out on the counter to prepare. Alice puts together a salad for us, and while the steaks and vegetables begin to sizzle, I decant the wine.

"I was wondering what you would like to do for your birthday. I would like to do something special for you."

"Oh, you don't have to do anything. I usually don't."

"So, let's change that. At least, let me take you to a nice dinner."

She says, "I don't want to celebrate this year."

"Whyever not?"

"It's a big number. I am not taking it too well, I suppose."

"Oh really? How old will you be? If you don't mind my asking."

"I will be forty."

I am glad that I am not facing her when she tells me this, as I believed she was several years older. I am not sure why exactly. She does not look older, but perhaps the fact that she is so controlled and stable in both her personality and her life, I have always thought of her as being older than she is. In addition, Julie was forty-five when she died, and for whatever reason, I have usually been involved with women older than me. I turned forty-one earlier this year, so it is odd to realize that I am the older one in this relationship. First time that has happened since university.

I turn to face her and smile. "In that case, we should definitely plan something special. No woman should have to turn forty without celebrating."

She looks doubtful, but says, "Alright. I trust you."

"I will come up with something. I promise."

We sit down at the table, and begin eating. I do not eat a lot of steak, but I was craving it yesterday, so picked up a couple. This is the first one I have eaten in months, and I enjoy it immensely. Absentmindedly, I wonder if my iron is low by how much I relish it.

The red wine is perfect with it, and I look across at Alice as we continue eating, and I find myself undressing her in my mind. The night we fooled around on my bed, I felt her under her shirt, but I have yet to see her body, and it is starting to drive me mad. Especially as I know that very soon she will be lying next to me in my bed tonight. I shake my head slightly, and try to get these thoughts out of my head as we finish eating. Alice has made it clear she wants to wait, and I need to respect her boundary.

I try to find something to talk about that will get me out of the thoughts in my head.

"So, where in Spain will we be staying?"

"In the south, in Andalucía. There is a small whitewashed village on the Mediterranean where Paul has his flat."

"Sounds beautiful."

"It is. We should see if we can find a flight into Málaga or Granada. Otherwise, if we fly into Madrid, we will have to take a long train or bus ride."

"Alright, I trust you to decide. Do you speak Spanish? You pronounce the cities with a Spanish accent."

"A little. I studied when I was young."

"Have you been to Spain before?"

"I have visited several times over the years. I have never stayed in Paul's flat with anyone though if that is what you are asking."

I smile as I hear the discomfort in her voice at my perceived jealousy. "No, I was not asking. Although, it is nice to hear you have not. We can make our own memories there."

She smiles, and adds, "I have stayed in Paul's flat several times before. But I have always gone alone."

"Oh."

"I have always liked travelling alone. It allows me to do what I like when the mood strikes. But…I am excited to know that we are going together."

"I am as well. Is there anything in particular we will do there?" I try to say this without innuendo, but it is impossible.

She smirks, but does not take the bait.

"Actually, I do as little as possible. I love sitting on the beach with a book, going to the tapas bars, and walking in the village. It is similar to here. There are not many activities or even many tourists as you find in the bigger cities, but the simplicity of life there helps me to slow down and enjoy every moment. The biggest difference is the heat in the summer there is stifling and the sea is much warmer and clear. But I hope October will be pleasant, while still being warm enough to enjoy the beach. I want to see you in that bikini."

"If you wear one for me."

"Believe me, sweetheart, I will."

This is the second time that Alice has called me sweetheart tonight, and I like it. It makes me feel treasured and reminds me that I am back in a relationship. Yes, it is awkward, and still rather platonic, but it is progressing. Slowly.

We clear the dishes, and move to the living room with our wine.

"It is rather late for a walk or to sit in the garden. We could watch some television or read. I have a few books or magazines if you did not bring anything."

"I actually brought my knitting. Would you mind if I got it out?"

"I did not know you knit."

"Yes, since I was young. One of the few things that my mum showed me how to do. I rarely make anything useful, but it helps me unwind at night. In fact, I have been known to knit row after row and then undo it and repeat, just for the mindlessness of it."

"I would love to see."

She goes into my bedroom, and I see her lean over her bag, and retrieve a ball of yarn and her knitting needles.

"I finished a new winter hat last night, and I plan to make a scarf with what is left of this yarn. It is an alpaca wool and very soft."

I reach over to feel it and she is right. It is a vibrant green and feels luxurious.

"It is lovely. I am impressed."

"Perhaps I will make you something one day."

"I would love it."

She sits back in the love seat, and I watch her for a few minutes. I ask her about how she starts it, and she explains how she casts on, and the basic knit and purl stitches. It sounds very complicated to me, but I watch her with fascination. After she does the first row, she no longer has to look closely at what she is doing, but instead continues to knit as she looks up to talk to me.

"Were you going to read?" she asks after about ten minutes. I realize by talking, I am not helping her relax as she says is her purpose for knitting.

"Oh yes," I reply as I reach over to the side table, and grab an old book that I am reading yet again. I love to read and rarely read anything more than once. Although I have a couple of favorites that I have read many times, those few are the exception. But since losing Julie, reading has become my comfort at night, and I often return to old favorites over and over again, as somehow the familiarity of the characters helps to soothe my heart and spirit.

I lean back in the love seat, and attempt to focus on my book. The room is quiet and the only noise is the clacking of Alice's knitting needles, and the occasional turn of a page in my book. I have all but forgotten the purpose of Alice staying tonight. I feel peaceful and content in this moment.

Sometime later, I notice out of the corner of my eye that Alice stretches her feet out in front of her, and grimaces.

"What's wrong?" I ask.

"My feet are sore. They often are at this point in the day. I stand on them so much in the shop."

"Why don't you take your shoes off then?"

"I will be fine."

"Alice, you are staying the night. I want you to be comfortable."

She is wearing all black today. Black shirt and a black skirt with basic black heels and stockings. The shoes are nothing fancy, but neither do they look comfortable. She gingerly takes them off. As she does, I hear her groan.

"Put your feet in my lap," I say as I motion towards myself.

"I think not."

"Please."

She does carefully. I set my book down, and reach for them. She jerks them back several inches.

"What are you doing?" she cries.

"I was going to rub them." Oh my, she is skittish.

"Why?"

"Because they hurt you. Don't they?"

"Yes, but..."

"But what?"

"I don't know. I have never had my feet rubbed."

"Ever?"

She shakes her head, but she has moved her feet back into my lap.

I reach first for the right one which is closest to me. It is stiff, as her discomfort is palpable. "Relax," I coax her, as I start to lightly rub.

She tries to as she sets her knitting in her lap, and leans back to close her eyes. As I massage the arch of her foot, she lets out a low moan, and I have to concentrate on what I am doing, as I am becoming aroused. I watch her, as I continue rubbing. I can tell she is relaxing more and more, as her hands are lying peacefully in her lap, and her jaw is no longer clenched. I venture up her ankles, her calves, and past her knees until I feel the lace edging of her thigh highs and a suspender belt under her skirt. My hand stills; it is my turn to groan. Oh god, I had no idea she wore stockings with suspenders.

Without opening her eyes, she says, "No, Hilary. Not tonight."

I feel chastised like a naughty child.

I move my hands back down to her feet, and after a few more minutes, she yawns.

"Why don't we go to bed? To sleep I mean."

"Alright. Do you want to use the loo first?"

She stands up, and gathers her things from the bedroom to take into the bathroom. I go into the bedroom and change into pajamas and robe. I sit on the edge of the bed waiting on Alice to come out, and I look outside the window. After she comes out, I go in, and within ten minutes we are back in the bedroom, staring at each other. She is sitting on the edge of the bed waiting on me.

"You could have gotten in the bed already."

"I wanted to wait."

I go around to my side, which is the right closest to the window. I untie my robe, and lay it across the foot of the bed. She stands and does the same.

We are both wearing similar silk pajamas. Alice's are green, while mine are black with white piping around the edge. Silently, we climb into bed, and I fluff my pillows into position.

The last time I slept in this bed with anyone else was with Julie. I try not to think about her. I really do. But it is impossible. I feel my heart grow heavy and sad, and I hurry to turn off the bedside light so Alice does not see my reaction.

However, Alice has learned to read me better than I give her credit for these past months. She turns her light off, and immediately reaches for me. At her touch, I begin to cry. I cannot help it. She moves to lie on her back, so that I can lay my head on her shoulder. I can feel the beating of her heart, and she holds me until I stop crying.

"I am sorry." I say as I wipe my eyes, and move away. I turn on my side facing her profile, so we can still talk. She turns towards me as well.

"No need to apologize."

"It's hardly how I had envisioned having you in my bed for the first time."

"Maybe not what you had envisioned. But I had a feeling it would be emotional for you, which is why we are just going to sleep tonight."

"I know."

"But…"

"But what?"

"I do want to do this," she says, as she gently leans over and kisses me. I feel her tongue glide into my mouth, and I happily receive it while sharing my own.

After she pulls away, she whispers, "Good night," and within a few minutes, her breathing deepens, and she is asleep.

***

The next morning, I convince Alice to stay long enough for a quick breakfast before Heather arrives. Afterwards, while she is in the loo, Heather comes in and we begin serving breakfast. As I am boiling more water for my guests, Alice comes out of the bedroom carrying her overnight bag and tells me goodbye.

The man, who caused me to feel so unsettled yesterday, checked out ten minutes ago without eating breakfast. He told me that he needed to be on his way, and I breathed a sigh of relief when he walked out the door.

I tell her that he left, and say, "I am sorry. I feel as though it was all for naught."

"Don't be silly. Of course it wasn't. You say that as though something bad should have happened to warrant me staying."

"I don't mean that."

"Hilary, I loved staying with you. I will see you soon, alright?"

I nod, as she kisses me gently goodbye. Heather walks back into the kitchen as we break away, and she says, "Well, well, well. Had a slumber party, did we? Now I know why you are flying off to Spain!" She says, as she winks at us, grabs the tea kettle and heads back into the guest dining room.

I cringe, "I hope you were not hoping to keep our relationship a secret. Because it will be all over St. Just by tea time today."

"Maybe I should go shout it in the roundabout. Save her the trouble."

I laugh.

She suddenly looks serious. "Hil, she could tell every last person on earth, and it would not bother me. Because I love you."

Without waiting for my reply, she kisses me softly once more, and walks out the door.

I am stunned, but find myself smiling the rest of the day.

October

Chapter 11

A week and a half later, and Alice's birthday has arrived. For days I tried to come up with something original and romantic. Knowing that Alice did not want to do anything to celebrate caused me to hesitate over anything lavish. But after talking to Grace last week, she encouraged me to ask Gus for suggestions.

When he came to visit me over the weekend, I discussed with him what to do, and he kindly offered to take us out on the boat for a sunset cruise. He told me that I could bring food and wine, and he offered to sit at the opposite end of the boat the entire time to give us privacy. I decided to contact one of my favorite restaurants in St. Ives, and they agreed to fix our meal in a takeaway picnic basket, and I have a couple of bottles of wine, a large blanket, and my scarf ready by the back door. I asked Alice to come here first so I could drive us, and to stay the night afterwards. My libido is active and high again, but the no sex mandate is still in place. Thankfully, Spain is less than three weeks away.

I walk back into the bathroom, and look in the mirror once more. I did not buy anything specifically for tonight, but I am wearing new black trousers, and a sweater that Alice gave me a few weeks ago. It is chocolate brown, and makes my eyes look darker than they are. I nervously brush my hair out once more, and I make a mental note to get it trimmed before we leave for Spain. I have not had it cut since before Julie's death, and the dead ends are terrible. I know Alice likes it long, so I resolve only to have it tidied. Going into the bedroom, I find my three-inch black suede heels, and put them on, hoping to be close to eye level with Alice.

I hear a knock, and call out, "Coming!"

I open it, and Alice is there looking beautiful in a black jersey knit long-sleeve dress that goes all the way to mid-calf while skimming all of her curves. She is wearing black stockings and low heels. Bless her. I can look her in the eyes with a minimal tilt of my head.

I cannot help wondering if she is wearing thigh highs and a suspender belt again, but I have to get that out of my head quickly.

"Happy Birthday, darling! Many happy returns!" I tell her without thinking, as I reach to embrace her after kissing her lightly on the lips.

I feel a lump form in my throat, as I realize this is the first time I have called her darling. It is what I called Julie all the time. It was my own special term of endearment for her. It is not that I have not called others over the years the same name and I often call Grace that, but I still take note that this is a line of demarcation I have now crossed.

I know Alice recognizes the line as well, because when I pull away, she caresses my face, and says, "Thank you, sweetheart."

I break the eye contact first, and reach for my things by the door.

"Did you bring a scarf or would you like to borrow one of mine?"

"I have one. Where are we going?"

"You will have to wait and see."

She picks up her overnight bag that she had set beside the door before knocking. "Shall I put this in the bedroom?"

"Yes, of course." I wave her past, and I wait for her to put it away after she rummages inside to find her scarf.

Within a few minutes, we are on the road to St. Ives, and she begins to pester me with questions. I cannot tell if she is nervous, excited, worried, or a mixture of all three.

I refuse to tell her anything though, other than to say that she will find out soon enough.

We find a space in the car park closest to the shoreline, and I gather everything and reach for Alice's hand to hold as we walk down the steep incline in our heels towards the boat dock. Evening boat tours are certainly more of a summer excursion for tourists. Nor are there many local people who hire boats in the evening this time of year, so as the sun sinks lower in the horizon, we are the only ones who are around the boat dock tonight. The wind is absent at present, and the waves are gentle. The air is crisp, but not cold, and I feel hopeful that Alice will enjoy what I have planned this evening.

When we reach the dock, I see Gus' boat at the far end, and I can make him out aboard, appearing as though he is rearranging everything in a hurry.

Alice sounds amused. "What is Gus doing?"

As I suddenly realize that she could get motion sick or something equally horrid that I never considered, I ask, "You do like boats, right?"

"Yes, of course."

I feel relief as I have not a clue what I would have done if she had said no.

We walk up to the boat, as Gus stands up and sees us.

"Hello, ladies! How lucky I am to be your host this evening." He jumps down onto the dock, and gives us both a kiss, and wishes Alice a happy birthday.

I look at Alice and say, "Gus is taking us on a sunset dinner cruise. Is that alright?"

"Sounds wonderful."

Gus helps us to board the boat. I notice he is wearing nice trousers and a button-up shirt for the occasion. He assures me that he was able to pick up everything as planned. When we walk carefully towards the bow of the boat, I see he has laid out a small shallow vase of yellow roses on the sunken table, and a candle with a white tablecloth underneath. There is an ice bucket for the wine which I place the bottles into, and we sit across from one another as he starts the engine and drives us out of the harbor.

    A short time later, he cuts the engine and drops anchor in a small cove. This is not the one he normally comes to for the seal tours, but that does not mean we will not see any. But this cove is the perfect location for viewing the sunset, and in the unlikely event there are any tourist excursions tonight, it will not be here that they travel.

    Gus immediately pops open a bottle of champagne. I see the label and gulp as I recognize it as being rather an expensive one. I arch my eyebrow at him when he pours two glasses for us.

Smoothly, he says for my benefit, "Hilary, I know you brought your own wine, but I hope you don't mind. Grace and I did not want to intrude on your plans, but we wanted to gift a bottle of champagne for Alice's birthday."

Alice says, "Oh, how kind."

We toast to our good health and Alice's birthday and clink glasses. The champagne is dry and crisp. He turns to gather plates, cutlery, and wineglasses and sets the table for us. It is difficult for me to sit still as he waits on us. I am used to serving others at home. When I spoke to Gus, my plan was for this evening to be much more casual. But Gus would not hear of it. He wanted to make it special for Alice as well as me, and in his mind, that entailed making it more formal. We were sitting in the garden last weekend having a row about it, especially as to payment, because Gus was refusing to charge me. I heard the video chat ring through the open window. While speaking to Grace, she made us agree to a compromise; I pay for all of the expenses including the petrol for the boat, and Gus gives his time and assistance as a birthday gift to

Alice. But now that apparently includes an expensive bottle of champagne. It is for Alice, so I decide to keep my mouth shut.

Now, I am here sitting across from Alice on the boat, and Gus is posing as tour guide, waiter, and host all at once. I am grateful that not only did I gain a friend in Grace last year, but one in Gus as well. But then I look across at Alice watching me, and I realize that I am grateful for her most of all.

Gus sets about serving us salads and bread with olive oil and balsamic vinegar. It is light and refreshing. The main course is a surf and turf, and the restaurant did an excellent job at preparing and packaging it well, so it would be warm and moist when we eat it.

Once Gus serves us our main course, he retreats to the stern of the boat where he eats on his own. The sun is within minutes of setting, and the sky is many shades of orange and red.

Alice says, "This is so thoughtful of you, Hilary. I am very touched."

"I am glad you like it. I wanted it to be special. I am sorry that I didn't remember last year."

"You didn't forget. I did not tell you."

"Yes, well, that still feels like my fault."

"Hilary, listen to me. You are not to blame for your grief. Grieving was what you needed to do then. It would have been wrong if you were not focused inward dealing with it. If you had not grieved hard and long, we would not be where we are tonight."

I stare at my plate, because if I look up, I know I will cry. "Thank you."

She stretches her long legs in front of her, and sighs.

I find myself asking as I look at her legs stretched out beside me and resist the urge to touch them, "How tall are you?"

"Five eleven…and a half."

"I just wondered."

"I am sorry if it makes you uncomfortable."

"I didn't say that!"

"Then why do you wear three-inch heels every time we go out?"

I counter, "Why have you started wearing low heels?"

She smiles, "Touché."

I explain, "Your height does not bother me; it is part of you. I wear the high heels though, because I enjoy looking at your eyes, and if there is too much of a difference when we are standing next to each other, I cannot see them directly as much as I would like." This admission causes me to feel embarrassed, and as I sneak a peek in her direction, I discover she has tears in her eyes.

"What a beautiful thing to say. I may never wear heels again."

"Do you dislike being tall?"

"I did when I was young. I got teased by the other children at school. My parents were always angry at me, because I was growing out of my clothes constantly, which fed into being made fun of at school. But as an adult, I am rather ambivalent about it. I know where to find clothes that fit now, and living alone, I rarely have problems having things out of reach. It no longer seems important how tall I am. But I would hate to think it bothered you for any reason."

"It doesn't. I find you very attractive just as you are." I feel my face heat, but I want her to know how I feel. We may not be planning to make love tonight, but I want us to be comfortable when we do in Spain. I hope as we become more connected emotionally, it will be easier when we connect physically.

We pause for a few minutes to watch the sun sink completely from view, as though the ocean is swallowing it whole. As the sky begins to darken, Gus turns on a strand of twinkle lights. This and the candle on our table add a seductive feel to our already romantic evening.

Gus comes over to our table and clears away our plates, and he refills our wineglasses.

"Is everything to your liking, my ladies?" he asks formally.

"Yes, Gus. It is wonderful," I tell him.

"Are you both ready for dessert?"

I look to Alice, "Are you ready for dessert, darling?"

"I wouldn't dare say no."

He bows to us like he is working at some posh restaurant, and goes to retrieve the cake that I ordered. It is a chocolate torte with raspberries. It is Alice's favorite dessert, and I hope she will be pleased that I remembered.

Out of the corner of my eye, I see Gus light a candle in the center of the torte, and he carefully brings it over to us and sets it down in the center of the table. The candle is unsteady in the light breeze that has started up, but it stays lit as we sing to her.

Alice watches us both, and with great concentration she pauses to make a wish and blow out the candle. We ask Gus to join us for dessert, but he refuses.

As we bite into the torte, it is so rich and decadent, that we do not talk for a while. After only a couple of bites, I cannot eat anymore. It is delicious, but I prefer desserts that are less dense. But Alice is enjoying it and that is all that matters. I settle back in with my wine, as she eats. I feel the alcohol as the breeze is kicking up, but I remain warm.

I reach into my pocket where the tiny silk pouch with her earrings lie nestled inside. As she swallows her last bite, I set it beside her hand on the table.

She looks down, and asks, "What's this?"

"Open it and see."

When she does, there is just enough light from the candle to see the stones sparkle.

"Oh, Hilary, they are lovely." She says, as she puts them on straight away. She leans over for a kiss, and before she pulls away, I whisper in her ear, "Happy Birthday, darling."

She holds my hand as she says, "I never imagined I could be happy turning forty."

At this point, Gus clears his throat and tells us it is time to head back, as there are too many clouds moving in and covering the moonlight. He needs to get us back to the dock, before it becomes too dark to see. As he turns the boat towards St. Ives, I move to Alice's bench seat to sit beside her, and we use the blanket to cover up, as there is now a chill in the air.

Gus drives slow, both to be safe with the darkening skies and to avoid the frigid breeze at high speeds. Alice and I snuggle beside each other under the blanket. Perhaps it is due to the alcohol, but I grow bold, as I move my hand under her skirt to graze her inner thighs. She is wearing thigh highs and suspender belt again, and as much as I would enjoy exploring, I force my hand to still. I know if I do anything more, I will not be able to stifle the groans that I am sure to release, and I would be mortified if Gus heard.

All too soon, we arrive back at the dock in St. Ives. Gus wishes us a good evening, but hands me a bottle of water as we disembark. I must appear confused, because Gus says quietly in my ear, "You probably need to drink some water and wait a bit before you drive."

I want to protest, but I see how uncomfortable he is, and I know that he would not say anything if he did not feel it was not necessary. I take the water, but as usual Alice is more astute than I give her credit for. Instead of asking what we are talking about, she simply says to me, "Hilary, let me have your keys. I will drive us back. I stopped drinking more than an hour ago." Gus looks relieved, and I am able to save face.

***

When we are lying in bed later that night, trying to fall asleep in each other's arms, Alice kisses the side of my forehead. She says, "Thank you. It was the best birthday I have ever had."

I am taken aback, "Really? Surely as a child or in university…" I trail off, as I remember how Alice's family treated her.

"The only one even close was in university with Ruth one year. It was before…the rape…when things were innocent I suppose. She took me to London for the day and we went on a pub crawl, and then to several discos. I had never been that drunk before. I woke up the next morning with a horrid hangover, and I swore to myself I would never drink that much ever again."

"And you actually kept that promise?"

"Yes."

"Well, I regret to say that I may flabbergast you in that department. I drink a lot if you have not already noticed. But I have a high tolerance."

"I have noticed."

"Does it bother you?"

"Should it?"

"I don't think so. A couple of months ago, I realized I was drinking even more than normal. I have gotten close to the border of having a problem in the past, but have not crossed it."

"I agree, Hilary. Yes, you drink a fair share, but I have never actually seen you lose control, even if you have been over the legal limit a few times. And it was my birthday, and I thought it was sweet that you went to so much effort."

I feel happy as I fall asleep wrapped in her arms.

Chapter 12

"Are you excited about Spain?" Grace asks me one day on the video chat later in October. We are both excited for different reasons. Alice and I leave tomorrow for our holiday, and I am trying to pack, while Gus is about to leave for the US by the end of the week to see Grace. But I am in the midst of chaos here, and I need help. I have things strewn all over the flat, and as I talk to Grace on my laptop that is on my dining table, I am trying to decide what to take. Every so often, I hold something up to the screen to get her opinion.

"Yes, of course, I am excited. But I am nervous, too. And at the moment, stressed."

"I understand. As long as you have some excitement though, all the other emotions will lessen once you are there."

"I hope so."

"What are you planning to do in Spain?"

I cannot help smirking, so I turn away from the screen briefly to hide my reaction. "Actually, the south of Spain is unusually warm right now for this time of year, so I think we will spend some time on the beach. The water will probably be rather cold, likely similar to how it is here in July, but for October, I can handle that."

"Oh, that will be lovely."

She is hedging. I know that she wants to ask something, but either is not sure if she should or is debating how to phrase it. I have a fairly confident idea what it is, but I have always enjoyed making Grace squirm a bit. She is still innocent about much of life.

I hold up my black bikini, and I ask her if she likes it.

"Yes, it's nice. Basic, but I am sure Alice will like it."

"Well, I am rather hoping she will prefer taking it off of me."

She is at a loss for words until I start laughing at her, and then she says, "Oh piss off!" She will fit in well here in England when she and Gus marry. She is finally learning to swear.

After I am able to stop laughing, I apologize. Laughing did help release some of the tension though.

But Grace knows me well and understands what is stressing me out even when I try to deflect the situation, "Spain is D-Day then."

"Yes, it is."

"That is what all this stress and anxiety is about…it's not about packing. It's about having sex with Alice for the first time."

"Yes."

She stares at me. I know what she is doing. She is willing me to elaborate without asking any direct questions. It is her counseling trick to find out what is really going on, instead of asking open-ended questions that would allow me to steer the conversation in a more comfortable direction.

I give up and sigh. "Alice has stayed a few times overnight, but other than kissing, and light touching, we have not had sex. And it is about to drive me mad! I would have weeks ago, but things kept happening. I kept crying or it was bad timing for some reason. Then, we planned this holiday, and Alice seemed to think it would be a good neutral place to make love for the first time. I think she is probably right, but as we have gotten closer the last few months, it is getting harder and harder to wait. I am so randy that I keep trying to touch her and convince her otherwise the last few times we have been together, but that woman has the patience of a nun. I keep undressing her in my head when I am alone and even when I am with her. I feel like a bloody teenager."

Now, it is Grace's turn to laugh, although she makes the effort to subdue it at first. Her shoulders begin to shake, before I finally say, "Oh, go ahead and laugh. It is funny." At that, she throws back her head and laughs until her eyes water.

I wait for her to stop laughing, before I speak again. When she does, she wipes her eyes and tries to focus. I say, "It's been sixteen months since I made love, and it was with Julie in London. That is the last time. I don't want to betray a confidence with giving details, but suffice it to say it has been even longer for Alice. I am afraid it will not measure up for either of us. Yet I do not want to compare anything. I know that I need to compartmentalize what I have experienced with Julie, just as I did with her in the early days in regards to my previous relationships. But this seems monumental. I was with Julie for fifteen years. I knew her body and what drove her mad with delight better than I knew my own sometimes. It seems overwhelming to not compare what I will experience with Alice, and yet I know it is paramount." I am now sitting at the table looking directly at Grace. No matter how uncomfortable this conversation is becoming for me, I need to voice my concerns and hopefully hear some words of wisdom to restore my confidence, even if calmness seems impossible.

But Grace bursts my bubble of hope when she replies, "Hilary, I don't have any words of wisdom. But nothing you have said surprises me. It sounds very normal, and I doubt Alice would be surprised to hear it as well. Can you tell her what you just told me?"

"Perhaps."

Grace hurries to add, "But don't tell her right before you go to bed. Talk about it somewhere other than the bedroom. Maybe on the plane if you have enough privacy."

I nod in agreement. She is right. I ask one last question, "What if I cry? I cried the first time we slept together in my bed, and we didn't do anything. What if I cry afterwards, or even worse, when we are in the process of making love?"

"You talk about it, Hil. Making love is the closest we ever get to another human being, both physically and emotionally. If you are being present in the moment, you can't control what emotions may occur. Trust Alice. I believe she loves you, and I think she can handle whatever happens."

I take a deep breath, and let it out, and suddenly I feel much better. I needed to talk to Grace who has no stake in the situation. Tomorrow, I hope to have the nerve to discuss it with Alice.

***

The next day, I take the afternoon bus into Penzance, so I can leave my car at home. Heather is staying in Grace's room at the B&B for the next four days running things for me, and arrives a few minutes before I head to the bus stop. Heather has met both Gus and Tabitha, and she knows to ring either of them if she needs help. It is not the same as when Grace has helped me in the past, but still I am grateful that I do not have to worry.

Alice and I agreed to meet at the train station, and when I arrive, she is there already. She is wearing brown trousers with a cream blouse and a dark green jacket. She looks very chic, and when I reach her, I notice that I can look her directly in the eyes. I glance down to see she is wearing ballet flats, while I have on my usual three-inch heels I wear when I am with her. Perhaps she did decide to not wear heels again.

I greet her with a light kiss on the cheek, and we board the train. We booked seats, but on a Monday at the end of October, there are few passengers going all the way to London today. We sit down, only to discover that there is not another soul in our compartment.

I sit back in my seat, and close my eyes. I did not sleep well last night. I must have tossed and turned as evidenced by how the bedding was in disarray when I awoke. By around four am, I could not fall back asleep. After a while, I gave up trying. Once the sky started to lighten, I walked down to Julie's cove and watched the sun rise.

I spoke to Julie for a long time. I told her that I am going to Spain with Alice, and that I hoped she would be pleased. I found myself verbalizing my worries and woes in great detail, and it felt like a purging. By the time I walked back, I was drained. But I always feel her presence there. Today, I needed to feel her and be at peace, before leaving with Alice. Perhaps it is mad, but I need her blessing and approval before I take this next step.

Now, with my eyes closed, I feel Alice next to me moving to get comfortable and arrange things for our several hour train ride to London. We decided to go to London tonight, and fly to Spain tomorrow morning. It will be easier than making the entire journey in one day. We will stay in a hotel close to the airport, and have dinner at a local pub.

Alice reaches for my hand, and says softly, "You look tired. Did you not sleep well?"

This is my opening to share with her my anxiety. I know the sooner I say it, the better I will feel. It will probably be as Grace suggests, and she will not be surprised anyway. Why is it always difficult to say the first words though?

I open my eyes and look at her. Oddly, she is the one who appears emotional though. I sit up straighter and clasp her hand tightly.

"What's wrong?"

"Nothing. I could not be happier. But I know this is a big step for you."

"Yes. Alice?"

"Hmm?"

"I want this holiday to be good for you, too. I am worried though. I was with Julie for fifteen years. It feels a bit like jumping into the deep end of a pool, and wondering if I will remember how to swim."

She smiles, "There will be a learning curve I am sure. For both of us. You may have been with the same woman for fifteen years, but don't forget, I have not been with anyone in almost a decade. I am nervous as well, but if you will be patient with me, I promise to be patient with you. But we won't know anymore until we experience it, will we?"

It frustrates me to ask, but I must. "What if I get emotional?"

Her eyes darken, as she replies, "Then I will hold you as you cry."

Chapter 13

Spain

Alice and I arrive at Paul's flat in the south of Spain by lunchtime the next day. It is stifling hot outside for the end of October, and we decide to take advantage of the heat and go straight to the beach. After changing into our bikinis and cover-ups, we gather a few things in a canvas bag, and walk the ten minutes to the coast.

We find a seaside restaurant for a light lunch of salads with olive oil and vinegar, appetizer of olives, and a traditional tortilla that we share. We drink a carafe of sangria, and as the breeze wafts through the windows, I finally feel as though I am on holiday. I have now gained back the stone that I lost over the last year, and I feel healthy and energized again. I even remembered to have my hair trimmed last week, and I know that Alice likes it, as she has touched it a few times already.

After lunch, we hold hands and walk down to the beach. Instead of stopping where the few tourists are sunbathing, Alice suggests that we walk further down. I follow her lead. It is hot; I never guessed that it could be so warm here this time of year. Alice assures me this is unusual and likely the last heat wave the country will have until spring. If the weather report is to be believed, in another two days, it will be much cooler. For this reason, we are taking advantage of the warm weather now.

"I wonder how warm the water is," I say.

"I am sure it is crisp."

"Nice way of saying it will be miserable."

She smiles at me, "Not if you get hot enough first."

She stops at the far end of the beach, where rocks as we have in Cornwall jut out into the water. She tells me this is where she always comes, because no one else ever walks down the beach this far. There is a small area of flat sand that we spread our towels on, and she smiles at me, as she suggests, "Why don't you lie down in the sun before you get in the water?"

"Will you join me?" I ask.

We take our cover-ups off. I am using my new pink dress as my cover-up, and I take it off to reveal my black bikini. Alice's bikini is dark green, and gives color to her pale skin. I do not say anything, because I am incapable of speech by seeing more of her body in this moment than I have ever been granted. She is tall and willowy. Although her breasts are not large, they are perky, and her hips have enough shape to be considered feminine.

It does not take long of lying in the sun, before we are both miserably hot, and we jump in off the rocks. The cool water feels refreshing, even if there is a bite to it. The Mediterranean is clear blue, and from where we are swimming, I can see straight to the bottom, another two or three feet below us. I have not swum in the sea in years. It is exhilarating.

But not as exhilarating, as what happens next when Alice swims up to me and casually unties my bikini top. I begin to protest, but who I am kidding? We are in the south of Spain, where even though this is not a nude beach, Alice tells me that it is not uncommon for women to go topless here. Even if someone did walk up, no one will care. When she slides it off of me, I breathe sharply in. She lies the top down on a nearby rock, and then reaches for me. I can taste the salt from the water as she kisses my mouth with such desire that I suddenly realize how much she wants me, and I can barely stay afloat. She realizes my distress, and backs me against one of the rocks, so that I can stay above the water with ease. As soon as she is assured that I am safe, she reaches for me again, but this time, begins to fondle my breasts that are bobbing to the surface. Every nerve ending in my body stands alert, and I am on fire. The chill of the water cannot extinguish what I feel. She leaves my lips behind, as she moves down to my ear, neck, before arriving at my chest. She begins to lick and suck and play with my nipples, and then every so often, she slows down to hold both breasts lightly in the palms of her hands. Each time she does this, I open my eyes to watch only to discover such a look of awe on her face that feels so vulnerable, I am not sure if I should continue.

When she pauses during one of these moments, I switch places with her. I lean against her on the rock, but I decide not to take her top off. I know myself well enough to know that if I do, I will not stop, and that will surely be more risqué than even people around here would tolerate. But I do kiss her, and fondle her through her bikini top until I can feel her nipples harden like small pebbles.

I have no idea how long we have been in the water, but I notice my fingers are starting to turn blue and look like prunes.

My voice is hoarse as I say to her, "Alice, let's go back to the flat. It's time we go to bed together."

***

The twenty minutes that it takes to dry off, dress, and walk back to the flat are the longest of my life.

The moment we arrive inside, we drop everything and I take her hand and lead her to the bedroom. It is the siesta hour. The building that this flat is in houses several other flats, and the occupants are all either out or sleeping, as everything is quiet around us. The windows in the flat are open to allow air flow, but the outside shutters are shut against the heat of the day. The bedroom has enough light coming through the cracks in the shutters that there is no need for additional. The bed is a four poster double, and has mosquito netting around it which gives it an element of drama and seduction.

    As I shut the bedroom door behind us, I push Alice gently against it, and I kiss her while touching her damp hair. My breathing quickens, as I pull her cover-up over her head. She is standing in front of me in her dark green bikini, and I realize that this is the moment I have been waiting for as I have undressed her in my mind the last few months. My hands are shaking as I undo her top, and it falls beside us, allowing me to see her breasts for the first time. They fit perfectly in my hands as I massage one with one hand, and suck the other with my mouth. She begins to moan and arch her back. Her hands and arms are clinging to my own, as if she can no longer support herself. I shimmy the bikini bottoms down her legs, and look at her body slowly in its entirety. She is beautiful; her pale figure looks like a Greek goddess.

In this moment, I pause with a sudden case of uncertainty. I want her desperately, but I am scared of what thoughts my head may punish me with later. I know Alice loves me, but I do not yet know how I feel about her. I care for her, and I have certainly lusted after her, but whether or not I can love her remains to be seen. It seems unfair of me to toy with her emotions by making love to her if I cannot at least commit to her in some way.

I do my best by being as honest as I can be, "You are beautiful, Alice, both inside and out. You are kind, decent, and ridiculously patient. I care very much for you, but…"

"But what?"

"Are you sure you want to take a chance on me? I don't want to hurt you."

She touches the side of my face and says, "I would take the risk, even if I thought it would be only for tonight."

She looks me in the eyes and I see them dilate, and I cannot wait any longer. I pull her to the bed, and have her sit down on the edge. I move to where I can stand between her legs, and begin to kiss her again. She pulls my top off and pushes my bikini bottoms down, and our warm bare flesh finally touches. I want to lose myself in the sensation, but I focus on her and work my way with my mouth from her lips all the way down to where I have to kneel on the floor to reach. She strokes my hair, murmuring sounds with no meaning and as her pleasure builds, her breathing quickens. I look up to see her chest rising and falling rapidly. As she climaxes, she arches her back and screams my name.

    I thought she would be too spent, but without saying anything, she moves a few inches further back on the bed, and motions for me to sit on the edge between her spread legs with my back to her chest. From this position, she can see to use her hands, and with her right hand between my own legs, and the other on my left breast, she appears confident in what she is doing. As she moves her hands, she kisses my neck and my ears, and occasionally, I turn my head enough so that she can snatch a kiss from my mouth. The difference now is that she is lethargic from being sated, and she is clearly enjoying drawing it out for me. It is driving me mad, but I know that is her intent. I want release badly, but she will not yet let me.

This is where my emotions begin to be tested, as before I focused on Alice's enjoyment. But now, to achieve my own, I struggle to lose myself. My brain is beginning to cycle on, and it is everything within me to resist conjuring Julie. I am thankful that Alice cannot see my face directly, as it is sheer willpower that keeps the tears at bay, but it is wearing me down.

I whimper at one point, and she whispers in my ear, "Relax, sweetheart. Trust me."

I realize that my entire body is tense and tight. In that moment, I make the conscious decision to listen to her and relax. I feel my body collapse against hers from its own emotional exhaustion. As soon as it does though, she speeds up with energy that I did not think she had left, which allows me to focus selfishly on my body and nothing else. As I find my own release, I arch my back against her, and cry out from the intensity.

She pulls me back against her, and as I fall asleep with our arms wrapped around each other, I hear her whisper, "I love you."

***

Later, the tears start. I wake up and the room is dark with pale shafts of light coming through the cracks in the window from the street lights outside. Alice is asleep behind me, and her breathing is deep. I look at the side table and can barely make out that it is gone seven. The flat is quiet except for her breathing, and I lie on my side away from her, and turn inward.

Making love with Alice was wonderful, and I intend on doing it again, but it was different. I had to concentrate to enjoy it, instead of it being full of ease. I feel as though I need to take a moment to acknowledge the difficulty, which will hopefully allow me to let it go. I will never make love to Julie again. The degree of intimacy we had achieved was a result of fifteen years together, and not likely to be replicated. Even if I can hope to reach that with Alice, it will be years in the future and have its own nuances.

It feels overwhelming to be starting over at forty-one. I am not sure what I thought would happen once I knew Julie was dying last year. In all likelihood, I never contemplated it, because I could not. But I feel my age now in ways that I never have before. Sex has more meaning and repercussions now, and I cannot continue in a relationship with Alice without a clear intention.

Alice is special. I recognize that she is kind and gentle, and will never intentionally hurt me, which is more than I can say about myself. She has been damaged and broken in her own way, and even though it has been many years, I know her past still haunts her. I respect her and her boundaries too much to not take our relationship seriously. Her heart is too fragile and precious to not treat with care.

As I allow myself to feel the fear and overwhelming sense of uncertainty for our future, I succumb to the tears. They are silent tonight. No sobs rack my body as in times past. But the tears feel like a cleansing rain in my soul. I will miss Julie forever, but I need and want to focus on Alice now.

Julie is my past, but she is gone. Alice is my present, and I know she wants to be my future.

I feel Alice shift behind me as she moves her arm around my torso, and leans over to kiss me, only to discover my wet cheek.

She moves back a fraction of an inch and with her lips right above my face, she says, "Oh Hilary, I am sorry."

I hurry to assure her that I am okay, but I cannot get any words out.

"May I hold you?" she asks.

I nod, and I turn over and rest my head on her shoulder. I had forgotten that we are both still nude until I face her. The intimate contact feeds my vulnerability, but it also comforts me. As I relax against her, I find myself watching the rise and fall of her chest in fascination. She idly plays with my hair, and as I stretch my feet out as long as they will reach, I can brush the bone on her ankle.

The tears have long stopped, and I feel marginally better.

"How are you feeling?" she asks.

"Better."

"Do you want to talk about it?"

I shrug. "I did not feel guilty as I feared I might. But I felt a change tonight. Recognizing that this is now a different time of life and how overwhelming it feels to start a relationship again at my age. It felt as though this was the final assertion that Julie is gone, and accepting that, while knowing I am lucky to be with you now."

She kisses my head, "I understand."

I look up at her face, "Darling, I don't understand how you understand me sometimes. I am a mess the majority of the time."

She smiles, "I love you."

I say with sincerity, "I don't know why."

She does not blink, and I can see the intensity from the small shaft of light coming in the dark room, when she answers, "Because you need loving."

Chapter 14

The rest of our holiday is much the same as the first day. When it is warm, we go down to the beach and brave the cool water to swim. We eat fresh seafood and drink Spanish wine. We make love at all hours of the day and night; often staying in bed for hours before and after talking, laughing, and sleeping side by side.

I am growing to have a deep fondness for Alice, but I am not sure if it is love. She does not pressure me to decide, but I have put pressure on myself to discern my heart. My greatest fear is that I will convince myself I love her merely because I do not want to be alone and I know that she loves me. While I feel sure Alice would be alright with this circumstance, she deserves to be loved and treated with affection. I could not live with myself if I used her selfishly for my own benefit without reciprocating her emotions. I know I love her as a friend, but I want to love her passionately as a long-term partner.

Whenever we are exhausted enough to sleep, I often find my mind returning to these thoughts. It troubles me, because I feel as though I should know by now. We may have only been dating for three months, but she has been by my side since Julie's death. But no amount of pressure will force my heart to decide. I need time, and I accept that I need time. For now.

***

On our last day in Spain, we decide to take an excursion to Granada to see La Alhambra. Alice has been before, and tells me that it is a requirement for anyone visiting the south of Spain. We hire a car, and it is lovely seeing the Sierra Nevada mountain range on the way. She drives, and I enjoy leaning back in the seat with the windows down, and enjoying the scenery.

"I know you have travelled to Spain several times. Have you been to many other countries as well?"

"A fair amount. During university, I went with Ruth on holiday with her family to ski in the Swiss Alps once. Another time, she took me to France and Italy. She and I also went to Madrid and Barcelona once. I mentioned to you that she had a trust fund, right?"

I nod.

"Well, she was incredibly generous with it. She always said that as long as she was happy, her parents would not care what she spent it on. Apparently, going to Europe with her girlfriend fell into that category."

"That's nice. Julie and I never travelled far. The furthest we ever went was Paris. We took holidays every year, but usually within England and Scotland."

"I have not travelled near as much since university. I have been alone so much of the time that it takes a special location to feel comfortable going without anyone else. This area often feels so secluded and has never felt awkward for me to come on my own. But I have to say, I much prefer being here with you."

She smiles at me with her hand holding the steering wheel loosely, and she winks at me. Today, everything feels easy and relaxed. I never want to leave.

We are not in a rush, and as we walk through La Alhambra with the horseshoe arches, and the Moorish architecture, I am in awe. The Court of the Lions is the show stopper, and it feels so pleasant outside today, as the heat of earlier in the week has dissipated. I love how in certain areas, the buildings that make up the palace overlook the city of Granada. The sky is clear, and we can see forever. However, my favorite place may have been El Palacio de Generalife and the gardens surrounding it. Everywhere we walk, we are greeted with flowers and a variety of greenery. But it is not the greenery of England. Spain is arid and dry, so the vegetation is completely different than anything I know about at home. In one secluded spot, Alice and I sit in a courtyard by one of the fountains. It is peaceful as I listen to the water cascade beside us and I feel the warm sun on my skin.

Running the B&B is not difficult work, but it is often time consuming. When there is high tourism in the summer months, it often means long hours on my feet, and that translates into exhaustion by the end of the day. I am not at my best emotionally when I allow that to happen. Being away from home for the past week has made me realize I need time away on occasion. Because Julie and I owned the business together, everything reminds me of her when I work. Combine that with living together, and I cannot do a single task during the day that did not involve Julie when she was alive. Many times I can block that out, and as time has gone on, I am able to do that more and more. However, being away from Cornwall this week has shown me the toll it has taken on my mind and body.

"I needed this holiday more than I realized," I tell Alice, as I sit back on the bench and close my eyes against the sun.

"I think we needed this holiday together," she replies.

"I don't want to go back yet."

"Neither do I. But we can come back."

"We can?" I ask hopefully.

"Of course we can. Paul offers me the flat at least once a year. I have never stayed that often, but I know if I asked, I could have it even more."

"That would be wonderful."

"Alright then. We will plan another visit soon. No need to be sad."

As we sit in the sun, a cloud floats across it and we are now covered in shade. I look at Alice's vivid green eyes, and she kisses me suddenly. It feels so natural. So right. As though the world has started turning on its axis again, after months of sadness and grief.

I feel happy. Because of Alice.

***

That night, we go to a local venue Paul suggested to see Flamenco music and have dinner. Alice wears her jade green dress with a cream-colored shawl, and I wear my cobalt blue one. It feels as though we have come full circle from our first date in the summer when we wore these dresses for the first time. We eat freshly caught prawns and mussels and drink Spanish wine, and when we walk back to the flat late that night, my senses seem heightened as we find ourselves under the influence of the alcohol trying to mimic the steps and sounds of the dance.

We fall into bed together soon after. Our lovemaking that night is slow and sensual. There is no hurry. Our hands and bodies create a dance of their own and we are each the conductor. I can feel her love for me in every touch and kiss she gives.

I cannot yet interpret my feelings for Alice. But I know one thing. We will have a future together.

November

Chapter 15

We arrive back in Cornwall late Friday night, the first day of November. I am tempted to ring Heather and ask her to stay overnight again as I would love to stay at Alice's flat for once. I know it is time to return to reality though. As I gather my things off the train to head in the direction of the bus stop, Alice grabs my hand to stop me.

"Where are you going?"

"Home. I took the bus here, remember?"

"I will drive you home, Hilary."

"No, we are both tired. I don't want you to have to drive back and forth tonight."

"Who said I would drive back tonight?" she asks me with a wicked grin. "Charlotte has already closed the shop for the day. Let me just make sure she has not left chaos for me to deal with before tomorrow first."

We walk the few minutes to her shop, and I wait for her to read a lengthy note from Charlotte behind the counter.

She opens the till, and rummages around and looks at a few credit card receipts.

She looks up at me and says, "Nothing too difficult. It can all wait until tomorrow. Let me go upstairs and leave what I don't need for tonight. You want to follow me?"

I leave my things, and we take the stairs. She wheels her luggage into her bedroom, and I watch her through the open door pull out a small bag from under the bed. She takes out her toiletries from her luggage to put in the smaller one, and then grabs a pair of pajamas from her wardrobe and a change of clothes for tomorrow. She is ready within a minute, and I feel a lightness in my chest as I did not realize how much I was dreading saying goodbye to her until this moment.

"Ready?" she asks.

"Yes, thank you."

"For what?"

"For not leaving me alone tonight." Becoming intimate this week with Alice has been wonderful, but also leaves me feeling vulnerable, as I know it would have been difficult going back to my monastic bedroom alone tonight. I know that she knows it as well, as she squeezes my hand tight and we walk out the door.

***

I relieve Heather as soon as I walk through my own door a short time later. As it is a Friday night, she is in a tear to see her boyfriend and is content with a curious glance and a wave of the hand. I am sure she will have plenty to ask when she returns on Sunday. I thank her at the back door, and close it to hear the bizarre silence of the house on a Friday night when the rooms are full, but the guests are out until late in the evening drinking at the pub.

I walk into the flat, and Alice is in the bedroom putting away her few things. We ate dinner on the train, but that was a couple of hours ago, and I feel peckish. In the kitchen, I grab a bottle of wine Heather must have opened this week and not finished, as well as some cheese, an apple, and a few biscuits.

"Would you like something to eat?" I call out to Alice.

"Lovely."

"Do you prefer wine or tea?"

"Oh, I think tea if it isn't trouble. Herbal if you have it. It is too late for caffeine."

"Not at all." I put the kettle on, and set out my choices of herbal tea for her. I pour the wine for myself, and put the wineglass with the food onto the dining table. She selects a berry tea, and I steep it for her, while I wave for her to sit down.

I join her at the table, and it feels good to be home. But more important, it feels good for Alice to be here with me.

I decide to ask her the question I have been mulling over all week, "Darling, what do you think about living together?"

She maintains a poker face as she asks, "In what way?"

"I don't know exactly. I know it would be challenging with both of our businesses…To be honest, I am not sure if I could live with you. Not without employing someone full-time to live here on the premises."

"I understand."

"I guess I am asking…would you care to move in with me? Or would that be too difficult with your own business?"

"Difficult, yes. Impossible, no."

"Would you consider it?"

"Yes, of course I will. The commute back and forth to work would not bother me. It is more about my own flat above. I am not sure that I would want to let it unless I knew we were committed in some way."

I want to shirk away from where this is headed, but I do my best to be direct, as I know I need to be for my own peace of mind.

"In what way would you need commitment?"

"I am not sure. I think I would need to know we were committed for the foreseeable future at least."

Oh, piss it. I cannot deal with any ambiguity in this, "But you wouldn't need marriage?"

She does not blink. "Not unless you want marriage again."

I feel a rising panic. "I can't. I'm sorry."

"I thought not. In that case, I will probably need to know that you are promised to me in some way without the marriage vows…" She reaches across for my hand, and says, "Sweetheart, we are both tired. Let's go to bed. We can talk about this later. We do not need to decide tonight."

Reluctantly, I agree.

She follows me to my bedroom, and finally, we do more than sleep.

***

It is early the next morning, and I wake to see light entering the window from the impending sunrise. I stretch my body languidly, and look over at Alice. She is still in a deep sleep. Last night was…special…and…unique. I find myself grinning like a Cheshire cat, as I managed to have sex in my bedroom without thinking of Julie. It was sensual, erotic, and all together wonderful. It feels incredible to be able to share my life again with someone. I can hardly believe my good fortune.

And yet, I take a moment to think of Julie. I know in my deepest core that she would not begrudge me in any way.

She was the kindest, most loving person I ever knew. If she is my guardian angel somewhere, I imagine she is sprinkling some type of fairy dust on me now that I would maintain my current sense of happiness. I know she would. With that, I release her once again from my mind, and I turn my attention to the lover in the bed beside me.

"Good morning, darling. Would you like breakfast?"

Without opening her eyes, she smiles, and asks, "What are you making?"

"Anything you want."

"I am ravenous."

I begin to snuggle in beside her, but she says playfully, "No, not again! I am exhausted. And famished. Food, please. Then, I have to get back to Penzance. It's Saturday."

I grumble without truly complaining, and pull myself out of the bed and go into the bathroom to ready myself for the day.

Within half an hour, we are both dressed, and I have breakfast ready for both of us, and everything on the counter ready to prepare for my guests as soon as Alice leaves. We sit down to eat side by side. It hits me that our week together is about to end. I struggle with a sudden sadness and this shocks me. After only a few months, I have gone from putting up with Alice to wanting to be with her as much as possible. It is a shift I was not expecting, especially not considering how our relationship began the summer before last.

"What are you thinking?" she asks as she sips her tea.

"I…I was feeling sad all of a sudden knowing that you have to leave for work. I am going to miss you today, Alice."

She looks as if she might cry.

"Please don't cry!"

She blinks rapidly, and says, "I am alright. You have no idea how much that means to hear you say that though. I will miss you, too."

I feel needy, but damn it, I cannot help it. "When will I see you again?"

She teases, "Sounds as though you want to see me soon!" But then, she becomes serious, and says, "Sweetheart, I need to get my flat and shop in order, do laundry, and go to the grocer's. Let's take the next couple of days to do that. Perhaps Monday as we usually do?"

I try one last time, "But the shop is closed tomorrow."

"Which is when I will do my laundry and get my flat in order. Besides, you will be working all morning getting the rooms turned over here. Patience, my dearest."

I give in. "Monday, it is." I feel marginally better, as I know I will see her soon. Yet, Monday feels very far away at the moment.

***

Despite the fact that I work the majority of the weekend, Alice's pronouncement that it would be enough to keep my mind off of her is not accurate. On Sundays, Gus often visits me after lunch with his family if I have not already been coerced into joining. They are always kind to invite, but I am not family and I always feel as though I am intruding.

Today, Gus is in the States with Grace. He left while Alice and I were in Spain. Tabitha extended the invitation to join them today, but I turned her down. For several months after Julie died and Grace went home, as soon as I would finish work in the mornings, I was so depressed and lonely I would go back into the flat, put my bathrobe on and have a lie down. Once Grace found out what I was doing, she sent Gus my way on a regular basis. Every Sunday and often another day or two in between, Gus would appear at my door. If it was a Sunday, he would wait in the living room for me to change again out of my bathrobe into clothes and escort me to Tabitha's house. It took me a long time before I saw the kindness meant and stopped being annoyed. A compensation of dating Alice has been that Gus' family does not seem to worry as much about me as they once did.

  On this Sunday, I am alone. Heather came to help with breakfast and the guests have since checked out. She left an hour ago, and it will be later in the week before I need her help again. Now that November is here, tourist season is slowing way down. For a brief moment, I consider reverting back to last summer and putting on my bathrobe. But I am not sad or depressed as I was all of those months ago. However, I am restless. I reconsider calling Tabitha about lunch, but I do not want to disturb her family. Grace told me before I left for Spain that Tabitha is indeed pregnant again, and morning sickness has hit her hard. I did not ruin Grace's news by telling her that I guessed Tabitha was pregnant before she knew for certain. Remembering how sick she has been confirms that she does not need me throwing her afternoon plans astray.

So, I do what Julie and I always did when we were restless; I decide to take a walk. I put on walking shoes, grab a jacket, and my wallet in case I decide to stop in at the pub later.

The weather this time of year has a bite to it, as the wind is strong and the skies grey and overcast. Rain comes often, but as I step outside and look around, I believe I will be able to avoid any long enough for a walk. I turn right and stroll through the village towards the Cape. It will be an easier journey as it is more level this way and with the cold wind, I do not fancy going down the cliff path and having the wind spray me with frigid water. I lengthen my stride and attempt to get my heart rate up so that I can burn off some of the restless energy I have accumulated. When I reach the Cape, I stop for a few minutes far enough away from the surf to avoid getting splattered. The waves are choppy and the sea looks dark and gloomy. I raise the sides of my jacket up higher around my neck, as I feel a chill even after walking. Before long, I am ready to turn around.

 I walk back the way I came. In the roundabout, I consider stopping in at the pub, but I have no desire to make conversation with anyone I may meet, and I am bound to know people if I go inside.

 I do not know what possesses me, but on an impulse, I decide to go inside the church. I am aware of the fact that I have not been inside since the day of Julie's memorial. In fact, that one day is the only time I have ever been into this church. Yet, I have a sudden desire to go inside. The door is unlatched, and I walk in across the old flagstones into the narthex. The musty smell of old churches, especially those near the sea is prevalent. I continue soundlessly towards the door of the nave. Before I allow myself time to think, I open the door and walk inside. No one is around. The room is dark other than the waning light from the windows and the chancel lamp burning at the altar.

    This is the first time since before my mum died that I have willingly entered a church. I have no idea why I am here, but I walk towards the front, and I sit down on the first pew where I sat with Grace and Gus on that horrible day last summer. I look around and I see familiar things that remind me of my childhood church. Candles, bells, kneelers, the cross above the sanctuary. If I close my eyes, I can almost hear my father's voice reading the Gospel on a Sunday morning from my childhood years before. Just as quickly though, I imagine hearing him tell my mum and me that he is leaving us for the young parishioner who had sought him out for comfort when her father passed away the previous year. Father issues indeed. I open my eyes, so that I can dispel those memories. They are no longer welcome.

    I finally allow my eyes to stray to the location to the right of this pew where Julie's urn lay on a stand during her memorial. The stand is not there now of course, but I can remember how it looked in my head. I can imagine its shape and the weight of it when I carried it down the cliff path later that day.

I sit back in the pew, and roll my shoulders. I am at a loss to understand what I feel. Sadness? Yes, there is still sadness. I miss her every day. Even on a day such as this, if she were here beside me, there would not have been much to talk about, but we would have been together. Uncertainty and fear for the future are still present. But I think the deep pain and depression are lessening. I no longer feel as raw as I once did. However, there are two positive emotions. Hope. I feel real hope my grief is lessening and that life could be good again. But the real surprise is the second emotion. Joy. For spaces of time this last week with Alice, I felt joy again. I felt a lightness of heart and spirit I no longer thought possible for me.

I hear a noise behind me, and I look over my shoulder to see Father Ryan enter the nave. He does not see me at first. I consider slumping down in the pew to avoid a conversation, but as he is headed straight towards me, I clear my throat to acknowledge my presence.

He turns his head my direction and despite his look of surprise at seeing me, the woman who never once attended mass with her wife who was a devoted member of his church, he smiles kindly.

"Ah, Hilary." As he shuffles towards me wearing his usual black ensemble with priest collar, he sits down heavily beside me. He has always seemed to me to be an old man, as he appears grandfatherly. I realize with a jolt that he is not much older than my own father, who I have not seen in more than a decade. He rests his elbow on the pew between us, and asks, "How are you, my dear?"

I take my time answering. I am not offended by his question. I can tell he genuinely wants to know, and not in a patronizing or pacifying way. Yet I do not know him well, so I am uncertain how much to say. In my present state, I am even unsure how I am. But I remember Julie viewed him fondly, and that is good enough for me.

"I am alright, Father Ryan. Thank you for asking."

"We miss Julie here. There is not a Sunday that goes by that I do not think of her sitting on the pew behind us."

"She sat close to the front?" I ask as I glance at the pew behind me, as if I could see the mirage of her myself. I know so little about this part of her life. All I can see is her urn sitting up front. I am jealous to know this man has happy memories of her living and breathing here.

"Yes, second pew on the Gospel side. Unlike many of the congregants, she actually listened and smiled during my sermons. A priest remembers that, I can assure you. It can be rather lonely up there with everyone staring off into space."

I smile, and I feel my eyes stray to where her urn sat. He follows my gaze, and surmises what I am thinking about, because he says, "I know you may not remember, but her memorial was lovely. Everyone had wonderful things to say about her, and even now I often hear her remembered with fondness…I have not seen you much around the village. I know you must have had a difficult time."

"Yes, I have." I know I am not making this easy for him, but I am unsure what to say to alleviate his discomfort. I decide to try though as I continue softly, "It has been the most difficult sixteen months of my life. There were times that it was as though the whole world had gone dark around me. I felt as if I had been lost on the moors in a storm, but sometimes the most terrifying part is that I did not care to seek rescue. Then, at some point months and months later, the clouds began to part at times, and I would see flashes of light. Consequently, I would feel guilty I had that one second of hope, and it would put me farther in the dark again. Until the next time. And somehow the flashes of light began to occur more and more often. Only in the last couple of months has the deep sadness and burden of grief started to lift, where I feel as though I can breathe again."

"What has changed in the last couple of months?"

I feel embarrassed to tell him, but he hears confession. Mine cannot be much different than others he has heard in the past.

"I have started seeing someone."

He does not blink, "Have you now? Who is she?"

There is an ever so slight emphasis on the feminine pronoun, but I know it is his way of confirming to me that he knows who I am. He once told Julie emphatically he has a gay nephew, and he wanted us to know that we were always welcome in his church. It never made a difference to me, but I know it helped to give Julie a peace of mind that had eluded her spiritually once we became a couple.

"She lives in Penzance. Owns a shop there. Julie and I patronized her store from time to time the last few years of her life. After Julie's death, Alice befriended me. We have been dating the last few months."

"I see. She knew Julie then?"

I feel defensive, "Yes, but we only knew Alice as an acquaintance then."

"Oh, I don't doubt that, my dear. I merely perceive that this Alice has been able to help you grieve because she, too, knew what a wonderful woman Julie was."

I feel tears fill my eyes. "Yes, you are right. She has been kind and patient to watch me mourn."

"She sounds special."

"Yes…she is. I have never known anyone so willing to wait on me to heal while I grieve. She says she loves me, but I cannot seem to discern how I feel about her. I know I care for her, and I find her attractive. But I do not know if it is love. And she is so kind and loving, that she deserves to be loved in return. Not simply cared for in a relationship."

He replies, "There must be a high level of unselfishness, mercy, and grace that allows a person to give and give to someone who is grieving. All while perhaps hoping for reciprocation, yet knowing it will be months into the future, if at all."

"Yes."

"How will you know if you love her?"

"I wish I knew."

"How did you decide with Julie?"

I shrug my shoulder in a flippant gesture. "With Julie, nothing was ever a conscious decision. I saw her and I was immediately drawn to her. It was effortless. One day without thought, I told her when I walked in the door from work that I loved her, and there was no doubt in my mind from that point forward. But I did not meet Julie when I was full of grief over another woman. I have never been in this position before."

There is a comfortable silence for a few moments as we both turn our thoughts inward.

"My dear, forgive me if this is forward as I do not know you well, but you appear to be a woman of conviction. I suspect a similar event will occur with Alice one day, and when it does, your confidence will expand and you will doubt no longer. But this grief journey that you are on is not over, I fear. It would seem that it is coming to some closure, but to expect yourself to be healed at this point is not fair to you or to Alice. Do not put pressure on yourself to figure your feelings out yet. It does not sound as though she is. Give yourself some more time." It is everything within me not to roll my eyes. He senses my frustration, but he adds, "I know it is not what you want to hear. However, I am encouraged you are finding your way again." As he struggles to his feet, he says, "Hilary, I will take my leave, but know you…and Alice, are always welcome here."

I meet his eyes and thank him before he turns to leave. I watch him shuffle off, before turning to face the front again. I find myself staring at the form of Christ on the cross hanging above the altar contemplating the selfless love that a person can have for another, hoping for it to be reciprocated, but with no guarantee.

December

Chapter 16

One Sunday afternoon in the middle of December, Alice surprises me by arriving at my door with a small suitcase in hand, instead of her normal overnight bag. I had seen her pull up in the car park and walk by my kitchen window as I was clearing away dishes from my lunch a few hours ago.

I dry my hands, and hurry to the back door to let her in.

"Darling, what a lovely surprise! I didn't expect to see you until tomorrow." I lead her into the flat away from any unsuspecting guests, before allowing myself to kiss her on the lips.

She laughs as she says, "It's good to see you, too, Hil. I'm not disturbing you?"

"Of course not, I am delighted to see you. I just returned from a walk with Gus down to the coast. Absolutely glacial, it was. I still feel cold through and through. I was going to make some tea to warm up. Would you like some?"

Now, that she has stepped away from our embrace to put down her suitcase and I have stopped talking, I realize something is wrong. "Alice? Why are you here on a Sunday? And why do you have a suitcase?"

"A few reasons actually."

"Alright. Do I need to be sitting down?"

"No, nothing bad for you."

I do not ask if it is bad for her, as I know the answer already. I feel a knot in my belly form because whatever it is, I know I will feel pain with her. I vaguely realize I am healing if I can experience emotion on her behalf, but I push it away and try to focus as I wait for her to continue.

She rests one hand on the back of the dining room chair, and begins by saying, "I have been considering your suggestion…of moving in together. I do not think I am ready to move in with you yet, but I thought it might be nice to begin keeping a few things here. Perhaps several changes of clothes and a few toiletries, so if I decide to stay on the spur of the moment or forget something one night, I will not inconvenience either of us. I know I normally stay on Monday nights, but perhaps through the winter months when business is slow, I could stay two or three nights in a row each week. Charlotte can mind the shop on Mondays, so I can stay here in St. Just the entire time. Just to see how it goes. If we get on. That kind of thing."

"What a lovely idea, Alice." I start to walk towards her suitcase to suggest finding a location to put her things, when I realize there must be something else. Something that is upsetting her.

I turn away from the suitcase, and ask, "There was something else, wasn't there?"

She looks anxious, as she says, "Yes, perhaps we should sit down."

I grab her hand, and we sit on the love seat.

"I had a nightmare last night." Before I can interrupt, she says, "No, it wasn't about the rape this time." I feel my body relax slightly. "But it unsettled me. I dreamt that you were gone. I came to stay one night, and you had disappeared.

Vanished. There were new owners, and they didn't know who you were. I searched and searched only to discover that you had moved back to London. When I found you, you said you did not love me, and you wanted nothing to do with me."

"Oh, Alice. I am sorry. That is terrible, and not true. I am right here, and I want you here with me." I wait anxiously for her to look me in the eyes, hoping she does not ask me if I love her. I realize I want to protect her, but whether I love her or not, I cannot say for certain. And if I cannot say it truthfully, I will not say it. Instead, I coax, "Please, darling, look at me."

She meets my eyes, and her dark green eyes are swimming in tears.

"Hil, I need you to promise me something." I swallow as I wait for whatever she asks of me. "I need you to promise me that if you ever decide you do not want a relationship with me you tell me, so that I have closure."

I am scared by this conversation, because I cannot imagine life without Alice. I am aware my fear must be a positive reaction, but I know this is a serious request. No amount of placating will help, so I take both of her hands in my own, and say while looking her straight in the eyes, "You have my word."

She closes her eyes, and as tears seep out of them, I wipe them away before pulling her to me. I have had my fair share of nightmares, but Alice's seem to be so vivid that she struggles with letting them go. She appears stalwart most of the time, but when events like this one occur that would hardly affect other people; I realize how sensitive she is inside. Once again, I feel a strange form of protection for her; as though I need to guard her heart. I just hope I do not need to guard her from myself. When she is able to rein her emotions in, I pull her to her feet and forgetting my tea, I suggest, "Let's find a place for your things, alright?"

It takes some rearranging, but before long, I have made room in the wardrobe and closet for her clothes, and I feel both tearful and happy when she puts her toothbrush in the holder beside mine. Damn, I have been lonely for a long time.

***

That night after dinner, I ask her if she wants to knit while I read a gardening book. I put her feet in my lap, so that I can read and massage them at the same time. I am unaware that Alice is watching me. Thus, she surprises me by saying, "You told me once that Julie had wanted children, but she couldn't have any. Did you ever want children?"

I glance up from my book, and say, "God, no. I have never been maternal. But yes, Julie wanted children desperately at one time, but couldn't." I stretch my legs out in front of me, as I consider telling Alice more. I see her out of the corner of my eye watching me, so I continue. "I actually offered to have a child for Julie when we were first married and had moved here. I am sure Cornwall is a child's paradise, far better to raise a child here than in London. I could have carried one. I had gone to the doctor, and we had picked a donor, but…"

"But?" she prods.

"But my heart wasn't in it. I knew Julie wanted one, and for her, I would have done it, but she discerned I was doing it for her and not for myself as well. She said after careful thought that as grateful as she was for my willingness, she only wanted to have a baby with me if I wanted one as much as she did. She showed me a great deal of grace in giving up what she wanted desperately for me. I felt a lot of guilt for a long time after, but I have never regretted it."

She says quietly, "It sounds as though you knew how to reciprocate grace to one another." I must show my confusion, because she continues, "I simply mean that she may have shown you grace then, but you afforded her the same when she decided not to seek treatment and you supported her when it was not what you wanted."

I startle at this thought, as I realize the final hold on me for that debt of selfishness might actually have been paid. I feel good knowing that at least once I was able to show Julie how much I loved her; just as she had shown me love all those years ago.

I am curious what made Alice ask me about hypothetical children. "Why do you ask?"

"I had wanted children once a long time ago. But now at forty, I know it is unlikely. I just wondered if it was a dream of yours or not."

I reach for her hand. "Oh, I am sorry. I hope I haven't disappointed you."

"I can't say that I am surprised. But I did want to know, so I can stop wondering."

I reach across and kiss her soundly.

I ask, "Are you really staying until Tuesday morning?"

"If you will have me."

"Let's go to bed then," I say as we stand up to walk into the bedroom together.

***

Grace comes to stay with me for a fortnight during Christmas. It is lovely to see her again. Gus is a constant presence at the B&B during this time, staying every night in their room upstairs. He says he is beginning to send his CV to finance companies. He has improved and increased his father's tourism business since he has been back in Cornwall, and is hoping to leave his father to run it again next year. Gus believes the slight increase in business will allow his father to save face, as they will need to employ someone to help him.

Things look good for Gus and Grace to marry in July. They are still in the midst of immigration procedure, but they are beginning to make tentative plans for the wedding. Due to the uncertainty of when the visa will be organized, the wedding date needs to remain flexible, so they have decided to keep the ceremony small and informal.

Alice and I have been enjoying our new routine as well. She comes to stay with me on Sunday afternoons, and does not leave until Tuesday morning. Charlotte runs the shop on Mondays, and after I finish working on Monday mornings, Alice and I spend the day together. As the weather has turned cold recently, we usually stay inside the flat. I have read through a stack of books this month, some old Agatha Christie ones as well as some I picked up in Penzance recently. Alice has been knitting every day. She has made several Christmas presents, a hat for Charlotte, Grace, and Gus, and something for me, although I have no idea what it is.

She only works on my gift when I am dealing with guests or cleaning rooms, and then hides it to continue working on when she returns home later in the week.

During the two days a week we live together, I am learning so much more about her, and I find it all fascinating. She has the most unusual callouses on the tips of her fingers where the knitting needles rub against them. I have witnessed her knit one evening, run out of yarn, and undo the entire piece for the sheer desire to continue knitting. She is the tidiest person I have ever known. Even here in my flat, as soon as she finishes whatever task she is working on; everything gets cleared away and put in its place. I worried at first that perhaps she felt uncomfortable here, but I remembered how orderly her own flat has always been, and I have let it be. We have started walking together in the village and on the cliff paths, which is something I always enjoyed with Julie. By doing so, it is allowing me to make my own memories with Alice in and around St. Just. On the occasional day that the wind is not gusting, we take a brisk walk around the village and stop in at the pub for dinner. I have not been back inside the church, but it no longer feels as though I am an outcast either.

Grace and Gus are going to celebrate tomorrow on Christmas Day with Gus' family, so Alice and I orchestrate our own celebration with them on Christmas Eve. Grace decorated the tree for me when she arrived a few days ago, and the two of us have worked in the kitchen all afternoon preparing dinner. Alice is working all day as it is the last busy shopping day of the year. I do not envy her that. Gus is watching his nephew this afternoon, so that Tabitha and Stephen can ready things for Christmas morning.

Since there are only four of us tonight, we are roasting the smallest turkey we could find, with stuffing and gravy, roasted potatoes, and Julie's recipe for Devils on Horseback, which calls for bacon wrapped around a date that has been stuffed with an almond and served with chutney. I think it will be enough food, without having leftovers that waste before we can finish them. In the last eighteen months since Julie passed, I have become quite proficient in the kitchen when it comes to serving my guests breakfast, but not so much when it comes to making lavish meals such as Christmas dinner. Living alone, it does not appear Grace has spent much time cooking either, as we are both checking the recipe cards constantly to avoid any major catastrophes. We have drunk our way steadily through a bottle of wine this afternoon which is likely not helping, but we are enjoying each other's company.

Grace stops at one point and asks, "Will you go into London with me next week? I think it is time to find a wedding dress."

"Of course. Do you have anywhere in particular you wish to look? Or any style of dress in mind? We could ask Alice if she has any ideas."

"She won't be offended, will she?" I must seem confused, because she continues, "That I am not asking her to find a dress for me?"

"Oh, don't be silly. She owns a women's clothing shop, not a bridal one. But she might know of some good places. I will talk to her."

"Alright. That would be lovely. I want the dress to be simple since I want to be married on the beach. No veil or train. I was going to ask…Hilary, would it be alright if Gus and I got married in Julie's cove and then, perhaps had a reception here in the garden?"

I stop stuffing the dates, and turn to her. I cannot help the tears that spring to my eyes, as I hug her as tightly as I can. I whisper in her ear, "Nothing would make me happier." When I pull away, she has tears in her eyes as well. I add, "It would make Julie happy, too."

***

Dinner is wonderful. The four of us eat until we can eat no more. Actually, I drink more than I eat, but that is not surprising. I do not worry as I once did though. I am tipsy, but I am not drunk. I drink because I enjoy it again, not to escape from my mindless depression as I did a year ago.

After we clear the table, it is time for Christmas presents, and Gus and Grace love the hats Alice knitted for them. I hand Gus and Grace a fancy card from the Italian restaurant that I took Alice to on our first date. I have arranged for Gus and Grace to have a special dinner there while she is here during the holidays, and then a night in my best room upstairs with the picture window and the clawfoot tub in the en suite. Grace starts to argue, but I will not listen, and she stops after she realizes it is futile. Alice hands me a wrapped package in green paper and sparkly ribbon. I know this is what she has been working on for months. I open it to discover a beautiful hand-knitted cardigan. The stitching is so small and perfect; the alpaca wool is soft and warm. It is a beautiful cream color with pockets and a wide neckline. On close inspection, I see tiny beaded seed pearls on the front in a whimsical pattern. The pearls add the perfect touch for it to be dressy with the right blouse and trousers. It will go with everything in the wintertime, and will help me stay warm in the flat on cold winter nights. It must have taken her weeks to make it. I am speechless.

"Alice, it's stunning." I am hesitant. It looks too perfect to wear.

"Try it on, sweetheart. I hope it fits."

I stand up, and pull it around me. It fits impeccably. It does not swamp me as most cardigans do, but instead is fitted to my shape. I do not know why I am surprised. She has dressed me in her shop for years. She knows exactly what size I am, yet the perfection makes me understand in a new way, just how well Alice knows me.

Grace is the first to speak. "Oh, Alice, it's beautiful. You did an amazing job. You look wonderful, Hilary." Alice looks pleased, but silently waits for my reply.

I find my voice, and turn to Alice, "It's fabulous, darling. I love it." I reach down, and kiss her firmly on the lips, and when I sit down beside her, I squeeze her hand. I feel overcome with emotion. If I speak anymore, I know I will cry. It's Christmas. There should not be tears. Alice senses my emotion, as she wraps an arm around me, and kisses my forehead. "I am glad you like it," she whispers in my ear.

I feel shy to give her my own gift. It does not seem like enough. I ask Grace to hand me the large package under the tree. I have given Alice every accoutrement one could need for knitting inside a basket that will be easy for her to take back and forth to Penzance. Knitting needles in different sizes and lengths with a new case to hold them, a variety of types of yarn, and several knitting patterns for socks, as I heard her say one day she could never get the hang of it, and planned to figure it out one day. How she can figure out how to put beads on a knitted cardigan and not know how to knit socks is beyond me, but I guess we all struggle with something. I realized one day that several of Alice's knitting needles were showing signs of wear, which gave me the idea for her gift, so I hope she will like everything.

    When Alice opens it, she smiles and says, "Oh, Hil, these are wonderful." She picks each item up for closer inspection, and exclaims over everything. I feel better, as I can tell by her reaction that she does indeed like her gift. "Perhaps I will finally learn how to make socks. They are not supposed to be difficult, but have always eluded me." She kisses me on the cheek, and then it is my turn to open again.

    Grace hands me a small box, and inside is a necklace of the Catholic St. Julia. I must appear as confused as I feel, because Grace begins by asking a question, "Hilary, do you know what your name means?"

I reply, "Yes…It means cheerful." For some reason, I feel a bit foolish saying this aloud as I could not have been a less cheerful person the last eighteen months if I had tried. Grace and Gus have been sitting in the low chairs across from the love seat where I am sitting with Alice, but she stands up and comes to kneel beside me and rests her hand on my knee.

Grace says, "Yes, your name means cheerful. In one of my groups recently, we all researched and shared the meaning of our names. I happened to look up yours, and I was struck by it. Then, a few weeks ago, I read somewhere that St. Julia was known for her cheerfulness. I don't know if it will mean anything to you or not, but I remembered that the name Julie is a derivative of the name Julia, and I don't know…it sounded like hope to me. As though, St. Julia and your Julie are indeed guardian angels, and you have a promise to be cheerful again one day." She smiles at Alice, and says, "Hopefully, sooner rather than later."

Bloody hell, Grace can make me cry at a moment's notice. There is no way around it. "Oh, come here, and give me a hug." She does, and when she pulls away, I tell her. "It's a beautiful sentiment. Thank you, Grace."

***

Later that evening in bed, I ask Alice about it. "Did it bother you that Grace gave me the necklace with the reference to Julie?"

She rests her book on her chest, and glances over at me. "Not at all, sweetheart. Julie is very much a part of who you are. If thinking of her as a guardian angel helps you to continue healing, and allows you to be cheerful again as Grace suggests, then I think it is wonderful."

"Do you like Grace?"

"I do not know her well, but you do, and that speaks highly of her."

"But you aren't jealous of her?"

"I wouldn't say that. To be honest, I am a bit. You have such an easy relationship with her. But as it is not romantic, it appears almost sisterly from my vantage point.

Which is completely different from our relationship. You both connect emotionally, but I am not content with simply that. I want your body, too, and as I am the one currently beside you in bed, I trust I don't have to worry."

    I laugh aloud at that and agree with her before turning out the light.

Chapter 17

A few days later, Grace is in my flat having a glass of wine with Alice and me before bed. Gus had to help his father with something for the business, so he will be along later.

Alice says, "Grace, Hilary tells me that you are both going to London tomorrow to look for a wedding dress."

She answers excitedly, "Yes! I have not wanted to jinx it by buying one too early, but I cannot wait any longer."

Alice smiles at Grace, "I understand. You have waited a long time."

"Yes, I am afraid to hope that it will work out this time."

"I believe it will," I say with more certainty than I feel. One of us has to believe for the other. It seems to be the way our lives have worked for a long time.

Grace smiles at me, and Alice continues speaking, "I have been considering where to recommend you look for a dress, but I wanted to know first what you are hoping to find."

Grace pauses before saying, "Well, I want to be married in Julie's cove." Another brief pause, as I can tell she is uncertain if it will bother Alice by referring to Julie, but Alice is unfazed. Grace relaxes, as Alice waits for her to continue.

"I am not very formal, and it will be such a small wedding. My parents are not even coming. So, I thought perhaps a non-traditional dress. White, but tea length and maybe a full skirt. No veil or train. I want to be barefoot, as well as my guests. I hope no one thinks it is strange or too American."

Alice is nodding at Grace while she is speaking. When she finishes, Alice comments, "Who cares what anyone thinks? Your wedding day is about you and Gus. No one else."

Grace blushes and says, "Thank you."

Alice continues, "All right. I will write down a few suggestions. You may have a bit of difficulty with the time of year you are shopping, but I think you are wise to go to London. You will have more options."

I watch the two of them together, and my heart swells as I feel happy they seem to get on. I know it has been uncomfortable in the past for them to form a bond as they both care about me in completely different ways, but I am thankful they push through the discomfort and make the effort for me.

***

Late the next afternoon, Grace and I have moved our way through the list Alice made me without any success. We are both becoming discouraged, while trying to stay positive for the other. When we think we may have to come back another day, we find the last store Alice mentioned. She said she did not think it would be open this time of year, as the owner often closes for an extended break over the Christmas holiday, but she mentioned if it is open, it might be our best place to find something suitable.

When we walk through the door in a side road off Oxford Street, the shop assistant is alone behind the counter. I notice the sign on the door says the shop will close in a half hour, so I hope she will be kind and gracious to Grace instead of suggesting we come back on another day when there is more time.

The shopkeeper looks up and smiles, "Hello. How may I help you?"

Grace is on a mission. Instead of walking around, she gets right to the point, as I have witnessed her growing frustration this afternoon. She explains what she is looking for, and the girl smiles. "I think I have something you might find suitable." She motions to both of us to have a seat, and she walks into the back of the shop. The thick carpet and cream-colored walls block the noise from life outside, and wrap us in a cocoon of silence. I feel my nerves begin to calm, as somehow I know this place will have the dress she desires.

The shopkeeper returns soundlessly as the carpet hides the noise of her heels. She is holding a dress that matches the exact description of what Grace told Alice she wanted last night. It is white and tea length, a full skirt, with a fitted boat neck. Elegant, while being perfect for a coastal wedding. She holds it up, and I feel Grace's excitement become palpable, as she bounces beside me on the sofa.

"Oh! It's lovely. May I try it on?"

The shopkeeper says, "Of course. Come through."

Grace follows her, and the shopkeeper returns a moment later.

"She will be out shortly."

I nod my appreciation. When Grace walks out a few minutes later, there is no doubt in my mind she has found her dress. Despite my opinion when I see her in it, her eyes tell me how happy she is as they sparkle and shine with unshed tears. I feel my throat grow tight as I understand fully how much being in love makes us beautiful.

I stand and join her in front of the full-length mirror. I move behind her as she looks at herself in it.

I find my voice to tell her, "You are lovely."

She whispers, "This is it, isn't it?"

I nod.

She takes a big inhale, and when she forces the air out, she smiles. "I love it."

"You should. It is perfect for you." She continues to stare at herself as though she cannot believe it is really her. "Grace?" I ask.

She looks up in the mirror to meet my eyes.

I gently turn her around to face me. "Grace, I wanted to ask last night, but hesitated in front of Alice. Why aren't your parents coming to the wedding?"

She drops her eyes, and says, "Come on, Hil. You can't be surprised. I have told you they are not involved in my life. My father has some big work project going on this summer, and my mother and her husband are taking his children to Disney World the week of my wedding." She swallows, and says, "But Walter thinks he can come. Molly is pregnant again, so she and my niece will not, but if she is doing alright, he said he will."

I want to throttle her parents, so perhaps it is best they are an ocean away at the moment, but it helps me make a decision. I struggle with how to convince her.

"Grace, look at me." She does, and I continue, "I know we have a rather unconventional relationship. I consider you a close friend. But as an only child and there being a significant age difference, I also find myself thinking of you as a younger sister at times. But right now, I want to be a mum to you. I had such a close relationship to my own mum it grieves me that you do not. Buying wedding dresses and planning wedding details such as your cake and flowers should be something your mum helps with, and I want to stand in the gap. Will you allow me to do so?"

"I don't know what that even means."

"For starters, it means that I want to buy your dress for you."

"No! I couldn't possibly let you do that. You don't even know how much it costs."

"It does not matter how dear it is. I want to buy it. And I want to do your reception for you as well. Cake, food, and whatever else you would like in the garden." I can see her thoughts warring in her head, but I continue, "Please…let me. I want to do it for you and Gus, but also in a way, it would be honoring to my own mum. She passed away long before I married, but I know she would have done the same for me."

A tear escapes Grace's eye, as she nods her consent. When she goes into the dressing room to take the dress off, I turn to the shopkeeper, who has been watching us discreetly behind the counter, and tell her that we will take it. She smiles and begins making out the handwritten bill on heavy cream cardstock.

***

Later, over a glass of wine in a nearby pub, Grace squeezes my hand, and whispers, "Thank you."

"My pleasure, darling. I cannot wait to see Gus' face when he sees you wearing it."

She smiles, but then her face crumples. She covers her face with both hands as she tries to calm down.

"Darling, what's wrong?"

"I can't stand leaving him again. It is so hard."

"But you still have another four days here. Why cry now?"

"Why not? I thought after the first year and he proposed and we started to get some green lights with immigration that it would get easier to say goodbye, because I know it will not be permanently. But do I really know that? It could always change. And meanwhile, I have to leave him, you, and Cornwall every time, and return to Nashville alone. I enjoy my job, but at the end of the day, it is only a job. It pays the bills, but I am lonely every time I return home. I never want to go out with friends or make much effort, because I know everything in my life is temporary. I have no roots there anymore. But I don't exactly have roots here either."

I nod in understanding. "I know. I struggle for several days every time you leave, and I can only imagine what you and Gus go through."

She says, "Gus is so secure. Not stoic exactly, but unwavering in his belief that everything will work out. Only once have I seen him get frustrated and that was months ago when he could not get in touch with his connection in the immigration office. Otherwise, he is the one talking me off the cliff when I have a bad day or feel alone and all I want is his arms around me." Grace meets my eyes, and continues, "The sex is still wonderful. Don't get me wrong. But I wonder sometimes if by having it, we have made it harder to part each time."

I reply, "Of course you have. But it is not realistic to have a committed relationship and go without sex at this stage. Not if you are to be married soon."

"I know. I know. It's just so frustrating," she says as she runs her hand through her hair. I take another long swallow of my wine and motion for another glass from the bartender, as I watch her.

She looks across at me, and with a curious glance asks, "How is the sex with Alice?"

I smile, and reply, "Good. Very good."

She teases, "Is that all you can say?"

"Alright, after the initial learning curve and getting past the unfortunate comparisons of Julie…fantastic. It's fantastic."

She smiles at me, and I feel excited at the prospect of seeing Alice tomorrow.

January

Chapter 18

Tourism is almost non-existent this time of year in Cornwall. There are the occasional people who stay one night passing through to somewhere else or couples who come for the weekend to get away from their fast-paced urban life. During the week though, there are days that go by without any guests. It does not help that the weather is far from ideal this time of year. The cold and rain combined with strong wind means that one must bundle up to brave the elements. In my flat, I wear my handmade cardigan from Alice every day. When I feel lonely at night, it makes me feel comforted as well as warm.

This January, I do not mind the weather or the lack of business. I do not remember last January. My only real memory about last winter is staying indoors the majority of the time and often having the television on for company. Some days, it was the only conversation I heard. I would watch whatever the BBC deemed fit to show, as I was too depressed to concentrate on reading, even books I had read before. This was the period of time when I stayed in my bathrobe and drank far too much.

This year, I am better. Not completely healed, but I struggle with that concept. Do I want to be completely healed? What does that even mean? Because if it means I have to move on and not think of Julie every day, I do not want to be. I want to maintain status quo. I am content with my semi-dysfunction. I am used to it. I can function, and I have a relationship. No, we are not truly living together, and I still have not determined my feelings for Alice, but I am better. I am not depressed, and the sadness is only present when I go to bed alone. And in the mornings if I wake up alone. And when I eat alone. Perhaps I do have room for improvement, but I am getting there. I know I am.

One week towards the end of the month, I look at my registry, and there is not a single booking for the next three nights. On an impulse, I ring Heather. She answers and within a few minutes, I make arrangements with her to check in for a couple of hours every day, collect the post, check messages, and ring me if we do receive any bookings. Then, I ring Alice.

"Daffodil Yellow. This is Alice Mills. May I help you?"

"Hello darling! It's me."

"Oh! How are you, Hil?"

"I'm well. I wondered…I know you just left here yesterday, but would you like a bit of company this week? I do not have any bookings, and Heather has said she could mind things around here for me until the weekend."

There is a fraction of a second delay, before she replies, "I'd be delighted. When will you come?"

I ignore the perceived hesitancy. "This afternoon?"

"Lovely. I look forward to it."

When I end the call, I have to focus on breathing, as I realize my anxiety has spiked, as I believe Alice's did just now. She said all the right words, but she sounded as I imagine I did…rather uncertain and hesitant to see how this change in our routine will affect us. Well, no escape now. I am committed, and I am excited, damn it. Nervous, too. I square my shoulders and go back into the flat to pack for the rest of the week.

***

It is not exactly awkward arriving at Alice's flat later this afternoon, but it is different. Alice's flat is so opposite of mine. Being on the first floor, it gets more natural light than my own, and she has everything decorated in rich creams and beiges with gold and silver accents. It feels luxurious, with a vintage flair everywhere I turn. After climbing the stairs, I walk through the main room into her bedroom and leave my overnight bag to deal with later. The room feels so warm and perfect, yet nothing personal is in view. I realize as I walk around that she does not have any pictures out, no glasses on the bedside table, no shoes on the floor, nothing to show that anyone is in residence. It could be a guest room in my own house, except it would be the nicest room if it was. I consider my B&B to be clean and organized, but Alice seeks perfection. The only thing out of place is my own bag by the door. I suddenly feel self-conscious, as though I have disturbed her sanctuary, so I move it from view around to my side of the bed, before joining her back in the shop. She closes up for the day, and as we had not planned this evening, I offer her dinner in the pub.

While Julie and I were known in St. Just as the local lesbians, we were always treated with respect and kindness. Within the first year, whatever interest people had, died down. We were simply Julie and Hilary there. Here in Penzance, everyone is kind, but curious. Alice and I have eaten in her local pub now numerous times together, and still, the regulars stare at us for much of the evening. No one is rude or unkind, but I can read the questions in their eyes. It has been my experience that people stare until they know for certain, and once they determine the answer, the novelty dies down.

Usually, I am not big on public displays of affection, but I reach for Alice's hand several times this evening, and meet several of the men's eyes at the bar while doing so. However, each time I do, she squeezes my hand and releases it quickly, but I do not pick up on her hint. After I pay the tab, I deliberately lean over to kiss Alice on the mouth before standing up.

When we step outside, Alice confronts me by asking, "Why did you do that?"

"What do you mean?"

"You know what I mean."

"I just thought it would be good for everyone to know, so they can stop staring and wondering."

"Did it ever occur to you that I might not want everyone to know?"

I stop short. "What are you saying? You surely cannot mean you are still in the closet here?" I ask incredulously.

"I haven't exactly advertised it. I own a local business in a small city where people are still rather traditional. Perhaps you and Julie got away with it, but that has never been my experience."

"But we have kissed before in other public areas around town and in St. Just."

"But nowhere I am known. It's not the same as my local pub three doors down from my shop and flat," she replies.

We have arrived at Alice's flat, and I follow her upstairs. She heads straight for the kitchen and puts the kettle on for tea.

"I know it has been a long time, but what did you do in the past? You have had relationships here before, haven't you?"

She is obviously annoyed as she speaks quickly, "My last relationship with the woman I bought merchandise from did not entail dating in public. Either I saw her here in the flat, or I met her in other locations outside Penzance. It was all rather clandestine. I told you, it was never serious. Before that, my last girlfriend was someone I worked with in London. She and I were together for a couple of years. We tried to make it work when I moved here, but within a year of travelling back and forth and no desire for either of us to move to live with the other, we broke up. That was all years and years ago, and I was so young and starting out in business, that I never dated in public here. I am sure people have wondered about me, but until tonight, I have never given them any proof."

I feel at a total loss of what to say or do. "I'm sorry. I didn't realize. I did not know you wanted to keep us a secret."

She sighs impatiently, "Hil, it cannot be a secret. I know that. But I just hoped to keep everyone guessing a little while longer. That's all. Forget it." The water has boiled and she pours it into an old chipped teapot on the sideboard, and carries it and two teacups to the dining table.

I am sorry if I put Alice in an untenable situation, but I also find myself feeling hurt, as though she has rejected me in public for all to see. I have not dealt with keeping a relationship secret in two decades. It feels foreign and leaves a bad taste in my mouth.

We sit down, and I watch Alice begin to drink her tea. I feel as though I may cry, which would only make a bad situation worse. I excuse myself and go to the loo. At least, I can have some privacy for a few minutes. I wipe the tears, blow my nose, and wash my hands, and when I look at myself in the mirror, I see a sad woman staring back at me. She looks overly tired, and the lines around her mouth and eyes are more pronounced. A few more grey hairs have appeared overnight as well. My perception of Alice's hesitancy on the phone earlier when I asked to stay this week makes all the more sense, as people will surely notice if I am here for several days. I will not put her in that position. I have not unpacked yet; I will go collect my things and head home. The thought of returning to my large, silent house tonight makes me feel sad, but better that than staying here.

While I am staring at myself in the mirror, there is a soft knock on the door. I grab one last tissue and try to wipe my eyes before opening it.

Alice is standing there, crying as well. Damn it.

She speaks first, "I am sorry. I realized when you went to the loo that I hurt your feelings. I am not ashamed of you or of our relationship. I recognize I have a lot of shame about myself still, but I am forty years old, damn it. We should not have to keep anything a secret. I need you in my life, and who cares what anyone else thinks? Will you…please forgive me?"

How many times have I hurt Alice? I fear to know the answer, so I muster more grace from within than I thought possible, and I tell her with more confidence than I feel, "Of course, darling. But I don't want to push you if you are not ready. God knows, you waited for me awhile. If you need more time, perhaps it is my turn to wait for you."

"No!" She steps forward and I look up into her eyes as I have already removed my shoes and she has not, which places me at a disadvantage. She turns my face to hers and kisses me, and says, "I have waited long enough for you, Hil. I am not waiting any more. I will just have to get over myself!" She laughs and I somehow smile back.

***

I wake up in the middle of the night to discover that Alice is not beside me. I turn over to read the clock and it's after four. I wait a minute or two in case she has gone to the loo, but when she does not return, I put my bathrobe on to go find her. The door to the loo is shut, and a sliver of light shows underneath. Just as I am about to knock, I hear retching sounds. My concern changes to alarm as I knock and ask at the same time, "Alice? Are you alright, darling?"

I hear her say, "Yes, I am fine. Go back to bed, Hil."

"I will not. Not until I am sure you are alright. It sounds as though you are retching."

"I will be fine."

She sounds weak. What the hell is going on? "Alice, I want to see you. Let me in."

I hear her sigh, before hearing the toilet flush and the door unlock and then she says, "Fine. Have it your way."

I turn the handle, and when I open the door, Alice is sitting on the cold floor wearing only her slip. She is flushed and beats of sweat are on her pale freckled skin. I kneel beside her. "Darling, are you ill? What's wrong?"

She makes eye contact, and says as though I am dim-witted. "Hilary, I told you, I am fine."

"Then what's wrong?"

She looks up, arches an eyebrow, and asks, "Presumably you have the same problem once a month?"

I suddenly understand, but my brain still feels muddled. "Of course I do. You know that already. But retching can't be normal."

"Of course it is. For me, at least. I have done it for years."

"Every month?" I ask disbelieving.

"Most months. Even when I do not retch, I feel queasy."

"Why haven't I noticed this already? We have been together at this time of the month before."

"Not on the first day. I have purposely been occupied the time or two you have wanted to get together."

"You are well by day two?"

She leans her head back against the wall and nods her head yes.

I do not know what to say. More than two decades of retching once a month seems absurd. I cannot imagine. I thought I had it bad because in the last few years mine come quicker than the average twenty-eight days. Now, I feel as though I won the lottery.

"Did you know it would happen this morning? Is this part of why you almost told me no yesterday on the phone?"

She does not deny the hesitancy I heard. "Yes, I considered it. I am a day early though. I had hoped it would hold off until you left."

"What can I do? What do you normally do?"

"Nothing. On days like today, Charlotte minds the shop, and I lie down with a hot water bottle all day."

"Alright, well, are you done retching?" She looks doubtful, so I tell her that I will get the hot water bottle ready. I go into the kitchen and turn the kettle on. As I stand at the counter waiting on the water, I yawn. I am tired. I pour the hot water in, and I carry it back to the loo. Alice has not moved. I hand her the hot water bottle, and I ask her if she wants her bathrobe.

She shakes her head no, while moving the bottle across her abdomen. She stretches her long legs out in front of her, and closes her eyes. "I am hot, but this feels good. Thank you."

"Of course." I sit down on the floor beside her, and her eyes spring open. She asks, "What are you doing?"

"Sitting with you, of course. I am concerned about you if you haven't noticed."

"I am used to it."

"I am *not* used to it."

"You should rest…you'll be getting yours later today, you know."

I think about it, and she is right, of course. Our bodies have synced together in more ways than one. "Oh, bloody hell."

She laughs, and says, "That's one way to put it."

***

Later in the morning, I go downstairs to the shop to notify Charlotte that Alice is unwell. Charlotte is in her early twenties, petite, and has long blonde hair. She looks up when I walk in, and before I can tell her that Alice will not be down today, she figures it out.

"Ah, it's that lovely time of the month isn't it? I thought so when you were the one to come down, and not Alice. No matter. Tell her that I will mind things. No need to worry."

I feel rather put out Charlotte knows Alice's body clock better than I do. Something that before today was previously unknown to me is common knowledge to her employee. I know this is because they see each other almost every day, and clearly Alice must depend on her often, but I head back upstairs feeling rather discomfited.

Alice has moved past the retching phase and is now in bed. I go to check on her. The blinds and curtains are pulled shut, and the sunlight is barely showing through a few chinks.

"Darling? Do you need anything?" I reach to feel the hot water bottle and it has gone cold. I pick it up, but she reflexively grabs at it. I realize she is barely awake. She squints at me, and I lean down to whisper, "Let me get more hot water. I will be right back."

When I return, she grabs the hot water bottle and puts it back on her abdomen. I start to leave the room, thinking I will read or watch television, when Alice says softly, "Hil, come back to bed. You have been up for hours. You need rest, too. I will be fine, and so will Charlotte."

I do not take any more convincing. I change back into my warm pajamas from the night before. I am exhausted. We sat on the cold floor for two hours this morning, until Alice's stomach settled. I held her hair back from her face while she retched twice more; afterwards wiping her face with a cold flannel. She never once complained. I understood that she really does deal with this every month. She was almost blasé about it. While she obviously does not feel well, she takes the day off, and waits for tomorrow. Meanwhile, I would not dare to complain after watching Alice this morning, but I can tell that I am about to join her in her monthly plight. Thankfully, I have never retched from it, but I do tend to have a great deal of back pain that sometimes causes spasms, as well as general exhaustion. As I sit on the edge of the bed and fling my robe towards the foot of the bed, I stifle a low groan, as I feel my back stiffen and protest.

Alice raises her head off the pillow behind me. "What's wrong?" she asks.

"Nothing. Bit of back pain is all."

I turn to get under the duvet rather stiffly, and she says, "Told you it would be today for you as well."

"Oh piss off."

She chuckles, and as she turns towards me, she flings her arm over my side and is asleep within minutes.

February

Chapter 19

February arrives in Cornwall, and while winter is here in force, and tourists are still an irregular occurrence, I am in a state of contentment. Alice comes to stay with me several days a week and I have gotten into the habit of going for a night or two to Penzance in the middle of the week if I do not have any guests. I will only be able to stay with her until the end of this month, as the rest of the year, it will be more common to have guests ring or stop by without warning looking for a room. I would like to ask Alice to move in permanently sometime in the spring, but I do not think it is fair to ask her until I can tell her in good faith that I love her. So, I continue to wait for an epiphany.

I have gotten used to being with her though. I love watching her knit, hearing the sound of her low chuckle, and the patient way she speaks and holds herself. She is controlled, but in a calm manner, and I realize she gives me this incredible sense of peace and contentment. The weekends when we both work the longest hours have become long and dull. I watch from the window on Sunday nights for her car to appear, and I cannot bear to say goodbye in Penzance later in the week when it is time to return home.

We have been discussing the idea of going back to Spain or possibly somewhere in the UK to celebrate Valentine's Day. I am full with guests on Valentine's weekend; it tends to be a busy time in the midst of winter as people want a romantic getaway, but I could get away the week or two after. Nothing has been decided though, and I am trying not to put pressure on myself. As long as I can spend some time with Alice, it will not matter where we are.

One Tuesday in the second week of February, Alice heads back to Penzance after our usual two nights together. I do not have any guests until the weekend, and while I had contemplated going to Penzance with her for a few nights, I have decided I should stay here and give everything a thorough spring cleaning before guests arrive in a few days. I have decided that if I can focus and get everything done in a timely manner, I might reward myself with staying in

Penzance tomorrow night. But first, I need to take care of my to-do list.

In years past, during the month of February, Julie and I would spend time cleaning gradually; only one or two projects a day as there was never any rush this time of year. But when there are no guests or activity in the house during the week, I often want to be anywhere but here. I wish that I could be comfortable here on my own, and perhaps if it was better weather where I could work in the garden, I could. But when I am alone staring at the four walls of my flat, it is hard to not become a bit sad and depressed again.

I walk Alice out to her car, and as I give her a lingering kiss goodbye, she gets into it and drives off. As I watch her pull out onto the road, I feel the chill of the wind cut into me, and I hurry back inside.

I return to my bedroom and change into work clothes, an old pair of jeans, a flannel shirt, and flats. I tie my hair up and go into the lounge, where I refer to the list I created last night. I need to take down the curtains in every room, and take them to the cleaners. The blinds and baseboards all have to be dusted. Then, the linen closet needs to be thoroughly inspected, and an order placed for new towels and sheets as well as guest toiletry items. Next, I must go through each room, checking the radiators, hot and cold taps, televisions, and radios to make sure everything is in working order. This is only my starting list. I know there will be more I add after I go through each room, but I decide to go to the garage to find the stepladder to take down the curtains first.

  I have been working for about two hours, when I have finished pulling all of the curtains down, and I have folded them neatly to fit in the car this afternoon to take them to the cleaners. They were a dusty mess, as I knew they would be. I have been coughing and sneezing all morning as a result. My stomach is beginning to grumble, and I am contemplating what I will make for lunch, as I begin to carry the curtains downstairs. On my third and final trip down, I hear the front door open, and I look up over the pile of curtains that I am carrying, feeling disconcerted, as I would hate to have a guest when every room is in disarray. I can barely see over all that I am carrying, but I can make out a woman coming through the inside door.

"Hello?" she asks in a soft timid voice that makes my spine tingle as I know I should recognize it, and I am scared to discover for what reason.

I manage to say hello as I carefully maneuver around the counter in the lounge, where I can deposit the load of curtains on the floor to deal with later. As I straighten up to look at my caller, I wish the ground would open and swallow me whole.

For standing there before me, looking as youthful and beautiful as she did the last time I saw her twenty years ago is Margaret. My first girlfriend, my first lover, my first everything. Somehow she looks the same as she did in university. Her hair is still long and wavy, a lighter brown than my own. I think I detect a few grey hairs, but that is the only indication of age on her person. Her blue eyes are still crystal clear and the marks around her eyes and mouth could only be considered beautiful and an affirmation of a life enjoyed. Her figure is still trim and petite as it was last time I saw her, and I find myself lost in memories.

In seconds, my brain cycles through flashes: a memory of her laughing at my disastrous attempt to dye my own hair in university, one of her wearing glasses late at night holding a cup of coffee as she tried to cram for an exam the next morning, one of her wearing her favorite old sleep shirt from a holiday to the States that said, *Virginia is for Lovers*, another of her looking sleepy and flushed after making love, and finally, one of her crying over me and the hurt and pain I caused her. My heart constricts as I think through this film in my head in moments that feel like a lifetime. She is staring at me, lost in her own thoughts, waiting on me to acknowledge her presence.

"Margaret." That is all I can say. I have no other words.

She smiles at me, "Hilary, it is good to see you."

I realize I am wearing my work clothes, hardly dressed as I would wish to be when seeing my former girlfriend from university.

"I apologize for my appearance. I have been doing a bit of spring cleaning."

"You look good to me." She says in her soft voice. I remember thinking that her voice sounded like warm honey, as though it was being poured slowly, and her words were sweet and too pure to rush through.

I swallow as I search for something to say. "I...I was just about to make some lunch. Would you care to join me?"

"I would love to."

I lead her back to my flat, and she follows me inside. I feel jittery and nervous, as though being in such close quarters will burn my skin alive with my lustful thoughts. Because no matter how much I now care about Alice, to deny the fact that my body is alive with former thoughts and memories of my life with Margaret would be a total lie. I tell her to have a seat, and I set about preparing sandwiches, cutting up fruit, and reheating some scones from breakfast. I ask her if she would like tea or wine, and she asks for a glass of wine. I open a bottle from the night before that I did not finish, as Alice so rarely drinks with me, and I pour the rest in two glasses. After bringing everything over to the table, I sit down across from her.

My curiosity is getting the better of me. "What brings you to Cornwall in the middle of winter?"

"I came to see you."

"I thought you were living in Italy, with uh…Eleanor, isn't it?"

"Wasn't it. Eleanor and I broke up before Christmas."

"I am sorry."

She becomes serious, "Not half as sorry as I was when I heard about Julie. I did not know until I moved back to England last month. I am so sorry, Hil. I cannot imagine what you have gone through." She leans across to squeeze my hand, and I freeze at her touch. It is both eerily familiar and foreign all at once.

"Yes, well."

"How are you coping?" She glances around the room. "I know Cornwall is not exactly the hub of the country. Are you keeping busy or retreating from life?"

I know she remembers how I would withdraw from people when life got stressful in university. When my mum became increasingly ill, I would throw myself into my studies and not go out with friends for long spans of time. Likewise, I would behave the same when I would have one of my few interactions with my father. I would feel lost, hurt, and alone, and in turn, I would create my own aloneness around me.

"I am not exactly busy this time of year, but I am staying active. She passed the June before last. I have had time to get used to it, unfortunately."

"I never met her, of course, but the few times we spoke over the years, you were always so happy. I know she must have been special."

I wonder what she means by this comment. Is she implying that Julie must have been special for me to have been faithful to her for fifteen years, when I could not for one year with Margaret? Even as I think this, I know it is false. Margaret never had a vindictive bone in her body. The vitriol is within me. The lingering hatred I feel towards myself for cheating on her all those years ago and becoming for a brief time like my father. Seeing her brings it all back, because although I know that we ended because Margaret no longer trusted me, it was also because I could not forgive myself for my actions, and if I could not or would not, there was no hope for us even if Margaret wanted to continue. Now, I find myself asking, why is she here? I can feel all of my emotions stirring in the pit of my belly, and it feels like I am spinning out of control.

When I do not speak, Margaret continues, "You were married for a long time, right?"

"Ten years. Together for five before that."

"I thought so. You met only a few years after university."

"Yes." I do not want to elaborate. It feels like a betrayal of Julie somehow. Margaret was my first love, the person I thought I would be with forever, and instead she broke up with me. Rightly so, I cannot fault her for it, but I had my heart broken for a long time afterwards. I do not relish opening up the emotions of that time, nor of Julie's passing. It feels far too vulnerable with someone I no longer know.

Margaret senses this, and lets me off the hook as she used to do, by deflecting the conversation, "Eleanor and I never married. We were together for seven years, but she left me for someone else before Christmas. I have not had a good track record, I'm afraid. I keep repeating the same mistakes as my mum. I thought by choosing women, I would protect myself, but that hasn't been the case." She struggles not to become emotional as she speaks in her lilting voice. I do not know what to say in reply, as I am part of her track record. I know she is not speaking out of anger or resentment, yet it is clear she is hurt, and so it still feels like a slap in the face.

Instead, I deflect the conversation myself by asking, "How is your mum?"

"Oh, she is on husband number five these days. This one is ten years her senior, wealthy of course, and they are currently living in Barbados. I have thought about going to visit this spring. England is already wearing me down with the weather. I have gotten used to living in the sun every day."

"Cornwall will not help your mood this time of year, I'm afraid."

"Cornwall was not why I came."

I do not know what is going on. Is she chatting me up? Or only trying to be friendly? Either way, I have no idea why she is here. We have already established that Margaret cannot bear to be cheated on. Clearly, I have crossed that boundary before. So what possible reason would she have to want contact with me again? Regardless of the answer, we have finished lunch, and I do have work to do today.

"Margaret, I have to take my curtains to the cleaners this afternoon. Are you staying somewhere in the area?"

"Here with you, if it would not put you out."

"No, I do not have any guests at the moment, but I just removed all the curtains this morning. I will not have them back up for a few days. I do have blinds, but they will likely let in a lot of light. I could perhaps put you in a room that does not get direct sunlight in the mornings."

"That sounds lovely."

"How long do you plan to stay?"

"I don't know yet."

"Right. Well, let me find you a key and get you sorted in a room."

Fifteen minutes later, we have carried her luggage upstairs and I have put her in the double room facing west towards the water. She has brought enough to stay a fortnight.

I load the car with the curtains, and I head straight to the cleaners. I am becoming increasingly agitated on the drive. Now that I am not in her presence, my brain is contemplating things that I previously could not when I was in survival mode. The number one thing I have realized is that I never told Alice about Margaret. I remember showing the picture album to Grace last summer, and telling her I would tell Alice, but I did not want to on our first date. Soon after when perhaps I could have shared my history, Alice shared her own past, and I never thought about it again. Until today of course.

I have a bad feeling in the pit of my stomach that I have to find a way to tell Alice straightaway. No matter how I tell her, I fear the consequences. Alice and I have never shared our lists in detail. I know about Ruth, but the other women Alice has been with are all nameless. She knows about Julie, but I have never shared about the others. But the problem is that I cheated on Margaret and with every other woman I have ever been with I always told them about Margaret out of courtesy, as a way to hold myself accountable to not repeat my mistake. By not telling Alice, I have opened myself up to having her not trust me. At the very least, it will be hurtful for her to know that I shared with everyone before her, but not her. I am not sure why I did not tell her. I do not think it was intentional. I think it has more to do with the fact that it has been so long ago and is no longer important to me. But it should have been for Alice's sake. I have been selfish, and I am afraid it will cost me dearly.

Chapter 20

I have wound myself up tight, because as soon as I return home from the cleaners, I ring Grace on video chat. I move the laptop to the dining table and sit in front of it. I did not tell her I wanted to speak today, so I wait anxiously, hoping she will answer.

The screen changes, and there she is in her office with a concerned look on her face. She is wearing her black dress from Julie's memorial with a long sleeve cardigan and scarf. How fitting for me to ring today, when this could be the death of my current relationship.

"Hilary! Hi! How are you?"

I waste no time with niceties, "I've screwed up royally this time, Grace. I need you to talk me off the cliff."

"Oh god, what's wrong? Did you and Alice fight?"

"Not yet."

"Don't keep me guessing. Spill it."

I take a deep breath, and I ask, "Do you remember me telling you about Margaret last summer?"

"Your first girlfriend in university. She broke up with you when you slept with your unethical boss for a job."

"She broke up with me when I cheated on her. Quit trying to skew the facts for my integrity. It did not exist at that point in my life."

"Whatever. So, what's happened?"

"Margaret is here."

"What?" she asks incredulously.

"She showed up out of the blue today. She is staying in the double room facing the sea."

Grace starts to stammer as she does not know what to say first.

I continue, "I don't know why she is here or how long she is staying. She apparently broke up with her partner before Christmas. She came back to England last month."

"Wasn't she living in Italy?" she finally manages to ask.

"Yes."

"What does she look like?"

"Is that all you can think to ask? I am in crisis, and you want to know what she looks like?"

"Yes."

"Oh hell, she looks bloody fantastic. She has not aged except for about two grey hairs. She could pass for late twenties. I do not know how she has managed not to get wrinkles in the Italian sun, but she is still beautiful."

Grace appears thoughtful. "Why are you in crisis, Hil? What does Alice say about her being there?"

I cannot meet her eyes. She says, "She doesn't know, does she?"

"No. I never even told her about Margaret."

"What?" again, the incredulity.

"I forgot."

"In more than six months of dating and living part-time together, you forgot to tell her that you cheated on your first girlfriend when you have told everyone else you have ever dated?" Now, I finally hear the judgment that I was afraid to hear when I first told Grace about Margaret last summer. But I deserve it and more.

"Hilary, why is she even there?"

"I don't know. I asked, and all she said was that she came to see me. She apparently just heard about Julie a month ago when she returned to England. Someone from university or London must have told her. We did have some of the same friends for many years. Any number of people could have told her."

"She wants you back."

"Oh, don't be silly."

"I'm not, Hil. And you know it. In your heart of hearts, you know it. Why else would she come all the way to Cornwall when she could have easily sent you a sympathy card? She broke up with her partner, and it has now been a respectable length of time since Julie passed. Did you at least tell her about Alice?"

"No. I barely told her anything. I was in shock seeing her."

Grace runs her hand through her hair and I hear her stifle a groan.

"You have to get rid of her, Hilary. Tell her about Alice and ask her to leave. And you have to tell Alice as soon as possible. Everything. And you need to pray hard that she forgives you." She softens her voice, as she continues, "I am sorry for the tough love, Hil. I…watched you struggle for so long without Julie, and now, you finally seem to be happy with Alice. I would hate for you to throw that away by something that should stay in the past."

I nod and exhale forcefully. "I know. That's why I rang you. I knew you would be honest. Do you think Alice will forgive me?"

"I don't know. I don't know her that well, or what the past trauma is that you have mentioned."

"But do you think she will?"

"I hope so, but if you are looking for honesty, I think there is a good chance it will take a while for her to move past this."

I say goodbye, and I go into my bedroom to weep.

***

    I do not leave my bedroom all evening. I forget all of the work that I had wanted to accomplish today. At one point, I get up to close the blinds, and I return back to my bed hoping this is all a bad dream. I hear a knock on the door later in the evening, but I ignore it. I know Grace is right, but I cannot get rid of her tonight. I am an innkeeper, and I have given her a room. I will try to get rid of her at breakfast tomorrow.

    I stare at the ceiling, and I consider my conversation with Grace. Margaret wants to get back together. I can feel it in the itching of my palms. I can hear it in the pounding of my eardrums. I can see it in the way she carries herself and the effort she has taken in her appearance. I can sense it like an animal. It feels feral and primal. There may be many years since our last time together, but I doubt anyone ever forgets what their first love was like, and when confronted with it after so many years, it is impossible not to wonder what it would be like to be with her again.

I can easily imagine what it would be like to go to bed with her. I did it often enough in those days. It was all so new and illicit; as we were each other's first. While it still feels exciting to imagine, it is not tantalizing. I do not feel trapped by these thoughts as though I must act on them to be free of them. Instead I shift to thinking about being in a relationship with her; surprisingly, I feel nothing. No desire to spend time with her. No desire to know her again. Nothing.

As my mind cycles through, I think of the other observation Grace made that she is right about…Alice. I am in trouble, and I know it. But I do not know what to do. At this point, it is too late to plan anything. I must come clean with everything the moment I can. And as Grace suggested, I need to pray and hope Alice will forgive me.

After a long time, I manage to get out of bed long enough to turn off the lights in the kitchen and living room before returning to bed. I ignore the grumblings of my stomach, as penance for my behavior. I try to get some sleep before dealing with Margaret tomorrow.

***

The next morning, I dress and prepare for breakfast as I would for any other paying guest. I remember that Margaret is allergic to eggs and prefers tea, so I prepare some oatmeal, fruit, and bacon, with a pot of tea. I have set a table in the guest dining room for her in front of the window, and as I bring in her pot of tea from the kitchen, I hear her come down the stairs.

When she enters the dining room, I am speechless. She is wearing a red cashmere sweater and black trousers. She has curled her long hair in soft waves, and I feel like she has cast a spell over me.

She smiles and says, "Good morning!" She looks over my shoulder and sees the table set for one. When she meets my eyes again, she appears hurt, "Am I not eating with you?"

I try for casualness, but fail as I say awkwardly, "No, you are a guest. I thought you would like overlooking the back garden."

"I would rather eat with you," she says, but she does sit down at the table and looks out the window.

I bring her plate and when I set it down in front of her, she says, "You remembered."

"I remembered what?"

"That I am allergic to eggs, and that I love oatmeal."

"Yes."

"I wonder what other things you remember about me."

"I couldn't say."

"I wish you would."

Yes, she is definitely chatting me up. The words, the smile, the eye contact, the coyness. Any hope that Grace was wrong yesterday is gone. I am uncomfortable directly confronting this though, so instead I try a different approach.

"Are you headed back to London today?"

"Why would I do that? I just got here."

Damn. "How long are you planning to stay?"

"As long as you will have me. I had hoped we could spend some time together."

"I am in the midst of spring cleaning. This weekend is Valentine's and all of my rooms are full."

"Are you full tonight?"

"No," I say quietly. I do not add that she is my only guest. She has figured it out.

"I had thought I would walk around the village today. Maybe down the cliff path. What do you say I do that this morning, and then we have lunch together later?"

I agree, because I do not know how to say no. She stands up to leave, and before she walks out of the room, she kisses me on the cheek, and whispers, "See you at lunch."

***

I throw myself into cleaning. Somehow I fool myself into thinking that if I can work hard enough and fast enough, I can drive this anxiety out of my mind. Instead, it seems to increase and rumble away as a volcano that is about to erupt. I accomplish a great deal by lunch, and when I hear Margaret knock on my door, I am ready for her.

When I open it, I say more brightly than I feel, "The sun is out today. Shall we eat outside in the garden?"

Within a few minutes, we are seated side by side on the garden bench, and as usual, I am coping by drinking wine. She chats for a while about her walk in the village and climbing down the cliff path by the cove. She has fallen in love with the natural beauty as do many of the people who visit for the first time.

There is silence, and I realize she has asked a question that I did not hear. "I am sorry. What did you ask?"

"I asked how you have managed since Julie passed."

I feel my neck tense at the question and a throbbing begins at my temples. "It has not been easy. It is one day at a time really."

"But surely it has not been as simple as that. I mean, you don't exactly have family anymore. And all our London friends say you rarely visit."

"Were you expecting to find me in a bathrobe and my hair not washed?"

"Be fair, Hilary. I am only asking because I am concerned. I was with Eleanor for seven years, and even two months after breaking up, I still struggle to get dressed in the morning."

"You fooled me."

She sounds exasperated, "All right. So, you are okay. You are doing well. Is that what I am supposed to believe?"

"Yes."

"Alright, well perhaps I should go back to London tomorrow."

Oh, thank God. "Yes, perhaps."

"I will see you later."

I nod, and she gets up and goes around to the front door.

I feel a little guilty at my refusal to engage in a meaningful conversation, but the relief at having gotten rid of her far outweighs the guilt. I decide not to return to work upstairs yet, as I hope she will leave for the afternoon again. Instead, I return to the cleaners. They told me they were slow yesterday, and thought they could have all of the curtains ready by this afternoon.

By the time I return home with them, I venture upstairs to get back to work. I walk softly by her closed door, but after a few minutes of working in the next room, I am confident she has gone out for the afternoon. After getting all of the curtains rehung in the vacant rooms, I focus on dusting.

As the afternoon sun starts to set and brightens the upstairs rooms facing west, I go downstairs to ring Alice. It is closing time for her shop, so I am confident I will reach her.

"Hello?"

"Hello, darling. It's me. Listen, I know I told you that I had hoped to come to Penzance and stay tonight, but I am knackered. I have not gotten near as much done as I had hoped, so would it be alright if I came tomorrow afternoon and took you to lunch instead?"

"Of course. Are you alright though? You do not sound well."

"I am fine, darling. Really, I am. But I do want to see you and talk to you soon. I…I miss you, Alice."

"Oh, Hil. I miss you, too. I look forward to seeing you tomorrow, alright?"

I ring off, and I sit down on the love seat for a few minutes. I have not exactly lied about anything with Margaret. Alice has never asked detailed questions about anyone from my past, but I know I have lied by omission nonetheless. Tomorrow, I will make it right. Somehow.

Because I miss Alice. I really do. And I think it is because I love her.

I say it aloud to try out how it sounds, "I love Alice. I love her."

It feels real. Authentic. I want her in my life. I need her in my life. I want her here every day. I want to see her smile, and hear her laugh. I want to gaze up into her eyes, and scan her long frame on the way up. I want to count the freckles on her face and chest. I want to hear her knitting needles clack back and forth while I read. I want to travel to Spain with her again and swim topless in the warm sea. I want to hear her fall asleep at night. Every night. I want to wake up beside her in the morning. Every morning. I even want to do the hard things like hold her hair when she retches every month and wake her up and hold her when she has one of her nightmares. I want and need her, because I love her. Pure and simple.

Feeling suddenly energized at the epiphany I have been waiting so long for; I decide to finish the room I was working on earlier before dinner. I work for about an hour before I hear the front door open and close and footsteps on the stairs. I am on my knees cleaning the baseboards, when I sense Margaret standing in the doorway.

I look up, and there she is. She is as beautiful as always, but I feel more confident now. As though I know who I am again and who I want to be with now. I no longer feel uncertain.

"Hello Margaret. Have a nice afternoon?"

"Yes, I did. The wind was not strong, and the sun stayed out all day."

"You were lucky."

"Yes."

"Oh, I was going to offer to hang your curtains back up for you. I picked them up from the cleaners this afternoon. If you like, I can do it now, and you will sleep better tonight."

She nods, and I stand up and collect the remaining curtains off one of the chairs. Normally, I would enter a guest's room to tidy each morning without thought, but this morning, I felt as though it would have been trespassing to have done so in Margaret's room.

She follows me inside, and I return to the other bedroom for the stepladder. When I walk back in, she is sitting on the edge of the bed watching me.

"I cannot believe that it has been twenty years since we have seen each other."

"Yes."

"You have not changed, Hil."

"I am not sure how to take that."

I look back at her to see her arch her eyebrow, and shrug her shoulder. "Take it how you like. You always were good at deflecting the conversation. If someone was not in your circle of friends, it did not matter what she did, you would not let her inside. I just…I never imagined that I would be one of those on the outside looking in."

I am working quickly and efficiently wanting this to end as soon as possible, but I do find it in my heart to feel sad for her. This is not her fault. I sigh, and turn around as I climb down the stepladder, "Margaret. It is not that I am not happy to see you. But it has been a long time. Maybe I haven't changed in some ways. But I am a different person in many others. I remember our time together fondly, but it has been too long ago now. We are worlds apart. We do not know each other anymore."

She stands up from the bed and walks over to me. "But we could try to know each other again."

"Margaret…" I am at a loss for what to say, but before I can try, she leans forward and kisses me. I am transported twenty years into the past, as I feel her searching me with her lips and tongue. It stirs my soul which causes me to feel exposed and vulnerable. But as her hands begin to search my body, I am thrown back into the present, and I find myself pushing her away.

"Stop!"

She looks confused as I gasp for air.

"Margaret, I can't. I am with someone again. I am sorry."

She becomes cross and begins crying all at the same time, "What? You led me to believe you were single again."

"I did not. I did not tell you anything really. I was caught off guard when you showed up, and I did not know why at first."

"But you think you know why now?"

"Yes."

She turns around and grabs her bag from under the bed, and begins to throw her clothes inside. "You think you are so bloody clever, Hilary Mead. I have wondered about you over the years. If you really changed, or if you screwed around on others. I thought to myself when I heard the news about Julie, 'Oh Margaret, they were married for years. She must have been faithful to Julie for all those years if they stayed together. She has changed. You are single now. She is single. Let bygones be bygones. Perhaps you can make it work after all these years.' Let me tell you…you may have made a fool out of me once twenty years ago, but I won't let you again."

"Margaret, I am sorry." There is nothing more to say.

She goes into the en suite and grabs her toiletry bag. Before she walks out, she takes one final parting shot, "I loved you once. But even after all these years, you are the coldest and most frigid woman I have ever been with before. I think I am actually glad you cheated on me now, because if you had not, we would probably still be together, and I need more in life than you." With that, she picks up her bag and exits dramatically as I have seen her do many times before.

I sigh, and pick up the stepladder to stow away before going downstairs to dinner. But when I walk out onto the landing, I am met by Alice standing in the shadows, crying. It is clear she overheard everything.

I go towards her, but she startles and says while holding out her hand, "Don't, Hilary. Don't say anything."

"But Alice, darling, please. Let me tell you what happened."

"Stop, Hilary. I think I heard enough." She is hurrying down the stairs, and I am following close behind. When she opens the front door, I follow, barely feeling the cold air that hits me. I look off to the right, and I see Margaret is almost to the village, where she can take the bus to the train station. At least she is gone now.

I have to hurry to catch up to Alice's long-legged stride. Just before she gets to her car, she turns around abruptly, and I stumble into her. She steps back as if I have burned her with my touch, and I almost lose my balance.

"I cannot believe that I thought I would surprise you tonight by coming to stay with you. What a fool I am."

I reach for her, but she jerks her hand away. "Please, Alice, let me explain."

She crosses her arms, and says, "Let's hear it then. Perhaps you better start with who you were kissing in there."

I feel as though I have been slapped, but I know it is no worse than what she is feeling. I force myself to meet her eyes. "Her name is Margaret. We went to university together. She was my first girlfriend."

"Why was she here?" she asks, her voice clipped.

"She turned up yesterday with no warning. She said she wanted to see me. It was the first time I had seen her since we broke up twenty years ago. We had kept in touch over the years, the occasional phone call or Christmas card early on, but in recent years, she had been living abroad with her partner, and we lost touch."

She remains silent, but is listening, so I continue, "She said she broke up with her partner before Christmas, and she moved back to London last month. She heard at that point about Julie, and she decided to come see me. I had no idea she was coming."

"So, she came hoping to get back together with you?"

"Apparently."

Softly, she says, "She had been here for over twenty-four hours, and you did not tell her about me until after she kissed you." It is a statement of fact. She heard everything.

"No, I did not." There is no point in trying to tell her how little I told Margaret about anything. Nothing will take away the hurt she is feeling right now. I need to own what I have done, and hope for the best.

"I *heard* the kiss. It was lengthy." The unspoken question of why is there.

"Yes, I was in shock at first, and it produced a lot of memories. But the moment I fully realized what was taking place is when I stopped it."

"She said you cheated on her."

I do not blink, as I admit, "Yes, I did. It is the one thing I have done that I am most ashamed of, perhaps until this moment with you now. I slept with my supervisor during my internship. She tempted me by suggesting she could get me a job, and I needed one. I did not consider how it would hurt Margaret. I slept with her one night, and then I was so consumed with guilt that I admitted what I had done to Margaret. We tried to move on for a long time, but she could not trust me, and I could not forgive myself. We broke up, and until yesterday, I had not seen her since."

She tilts her face and says a bit sarcastically, "Forgive me if I am wrong, but is that not something you would consider important to share with me before now, as we are sleeping together?"

"Yes, I meant to. I told Grace last summer before you and I started dating and…"

She cuts me off, "You told *Grace*?" she asks incredulously.

"It was before our first date. Grace and I were looking at old photo albums, and there were a few pictures of Margaret in one of them. I told her, and she said that I should tell you. I agreed, but I did not want to on the first date. Then, we started dating, you had your nightmares, and I simply forgot. It has been twenty years. I do not think about it like I used to."

"You forgot? Yet presumably, you told all your other partners before me?"

"Yes."

"Before you slept with them?"

"Yes, early on. I have no excuse, Alice. I am terribly sorry. I can't imagine how hurtful it is to hear this, in addition to walking in while I was talking to her."

"Oh, I will never forget it, Hilary. That's for damn sure." She moves to open her car door, but I put my hand on the door to stop her.

"Please, don't go, Alice."

She turns back around, and I swear she is another two inches taller as she uses her height to her full advantage while towering over me, "What the hell do you want me to do, Hilary? Do you want me to say it doesn't matter? That it doesn't hurt like hell to think that I have put so much of myself into our relationship, only to discover you continue to keep things from me that all your other lovers knew and got to decide beforehand if it mattered to them? That even Grace knew? Do you want me to say it doesn't feel defeating, as though I have waited and waited on you to be whole again, hoping I could love you enough to get you out of your grief? And what? Where am I now? You still don't even know if you love me!" The tears are pouring down her face, and I can barely hear her as she says, "I have loved you since I first laid eyes on you, hoping and wishing that one day you would notice and love me for me, and not just because I am here and Julie isn't. But I…I know better now. I think you shut off your ability to love the day Julie died. I understand. I do. It's protective, but I can't live like this anymore, wondering if you will ever return my feelings…Goodbye, Hilary."

I want to tell her that I love her, but somehow I know even if I did, she would not be able to hear it right now. She would think I am simply trying to placate her with what she wants to hear. I would hate for tonight to be her first memory of me telling her I love her. Instead, I am frozen in place as she gets in her car, and drives away. I watch until the car is lost from sight. I have no idea how long I linger in the car park, but I realize when the night becomes silent that I am not wearing a coat. From outside my body, I understand that I am chilled through and my tears are ice-cold on my cheeks. I stumble back inside my lonely flat.

Chapter 21

Somehow I manage to serve my guests over Valentine's Day weekend. Vaguely, I am aware that I am going through the motions. By now, I have had a great deal of experience in working while grieving. Having guests come for a relaxing and romantic weekend seems like an odd form of irony I do not wish to consider. So, I do not. Instead, I shut down my emotions to get through the weekend. I try to ring Alice a few times, but she either does not answer or hangs up when she realizes it is me.

The B&B is vacant the following week, and I stay in my bathrobe for four days straight. Grace rings me every day, and I answer long enough the first day to tell her the sordid details, and I have refused to answer since. I expect Gus to show up at any moment, as I know she will be after him to check on me.

But until then, I lie on the love seat watching television for hours every day. I eat little and drink a lot. I have cried so much my eyes hurt and stay bloodshot. I am back to not caring about anything. I am in my own selfish bubble again. It may not be cheerful, but it is comfortable. I know what to expect in this place. I know what it is to be alone and feel lonely, and now that I am here again, it cannot get any worse.

On the Thursday night of this week, I hear the front doorbell. I know it is Gus. Damn. I was hoping he would wait until the weekend when I would be more presentable for guests. I have not washed my hair all week, and I am still wearing my pajamas from Sunday night. Oh well, I remind myself that I do not care.

I stagger to the front door. It is the furthest I have walked since Sunday night, and I have already had a glass or two or three tonight.

I open the door, and turn around and walk back to my flat.

Gus follows me, and I return to my spot on the love seat and my glass of wine. I refuse to pretend in front of him. He knows me too well to try. He and Alice have seen me at my worst. He sits down on a chair across from me, and does not say anything.

"I would offer you wine, but I think I have about finished this."

Am I slurring?

When I see the emotion in his eyes, the sadness and concern are too much. I cover my face with my hands and begin to sob.

He moves beside me on the love seat, and rocks me back and forth as I sob loudly. Through my tears, I tell him, "I fucked up, Gus. I fucked up. She will never forgive me. I really do love her. I know I do now, but it's too late. It's too late. And now, I am alone again."

He smoothes back my hair, and lets me rest my head against his shoulder as I continue to cry. I wish this was a novelty, but Gus has been here with me before. It has been awhile though.

I push away much later, and reach across to the end table for a tissue. I blow my nose and wipe my eyes. I have cried more in the last year and a half than I thought was humanly possible for an entire lifetime. I am weary from it.

"Have you told her how you feel?" he asks finally.

"That I love her?" He nods. "No, I never got the chance. I told her about Margaret, and then she said she could not wait around for me to decide how I feel. I hardly thought it appropriate in that moment to try and convince her otherwise. I have tried to ring her multiple times since, but she hangs up or does not answer."

"Do you think it would help to go see her?"

I shrug. "Perhaps. But I don't think I have the nerve. I am already on the verge of a breakdown. I do not know if I could bear it if she rejected me in person."

He does not disagree with me. He sighs, and says, "Well, you know the drill."

It is my turn to sigh. Indeed, I do. Last year when I was in the midst of ongoing depression, Gus would often show up. If I was in my bathrobe as I am now, he would wait on me to shower, dress, and then take me to the pub, where he would try to force me to eat as much as possible.

I stand up, and walk to the bathroom. Before closing the door, I look behind me to see Gus stretching out on the love seat and reaching for the television remote.

***

Later that evening, Gus walks me home to make sure I get into the flat alright on my own. At the door, he says goodnight. Before he leaves, I tell him, "Thank you, Gus. You are a good friend."

He stoops down to kiss my forehead, and says, "I care about you, Hilary. I may have started checking up on you last year because Grace asked me to, but I honestly care about you now. I believe this will all eventually blow over, and Alice and you will make it work. Have some faith."

I say sadly, "You will have to have it for me. I cannot anymore. It hurts too much."

"I know. I will pick you up for Sunday lunch."

I sigh, "I guess I am back to being the aunt who needs looking after."

He looks confused, "Whatever gave you that idea?"

"Just my perception."

"Hilary, we are only nine years apart. If anything, I view you as a sister. Sometimes a sister who needs looking after, but I am used to that with Tabitha."

"I never had a brother."

He kisses my forehead once again, and says, "You do now."

I nod, and close the door behind him before he can see the tears in my eyes.

***

It is the last week of February, and two weeks since the row with Alice and the demise of our relationship. I decide to try to see her. But I can only risk rejection once more.

I wait until late one afternoon when the shop is closed, and Alice will be there alone. I knock on the door leading up to her flat. After a moment, I hear footsteps on the stairs.

Alice opens the door, and tries to shut it as soon as she sees me. I stick my foot into the doorframe to stop her. It is fortunate I am wearing sturdy shoes, or it would hurt.

"Hilary, please move your foot."

"Please, Alice. I miss you. Can we talk?"

She will not meet my eyes. "I have nothing to say to you, Hilary. It's over."

I know it is too late to tell her I love her now. I waited too long. She is too hurt, and I am too foolish thinking she could forgive me. Alice had a toxic, abusive family. She cut them out of her life, and she is doing the same to me. I have become a toxic cancer to her. She probably believes it is far better to be alone than to deal with me.

I want to say something, anything to make her listen, but when she finally looks up and makes eye contact, I see the pain in her eyes and I know I caused it. When she whispers, "Please leave," I cannot deny her request any longer. I slowly remove my foot, and the sound of the door closing in my face plays over and over again in my head, as I turn to walk back to the car.

She is right. It is over.

March

Chapter 22

A few weeks later, and I am barely functioning. I am back in the midst of deep depression, but it is a different kind. When Julie passed, I knew she was never going to come back. She was dead. She could not. But I also knew if she could have chosen to stay with me, she would have. By demanding I spread her ashes all along the cove, it was her final way of promising that she would be with me always. But with Alice, there is some kind of twisted masochistic notion that allows me to continue to hope she will have a change of heart and walk through my door again. Even though I know Alice better than that. She is calm and controlled. Once she makes a decision, I have never known her to go back on it. And she has a history of cutting people out of her life. I detest I am now relegated to being one of those people that needs to be culled.

But spring is coming to Cornwall, and with the longer days and the slightly warmer weather, I am forcing myself to spend some time in the garden and on long walks. I recognize I am doing it in preparation for Grace's visit in a few days. If I did not know she was coming, I would be sitting in my bathrobe again, but I know if I allow myself to wallow in despair, things will be worse when she arrives. For the first time I attempt to put on a mask to hide behind, instead of letting others see the pain that is still lurking inside. I tell myself it will be better to pretend that I have control over my life now, than have Grace try to fix it for me.

***

Later in the week, I am preparing lunch for Gus and Grace. They are due from the train station at any moment. I have been avoiding Penzance ever since Alice and I split up, so I let Gus collect her on his own. I gave an excuse about letting them spend time together first, but he knew the real reason.

I have made a cold pasta salad, some fresh bread, and cut up some fruit. There is fish I can fry up if Gus needs more, but I do not think I will manage to eat what I have prepared, and Grace has told me she is being careful with eating too much before the wedding. This is her last planned holiday before moving here this summer. They are not sure where Gus will find a job yet, but they are hoping it will be within a short drive of here. I am hopeful for them, but a bit apprehensive as well.

In my present state, it is far easier to be miserable when Grace is far away. If she can be here within a few hours, I have no doubt she will find plenty of excuses to pop down at the weekends if she still perceives I am in the depths of depression. It will be harder to pretend I am alright. Who am I kidding? She will come all the time. It is not that I mind. I love Grace, and I am grateful for her friendship. But I am weary of being on the receiving end of her care and concern. I am forty-one years old. I should not have to be looked after by a woman fifteen years my junior. It does not seem proper. Yet, I remember Julie asking that of Grace, and knowing Grace promised her that she would do what she could for me. I know it is their way of taking care of me because they love me. A joining together beyond death. I touch the St. Julia's medallion that I have recently taken to wearing since Alice split up with me. I had worn it several times since Christmas, but was self-conscious of it. But after that terrible night when Alice drove away, I saw it on my bedside table, and I put it on and I have yet to take it off. Somehow it seems comforting; a reminder that I am not completely alone.

I hear the crunch of tyres on gravel and look up to see Gus and Grace arriving in his father's car. I dry off my hands, and hurry to the door.

By the time I walk outside, Grace has reached me and wrapped me up in such a tight embrace that I can barely breathe. "Hilary! How are you?"

I avoid her question by saying, "Oh Grace, it is good to see you."

"You look terrible again. I have half a mind to go talk to Alice myself."

"Please don't. It will be far better for all of us to accept it is over. Come inside. I have lunch ready."

***

After lunch, the three of us walk down the cliff path. This is the first time I have been in a while. Somehow it feels shameful to admit to Julie how screwed up I have let my life become. As I always talk to her when I come down here, I have avoided coming. I have been walking every day, but I try to fool myself by thinking if I walk anywhere but in her cove, I can pretend she will not know. I am aware of how illogical this sounds, knowing that she is dead and no more, but I have retained this belief in her presence guarding me. Therefore, I would hate for her to think she has failed, as I am a miserable mess once again.

When the three of us reach the bottom of the cliff path, we stand in silence watching the waves, hearing the birds call to one another, and smelling the salt air. Out of the corner of my eye, I glance at the cove a bit further down, and although I feel the pull of it, I do not want to go alone. Grace sees me struggle and suggests, "Do you want me to come with you?"

"Would you?"

"Of course." She glances back at Gus, and says, "I would like to see again where I am going to say 'I do.'"

We walk slowly towards the cove together. Knowing that Gus and Grace will marry here in about four months' time is comforting, as I know this spot needs to have happy memories occur here again as they did once for Julie and me.

When I reach the largest rock that I sat on before spreading her ashes on top of and around its base, I contemplate another day further in the past. The day I proposed to her, roughly twelve years ago. We were here on holiday, and she wanted to climb up on this rock that I am now sitting on, but she was too weak. I knew how badly she wanted to, and I somehow managed super-human strength, and half-carried, half-pushed her to the top. The result was that my back started to spasm when I reached the top behind her, and she was upset I had pushed myself to help her. She said, 'Oh Hil, you always think of me to the determent of yourself. When we get back to London, things are going to change. I am well again. I will get my strength back, so you need to start taking better care of yourself. I want you to get more sleep, eat better, and exercise. You have taken such good care of me the last two years, and I am healthy again. I could not have gotten better without you, Hil. I love you.' I had caught my breath at that point, and I remember looking back at her as she was watching me, and she looked so frail and small, but also happy. Her long blonde hair was flying everywhere, it was before we had a plethora of scarves, and her cheeks were rosy. All I could think was what I said to her, 'I love you, too, darling. Marry me. I cannot imagine life without you, nor do I want to.' She laughed at first, and then realized I was serious. 'You always were daft, Hilary. We can't be married.' I said, 'I don't care if it is legal. But I want to promise to you in front of our friends as witnesses that I love you, and I will love you until death parts us.' She said, 'Oh, I see.' To which I replied, 'Is that a yes?' She answered, 'Oh, it most certainly is a yes.' We kissed and that night our lovemaking was the most satisfying it had been since before her illness.

Yes, this sacred place needs happy memories once again.

I startle out of my reverie when Grace asks, "Are you alright, Hil? You look as though you have seen a ghost."

"Yes. Just lost in memories."

"Good or bad ones?"

"Good, but sad. If that makes sense."

She nods yes. Gus clears his throat, and tells us he is going to take a walk down the coastline. I know he is giving us some privacy, but honestly, I had sunk so far into my thoughts, I had forgotten they were both there.

"Do you want to talk about Alice?"

"You know everything already."

"You told me what happened the night Margaret was here, but Gus said you tried to go see Alice a few weeks ago?"

"Yes, it did not go well."

"Well?" she arches her eyebrow at me.

I sigh and stretch my legs out in front of me on the rock, and lean my hands back behind me. "She tried to slam the door in my face, but I stuck my shoe in between the doorjamb, and she asked me to move it and I did."

"That surely cannot be all that happened."

"I did ask her to please let me talk to her, but she said no, that it was over, and could I please move my foot?"

"You didn't explain to her that you never cheated on anyone else after Margaret?"

"Grace, what difference does it make?"

"I think it is an important piece of information!"

"Perhaps, but at the end of the day it was not what the information was. The fact remained I kept something from her that I had never done in any other relationship."

"You really love her, don't you?"

"More than I ever thought possible again."

"And you can't tell her that?"

I look away from the sea and meet her eyes and reach for her hand. "No, I cannot. It hurts too much. I did not realize I loved her until it was too late, and knowing Alice as I do, I really believe it is too late. I have tried, and if she has decided that it is over, it is. The sooner I accept it, and move on, the better."

"But you haven't accepted it, Hilary. If you think you have, you are lying to yourself."

"If I tell myself the lie often enough, perhaps I will believe it."

I realize she is crying, and I turn towards her and ask in disbelief, "Why are you crying?"

"I feel awful. You were getting better, and…I feel as though I have failed both you and Julie."

"What on earth do you mean?"

"You know exactly what I mean. The promise I made Julie to look in on you, encourage you to love again. I should have asked you if you told her about Margaret months ago."

"Oh don't be absurd! That is ridiculous, Grace. You really have to get past this nonsense. You of all people, being a therapist, should understand you cannot be responsible for another person's actions or lack thereof."

"Maybe so, but I feel partly responsible. You won't let this turn you off finding love again, will you?"

"I think it is unlikely there are many other lesbians my age in this area. But if there are, I promise, I will give someone else a chance down the road."

"And you have never, ever fancied a man?"

I laugh aloud, "Now, we really are in fantasyland. No, I am a lesbian through and through. I would rather be alone than consider being with a man. No offense."

"None taken. I meant no offense at the suggestion. I hate for you to be alone though. I know some people prefer it, but I do not believe you are one of them."

"No, I am not, but I will learn to manage."

At this, Grace tilts her head against my shoulder, and I put my arm around her. We sit there in silence until Gus comes back a few minutes later, when we climb down from the rock, and make the long walk back up the cliff path.

***

A few days later, Grace and I are discussing wedding plans. She has a notebook that she has created a variety of lists in, and she is trying to work her way through the items that need to be taken care of while she is here this last time.

She looks up at me, and bites her lip before saying, "I hate to ask, but did Alice ever find you a dress for the wedding?"

I had completely forgotten about finding a dress. "Oh, no, she didn't. I know she was looking though. I suppose I could check with her to see if she found something."

"You don't have to."

"No, I should ring her before I look elsewhere. Knowing Alice, I would not be surprised to find out she has still been looking for me."

I stand to go ring her.

She looks up, and asks, "Are you going to ring her now? There is no rush."

"Better to get it over with." I go out to the telephone in reception. If I am in a public space, I will hold my emotions together better than if I ring her from the flat.

It is Charlotte who answers. I breathe a sigh of relief, but I also feel sadness that I will not hear Alice's voice.

"Hello Charlotte. This is Hilary."

She lowers her voice and answers, "Hello Hilary." Alice must be close by.

"Look, Charlotte. You don't happen to know if Alice found me a dress for Grace's wedding, do you? She promised to find one, but in our present circumstances, I am wondering if I should look elsewhere."

"I am not sure, but I will find out and ring you later, alright?"

"Yes, thank you."

I tidy up the front desk for a few minutes, delaying when I return to the flat and have to report to Grace. I decide that if Alice did not find something suitable, I will use it as an excuse to go to London next week after Grace goes home. It will help me to have something to look forward to when she is gone and I am alone again.

When I have organized the counter, and checked the registry to remind myself of the guests arriving in the next few days, I am ready to return to the flat, when the phone rings.

"Seaside B&B, Hilary Mead-Harrow speaking. How may I help?"

It is Charlotte and I can tell she is ringing from outside on her mobile as I hear wind gusting in the background.

"Hilary, listen. I went on break to ring you. I don't know what the hell happened between you two, and I am not asking for details, but I do wish you would get it sorted out. Alice is miserable to be around right now. I am not sure how much more of her I can take."

I am taken aback by the directness of this conversation, as I have never spoken to Charlotte for more than a brief greeting. However, I remember from the day Alice was ill that Charlotte knows Alice well, so my guess is she knows far more about me than I realize.

"Charlotte, I don't think we should discuss this."

"Like I said, I am not asking for details, but in case you were wondering if she missed you or was upset, she is. It may be hard for most people to tell, she is so bloody controlled most of the time. I admire her for that normally, but right now, it is obvious to me that she is faking it. My mum always says that I pick up on what is going on with people. I always say it is the little things you have to watch. With Alice, she never smiles anymore. And would you believe it, but her posture is horrid. You would think she has shrunk two inches in the last few weeks."

"I see."

"Anyway, like I said, I do not need to know details, but if there is any way you can fix it, I think you should."

"I have tried. I do not think it is fixable."

"That would be sad. You two seemed very happy together if I do say so myself."

"Yes."

"Oh, I almost forgot! Yes, Alice did order you a dress a month ago. A bright red one. She said you had a red silk shirt the same color she wanted to match. Anyway, it came into the shop a week or so ago, and it was behind the counter until yesterday. She has moved it somewhere, but I haven't a clue where. I do not have to ask her, do I?"

"Of course not. I will figure something out. Thank you, Charlotte."

"My pleasure."

I ring off, and I have no idea what to do next. The fact that Alice did order me a dress, and one to match the silk shirt she gave me because the color suited me, makes me feel sad in an unexpected way. It was lovely being known and found attractive by Alice. I have no doubt the dress will be perfect for me. I simply need to find a way to get it from her with as little drama as possible. For Grace's sake.

***

The next day, I am standing in front of Alice's shop, *Daffodil Yellow*, with Grace beside me. Once I told Grace what Charlotte said, it only made sense to have Grace come with me. The dress is for her wedding, and I could not bear to do this on my own.

I take a deep breath, open the door, and walk inside. I see there are several customers throughout the shop, and Alice is speaking to one of them towards the back. I am a bit disconcerted to realize Charlotte is right. Alice seems to have shrunk since last I saw her. Her shoulders are more rounded, as though she is trying to protect her heart. It is too late for that, I am afraid. She feels my eyes on her, and looks up while stopping mid-sentence with what she is saying. Our eyes only meet a moment, but I think I see hers blink rapidly, before turning back to her customer.

Charlotte sees me, and heads our way.

"Hello Hilary. How may I help?"

I decide that for Charlotte's sake, it is probably best to act as though she and I never spoke yesterday.

"Hello Charlotte. Alice had said she would find me a dress for Grace's wedding, and I was wondering if she was able to yet."

She plays along, and says, "Let me ask." I watch her walk across the shop to Alice, and they speak too softly for me to hear. I feel the tension in my body as I wait beside Grace.

Charlotte returns to us, and says, "She does have a dress for you. If you will follow me to the changing room, you may try it on."

Charlotte leads us towards the other side of the shop away from Alice. I can feel her eyes on me as I walk towards the back with Grace following close behind.

"I will put you in this changing room, and if you will give me a moment, I will locate the dress for you." She disappears, and I stand in the doorway of the open changing room, while Grace stays just outside the door looking rather bleak. I feel wretched this situation is because of me.

"I am sorry. Shopping for your wedding should be happy. Like the day we found your dress. I feel terrible this is not a continuation of that day."

"I am the one who is sorry, Hilary. You both look like the most miserable people in the world."

I hold up my hand. "Stop while you are ahead. I cannot bear to hear anymore just now."

She knows that I am not being harsh, only desperately trying to keep it together.

Charlotte returns with an opaque garment bag that she opens in front of us, and shakes out a long, beautiful red chiffon dress with a low neckline and spaghetti straps. It is breathtaking. I am speechless. I take it from her, and close the changing room door behind me.

I wriggle out of my trousers, shirt, and jumper. It is rather chilly for early spring, so it feels odd to be trying on a dress meant for summer. I know that at this time of year, Alice must have searched high and low to find it, especially as it is a dress that could be worn anywhere, not specifically a wedding. I am glad I thought to wear basic black heels, as at least I can see how the dress should fall. When I turn to look in the mirror, I have no doubt this is the dress. The color makes my dark hair appear deep and rich, far better than it normally looks. The bust line is flattering, and the texture of the chiffon feels cool to the touch. I adore it.

I open the door, and Grace puts her hands to her mouth. "Oh, Hil, it's beautiful."

"Are you alright with the color? It's very bright. I do not want to stand out in your wedding pictures."

"Oh, don't be silly. It is perfect for you."

I hear footsteps, and it is Alice, of course. She is standing stiffly at the entrance to the changing rooms. She does not smile, but I detect a shift, as she assesses the dress to her own critical eye. She finally speaks, "It looks good. It only needs slight alterations. Those can be done soon, unless of course, you think you will lose more weight."

I misunderstand at first, "I think I will be fine." She flinches, and I realize she is wondering if I will lose weight as I did after Julie's death. It may appear to Grace a bit twisted of her to hope I would lose weight again due to our breakup, but I understand. Everything in our relationship has been a comparison with the one I had with Julie. In a depressing way, Alice must believe if I manage not to lose weight, she does not mean as much to me. Which I know is false, but she does not.

"Yes, well, if you will permit me, I will get some pins."

Oh, dear God, she is going to pin everything herself for the alterations which means she will touch me. I feel my face grow warm, and Grace moves in front of me. "Breathe, Hilary. It's okay, I am right here." I do, and by the time Alice returns, she motions for me to stand on a step in front of the three-way mirror. Grace stands behind me, and I watch her face as I try not to watch Alice.

"What shoes are you wearing?"

"My basic black heels."

It feels too risqué to raise the dress up enough for her to see.

She continues, "Are they the same height of what you will wear to the wedding?"

They are three inches, and a fairly safe bet. Besides, once we are in the cove, everyone will be barefoot according to Grace. If I have to hold the dress up to keep from stepping on it, so be it.

"I believe so."

She does not ask anything else, as she kneels in front of me, and begins to place pins all around the hem. I watch her nimble fingers work; she has great dexterity. I am reminded of her knitting needles, and my heart sinks as I realize I may never get to sit with her and hear them clack together again. As difficult as it is to watch her kneeling in front of me, it becomes far worse when she stands up and begins to feel along my bust line. I feel faint, as I know that I am not getting enough oxygen. Apparently, the fact that I am holding my breath is affecting her work, because she murmurs, "I realize this is not pleasant, but I need you to breathe normally." Grace nods at me in the mirror, and I meet her eyes as I try to breathe in and out while Alice finishes. The moment she does, she steps away from me, as though I am dangerous, and says, "Right, well, if you will leave it with me, I will see it gets altered and sent on to you within the next few weeks."

"Thank you." She nods and leaves the corridor. I change back into my clothes, and I leave the dress with Charlotte, but not before telling her to post me the bill for the dress with the alteration fee.

***

A few days later, and Grace and I walk into town to meet Gus and his family at Tabitha's house for Sunday lunch. Gus opens the door for us, and I am enveloped in hugs from everyone and questions as to my well-being, to which I smile and tell them I am well. It is a lie they all accept, but thankfully, they understand I am doing the best I can.

Tabitha is enormously pregnant at this point. She is due on my birthday, May 1st, but I highly doubt she will make it that long. She has a great deal of swelling, and the doctor says the baby is already dropping. She says she is trying to stay off her feet as much as possible, but as I watch her bustling around her kitchen, and see Stephen Junior running around beneath her, I wonder what her definition of staying off her feet means. Grace and I jump in to help her and Gwen, and within a few minutes of arriving, we are all sitting down at the large farmhouse table in the center of the room.

As usual, I am the only one not paired up. I try not to feel sorry for myself, as Angus now has Gwen with him for Sunday lunches, and with Grace in town, she is next to Gus. I try to focus on the fact that oddly enough, these people seem to enjoy my presence, and I should be thankful. We begin eating the fish, vegetables, and salad that Tabitha has prepared, and I am content to listen to the conversations around me. Angus has been working with Gus as of late. He works part-time hours, but seems to be enjoying it. He dotes on Gwen, and she seems like the quintessential, kind Cornish lady. Stephen is quiet as usual, which could be due to some type of social anxiety. Grace has often speculated to me what is wrong, but I think he is clearly introverted and this many people in one room cause him to retreat internally. Grace and Gus are sitting to the right of me on the same bench, and I can feel it move and shift as they feel each other up under the table during the meal. I try to ignore it, but when Grace jerks unexpectedly at one point, I have to look down to avoid laughing. She knows I know, because she will not meet my eye for long afterwards.

"Hilary, how is business going this time of year?" Angus asks me towards the end of the meal. I know he has noticed that I have barely spoken, but I prefer not being the focus of conversation. But I know he means well, so I try to engage.

"It has been very slow since Christmas of course. But now with the warmer weather, I have a fair amount of bookings coming in. I am nearly full most weekends for the foreseeable future. However, during the week, it is still slow.

It will be later in the spring before I have many guests stay throughout the week."

"Gus and I have seen a definite influx in tourists the last few weeks ourselves, haven't we, Gus?"

Gus nods, and Angus continues. "I always think it is nice to have the slowness of the winter months though to truly appreciate the tourists when they come back in droves." He chuckles, and I agree.

The conversation shifts to fishing and Stephen manages to mumble a few words. Before I know it, we are finished eating. I help the women clean the kitchen, before we all insist that Tabitha have a lie down. Gus and Grace offer to take little Stephen off on an adventure for a few hours, and before I know it, I am walking back to the B&B alone.

I lengthen my stride as I attempt to enjoy the sunshine. Even though I no longer need to travel to London next week to find a dress for the wedding, I resolve to go soon. I love Cornwall, but I need a change of scene, even if only for a few days. As I consider the possibilities, I realize I could look in London for decorations for Grace's reception in the garden, as well as purchase items for the B&B that I had meant to do last month. I am stuck in a rut here, and I fear ever getting out of this second round of depression. I know it has only been a month since I lost Alice, but it seems a lifetime ago. Seeing her this week stirred up deep emotions, and made me understand I do need to accept that it is over. If I could only figure out how.

***

Gus rings me early on the last day of the month to tell me that Tabitha had a baby girl who she and Stephen have named Sophie Grace. The swelling I had witnessed last I saw her had been due to preeclampsia. After monitoring both her and the baby closely, the doctors decided this morning they could not afford to wait any longer, and delivered the baby by emergency caesarean. He tells me that although the baby is small and on a ventilator, they believe it is temporary, and she will be alright. I promise to make the drive to Penzance to see Tabitha and the baby tomorrow.

He sounds anxious on the phone, as though he has a lot of pent-up energy that he does not know how to release.

"Are you alright, Gus?"

"Yes, I am now. It got scary early this morning though."

"I see. Do you need anything?"

"No, some of the ladies from the village have already taken some food to the cottage for Stephen and Stephen Junior, but Tabitha and the baby will be in hospital for some time yet."

"Have you spoken to Grace?"

"Yes, it is the early morning hours there, but she told me to ring her as soon as the baby was delivered. Hopefully, she is asleep by now."

"Good. You need to get some rest, too. Alright? And let me know if you need anything."

"Will do. Bye now."

I replace the receiver, and resolve to keep my promise to visit tomorrow.

***

The next afternoon, I find myself standing in front of a window in hospital looking at tiny Sophie Grace in her incubator. She is hooked up to oxygen as well as several monitors, but she looks to be sleeping peacefully. She has a head full of black hair, and I wonder what color her eyes will be. She appears the image of her mother here, but I know she will change a great deal as she grows.

Gus told me that Tabitha gave the baby's middle name to honor Grace. I am so pleased. Grace will be delighted, and I feel a strange sort of anticipation as I consider for the first time being a part of the lives of Grace's children one day.

After gazing at her for a few minutes, I turn to find Tabitha's room. When I enter, she is sitting up in bed staring out the window. She sees me, and smiles.

"Oh, Hilary. How lovely to see you."

She looks tired and drained, but also has that quiet strength and tenacity that a new mother exhibits. She has gone through a lot these past months, and a terrible scare within the last two days, but she is calm.

"Hello, Tabitha. How are you feeling?"

"I am alright. Bit of pain today, but I will be fine."

"Gus told me about the cesarean, but the baby will be alright."

"Yes, she is on supplemental oxygen right now, but the doctor says she is breathing on her own. They are monitoring her and performing a lot of tests, but if all goes well, I hope to be home within another week or so. There is some concern about her making enough red blood cells; the doctor says she will need a blood transfusion if not, but they are waiting to see if her body will be able to do it on its own with all the other strain it is under. She is O+ unfortunately like me, but I am not sure I can give with all the strain my own body is under at the moment."

"Would you like me to donate? I am O+."

"Are you serious? That would be amazing. We might not need it though," she adds doubtfully.

"No matter. I will donate today, and if she does not need it, I will tell the nurse to give it to the blood bank."

Tabitha is fighting tears, and I can barely deal with my own emotions today, so I quickly stand, kiss her forehead, and say, "You need rest, dear. I will find a nurse on my way out. Let me know if you need anything else."

She nods, and I turn to leave.

A half hour later, my good deed accomplished, and I am headed home to St. Just. Visiting Tabitha and her new baby, I am reminded life continues to happen around me, while I remain stuck. I told Alice the truth when I said I never wanted children, and yet, for the first time, I feel the loss of them as I know that children are the legacy people leave behind. If something happened to me tomorrow, the only thing I would leave behind is the B&B to Grace. Which I know she would appreciate, but it is hardly something to think of as lasting for future generations.

April

Chapter 23

It is now the middle of April, and I am in Julie's cove on the largest rock alone. Now, a month after Grace's holiday, I am back in my deep depression, no longer having to pretend to anyone on a daily basis that I am well. I play with my St. Julia's medallion as I process my emotions. I need to get outside my head, so I force myself to speak aloud to Julie for the first time in a long time.

"Darling, I am drowning here. I saw Tabitha's baby again yesterday. They are home now. Little Sophie Grace is still so small and helpless, even though she is slowly gaining strength. I am reminded of how badly you wanted a child, and I wonder if we had a baby all those years ago, if it would have helped me. Perhaps I would be so focused on him or her that I would have healed by now, or at least not be so lonely. It sounds selfish I know, but I am selfish. All I think about is how much I have lost. I have lost you and now, I have lost Alice.

I am not getting better, Julie. I have been slowly sinking further into despair. I…I think…I want to die. I wish I could. I don't want to kill myself, but I would not mind dying accidentally…or even allowing an accident to occur. I have thought about it a great deal lately. Around here on the farm roads, I could easily crash the car into a stone wall or a bridge. Sometimes when I am drinking late at night, I think about drinking myself into oblivion and perhaps taking a few pills. If I do it, I need to make it look like an accident; otherwise, Grace will never forgive herself.

But, Grace could inherit the B&B. You would not mind that, would you, darling? She seems a fitting person to have it after us. All those years ago, using our inheritances from our parents to buy the property, I always felt that we had honored them, and that they were a part of our lives here together. I think by having Grace inherit the house, it would honor the two of us. Even if she decided not to keep it, she and Gus could have a bit of capital to start their life together."

I look out at the distant breakers in the water, and I wish I had the courage to walk into the sea and drown. That would be symbolic, a joining together of Julie's ashes and my body. However, in the back of my mind, I know I do not want to die in that manner as I cannot bear the idea of going mad like Ophelia. Drowning always seemed too melodramatic; such a waste. Yet, my depression has taken on a physical pain of its own, and I cannot continue to live like this. But I do not know any way to stop it either.

I sigh. "Don't worry, Julie. I am too much a coward to go through with anything. At the very least, I have to find a way to make it through the next three months. I refuse to ruin Grace's wedding."

I continue my purge of thoughts, "When I contemplate ending things, I do not think about what it would be like to die. Instead, I consider what it would be like to see you again. But then, I realize even if I could hope to be with you in heaven, I know you would be pissed off with me for ending my life when you could not extend your own. I would hate to row when I see you again.

I don't want to be alone. I hate it. Grace wants me to find someone again, and I tried to assure her I would be open, but I am only trying to placate her. I do not know of another single lesbian my age for a hundred kilometres. I suspect that is a convenient excuse, as I doubt I would even have the desire to try again. It hurts too much. I am broken."

I sit slumped on the rock. I feel numb. I can no longer cry. There is nothing left inside of me.

I hear myself whisper in a strange voice, "I am scared, Julie. I am lost, and I am afraid I will never be found again."

Chapter 24

The following Sunday evening, I am packing for a short visit to London this week. I need to purchase linens and towels for the B&B that I never got around to doing at the end of winter, as well as look for items for Grace's wedding reception in the garden. I should have made a trip weeks ago after Grace left in March, but I never had the motivation. Yesterday, I decided that although I no longer care about myself, I do care for Grace, and I need to take care of what I have promised her.

I have not gone anywhere today, as Sunday lunches have been suspended temporarily while Tabitha and the baby grow stronger. Gus has mentioned to me that if he can get away tomorrow, he will check in before I leave town and perhaps take me to the pub. I have asked Heather to run the B&B while I am gone.

I rang Grace last night to tell her that I was finally going to make the trip to London, and while we were speaking, something changed in the way she looked at me. I could not quite pinpoint it, but somehow I think she knows how much my head is torturing me right now. I know I look haggard again, and I am drinking too much, and eating too little.

Right before she rang off, she said something odd, 'Hilary, you are a child of God and well-loved by him, by Gus, and by me. You may feel alone, but you are not. Please do not forget that.'

Yes, I suspect she knows the thoughts in my head.

After sorting laundry to wash tomorrow for the brief trip this week, as well as preparing a list for Heather of things I need her to mind, I gather my formal stationary that I rarely use anymore, a nice ballpoint pen, and sit down at the dining table. I have not written a proper letter in years, but I have been writing this one in my head for days and need to get it out.

Dear Alice,

I never thought I would be writing a letter such as this, but I cannot help myself. It has been two months since we split up, and still I find myself aching for you. I long to touch you, kiss you, hold you. I reach for you in the middle of the night, only to feel emptiness both beside me and inside my heart. It is a physical pain, as well as an emotional one.

I know you feared being compared to Julie, and doubted I was capable of love after losing her. In the beginning, that was perhaps accurate. But in the months since our holiday in Spain, I found myself emotionally connected to you in ways that were completely new, different, and separate from anything having to do with Julie.

You became special to me in your own way, Alice. At first, I struggled with knowing if it was love. I needed to be sure before I told you, because you were too special, for me not to take our relationship seriously. I knew you loved me. You have no idea how much that knowledge kept me going at times. I feared taking advantage of you. You deserve to be loved in return, and I promised myself that I would not continue long-term if I was not going to be committed and love you as much as you loved me. I kept telling myself that I needed more time to determine my feelings. What a fool I was.

Twenty years ago, I did cheat on Margaret. I have taken full responsibility for that action, and I have lived with a great deal of guilt over the years. But I have never cheated on anyone since. I did tell all of my other partners early on as a way to stay accountable, because I was young and immature in my twenties, and terrified of repeating the mistakes of my father. But by the time I was with you, I became a different kind of fool, because after being successfully married for years, and then dating you, I could not comprehend cheating ever again, and so the importance of telling you about Margaret never surfaced. I realize when you overheard Margaret and me that night you could not have known that I was not seeking her attention. For what it is worth, I would never have cheated on you with her. But there was no way for you to know that. I do want to apologize and tell you how sorry I am. I realize how selfish that was of me not to tell you, and I know I hurt you deeply.

I did love you, Alice. I do love you. I regret I never told you to your face and that it took me so long to discover my feelings for you. Ironically enough, it was the day you found out about Margaret that I realized how much I loved you, but I knew it was not the right time. Faced with Margaret, I realized how much I missed you. It was all the small things that you say and do, and the person you are. Somehow those little things built up, and it became love that billowed and spilt out around us. I suspect I will love you forever, and always wish that I could hear your knitting needles clacking back and forth at night on the love seat, and your low laugh when you find something funny.

I wish you happiness, and I hope you find someone who can love you as much as you deserve to be loved. I am sorry that I could not be the person you deserve.

Know that no matter what happens, I will love you always,

Hilary

I sit back from the letter and stare at it. I have no intention of posting it. I know that I simply needed to get my thoughts down on paper. I do not think that it has helped, but in my current state, if anything were to happen to me, perhaps

Grace will find it and give it to Alice. After all, I would like her to know how much I love her.

Chapter 25

On Monday, I work on completing last minute tasks before travelling to London tomorrow morning. I finish laundry and packing, and I organize the kitchen and reception for Heather. There are only a handful of guests all week, but I try to have things ready in case anyone stops by looking for a room. I go to the grocer's and purchase what should be enough food for those guests who have booked, as well as any potential guests who have not. On an impulse, I buy a fresh pasty for my lunch. I manage three bites, before my stomach begins to protest and I throw the remainder in the bin.

Later in the afternoon, I hear a car pull up in the car park. The front doorbell buzzes a few minutes after. I go to see who it is, only to discover the detestable man who stayed here last autumn.

"Hello again. I doubt you remember me."

"I do actually."

"Oh, well, that's nice. I'm just travelling through again. Wondered if you had a room for the night. Anything will do."

"Yes, come through to reception."

He follows me inside, and I swear I can feel the hair on the back of my neck rise. I consult the registry, and put him in the room facing the sea that Margaret stayed in. Incidentally, it is the room farthest from my own. Whether it is subconscious or not, I do not stop to consider.

"If you will write your name on this line, and sign here."

He gives me his card to pay, and I swipe it before setting it on the counter.

I turn to kneel underneath the counter where I have the keys in a small lockbox, and collect the one for his room. When I stand back up, I realize he is staring at me. He is stocky and muscular, rather intimidating, especially with his crooked nose that has been broken one too many times.

I turn the registry back around; *Eddie Smith*, it reads. Yes, of course. Strange I did not remember it even months later.

I place the key on the counter, and tell him where to find his room. Once again, he grumbles that I will not show it to him personally, but I cannot bear to be near his leering eyes one second longer than necessary. He makes me feel as though I should go take a bath. As soon as he begins to climb the stairs, I take my laptop off the counter, and return to the privacy and safety of my own flat. I will quarantine myself here the rest of the night.

***

Several hours later, the phone rings, and it is Gus telling me that he is about to leave his father's house to catch the bus to St. Just. He says he will come to pick me up and we will walk to the pub. I breathe a sigh of relief that I will not be alone tonight.

I finish the last bit of my packing, and less than a half hour later, I hear a knock on my door. I wish I had thought to glance at the clock, because I would have known it was too early for Gus to have arrived.

I open the door without thought, only to discover my guest, Mr. Smith, leaning against my flat door, obviously drunk. I immediately try to shut it in his face, but even in his drunken state, he is too quick and moves inside.

"Hello there, pretty lady. I wondered if this is where you got off to earlier. Nice place," he says as he looks around the kitchen.

"Please leave." I motion for him to go back through the door, and hold it open for him.

"I don't think so. I want to stay here with you for a bit."

"You are not welcome. Get out."

He takes a step towards me, and I try not to visibly cringe, as he takes the door handle from my hand, and shuts the door. He pushes me back against it, and I maintain eye contact, as I am trying my best to not convey how terrified I feel.

"There now. What is a beautiful woman like you doing all the way out here in the middle of nowhere all alone?" He asks as he reaches up to touch my face.

I flinch, but refuse to answer. Although I am now trembling, I keep staring at him. I am willing him to look away first; all the while wishing I had thought to move the cricket bat by the door instead of having it still lie under my bed.

He is towering over me, but still a couple of inches away, and so carefully, I move my left hand to the door handle without detection, thinking if I can catch him off guard, I can open the door and leave the flat myself. Even if he chases me, perhaps I can get far enough away to attract attention. I grab the handle, pull it open and move to the side all in one motion, but he is too quick and too strong. He grabs my wrist in a vise, and in one movement twists it while forcing me bodily back around against the door. I hear a sickening crack as my wrist breaks in the strength of his grip. A second later, white, hot searing pain radiates from my wrist down to my fingertips and up my arm. The pain appears to take a shape of its own, as it forms as spots behind my eyes. I feel his hot breath in my ear, as he says without emotion, "Now, that was foolish. You have gone and broken your wrist. All I wanted was to give you a bit of attention, and you go and try to get away."

Tears begin to pour down my face and I whimper as I hear myself beg him to let go of my wrist in a voice I barely recognize. "Please, let go. I beg you."

He asks, "Are you going to cooperate?" I nod. Anything for him to let go.

He drops my wrist, and I immediately cradle it with my right hand, as the motion of him dropping it suddenly causes me to gasp, and almost lose my stomach. He backs me against the door again, and he begins kissing me, and groping me through my clothes. The roughness of his tongue and facial hair stubble, cause me to gag, but I do not resist. He moves down my neck, and bites and pulls and claws his way down to my breasts, which he begins to manhandle through my clothes. It is awkward to hold my wrist motionless while he is groping me, but I attempt to hold my breath to maintain stillness, hoping that he will not force me to let go with my good hand. I have no physical or mental strength to fight him at this point; my only focus is to keep as still as possible.

As he moves lower, he becomes frustrated that my arms are in his way. He pulls my right hand away from my left wrist, which causes me to groan as my left wrist is jolted, and pins my right arm above me. My left hand now hangs limply by my side. I can see in his eyes that he knows he has broken me, just as he broke my wrist. When he recognizes there is no threat from me, he drops my right arm. He rips the buttons on my shirt open and begins grabbing my breasts, stomach, assaulting every square inch within reach. I hear the lace rip on the cup of my bra as he cannot seem to be bothered to unhook it, but I do not even look down to see. All I can think about is the pain in my wrist.

I begin praying for the first time in ages, although it could hardly be considered more than a brief plea. Yet I find myself asking God to let him finish quickly. Somehow I think it would be cowardly to allow myself to blackout from the pain, so instead I focus on it with each breath I take, hoping and praying it is over soon. He is trying to undo my trousers, and getting increasingly frustrated with the double button enclosure. He turns me around to force my front against the kitchen door; the movement of my wrist with the motion of turning around is sheer agony. But the pain is almost preferable to what he is doing now. He shoves his hand down my trousers, while with his other he begins to push them down. I want to retch from the pain and indignity that I am suffering as his hand finds what he seeks, and I feel my tears coating the door as I try to keep as immobile as possible. Before he muscles my trousers all the way down, I hear a noise behind him, and suddenly, he is pulled off me, and I collapse to the floor.

    I grab my wrist and turn around in time to see Gus hitting the man in the gut, which angers him as he yells a cry of indignation and swings at Gus, but Gus is ready for him and ducks, and then with a left hook, sends the man reeling. With a dull thud, his head makes contact with the kitchen countertop. When he hits the floor, he is out cold, whether from Gus' hit or the contact with the countertop, it does not matter.

I sit in shock against the door, as Gus confirms that the man is not going to stand back up and attack either of us, and then comes to check on me.

He is out of breath, as he says, "The front door was open, but when I got to your door, I heard you crying and heavy breathing, so I came around outside, and thank God, you had left the window open. I stepped over the sill, and came up behind him." He notices me cradling my wrist for the first time, and my shirt open for anyone to see. He says angrily, "That bastard hurt you. Oh, Hilary, I am sorry. Let me see."

I do not want to take my other hand off of my wrist, but when I do and look at it for the first time, there is no doubt it is broken. It is lying unnaturally, and has already swollen and turned a rainbow of colors. Gus looks as though he may be sick.

He swallows, and says, "I need to ring the police, and you need to be taken to A&E." He looks up again, and realizes my shirt is still lying open. I notice what he has, and try to move the torn cup to cover my breast while also attempting to button it, but cannot one-handed.

"Would you button it, please?" Gus looks uncomfortable, but reaches up to do so or at least the few buttons remaining. I am mortified, but I motion to my trousers. "The button there, too, please." He obliges, but without making eye contact.

He looks back at the man, who has not moved, but says to me, "I am not leaving you alone in here with him. Can you walk with me to reception so that I can ring for the police and ambulance?"

I nod, and he helps me to stand. But the moment I do, I feel lightheaded as the room begins to spin and I find myself retching all over the floor.

I am still crying, and I sob, "Oh, Gus, I am sorry."

He tilts my face up to him, and he looks the angriest I have ever seen him, "Don't you dare apologize, Hilary. Don't you dare. You have done nothing wrong, do you hear me? That bastard is to blame. Not you."

***

Several hours later, Gus and I have given statements to the police and I have been taken to hospital. Mr. Smith was also taken to hospital and evaluated. He had concussion from the hit against the countertop, but after he is cleared, I am told he will be taken into custody. I am hopeful I will never have to see him again, even if and when his case is heard.

I am in x-ray, where we are awaiting results. The doctor would not say it was broken without seeing an x-ray first, which is absurd, but I understand it is likely he needs to see how the break appears to know how to set it. Holding my wrist in certain positions for the x-ray was so painful that I feel queasy at the thought of the bone being set. But I want to get it over with tonight. Gus is beside me, and has his arm wrapped protectively around me.

"Mrs. Mead-Harrow?" the nurse calls from the doorway. Gus and I stand, and make our way to the examining room. I sit down on the table, and Gus hovers by my side.

The doctor enters, and with no preliminaries says, "Yes, Mrs. Mead-Harrow, you were right. It is a bad break, but it is clean, and will not require surgery. I am going to give you a bit of numbing medication at the site, and then attempt to set it. You will wear a small plaster cast for eight to twelve weeks. In light of the trauma you have experienced tonight, I am recommending you stay the night in hospital, so we can monitor you, and I will discharge you in the morning."

He sits down on a short stool and moves to get into position in front of me. He picks up the injection that presumably has the numbing medicine, and before taking the cap off, he looks up at Gus, and says, "Mr. Mead-Harrow, if you will hold your wife as still as possible."

Gus does not correct him. I cry both from the pain as well as from the gentle kindness radiating off Gus as he holds me as tenderly as he can. I am surprised at the stab of jealousy I feel towards Grace, because she has found such a wonderful man to care for her.

Chapter 26

The next morning, I wake up disoriented and uncertain of where I am. I feel pain and look down and see a plaster cast on my left wrist, and I remember everything. Instead of travelling to London this morning, I am in hospital because my guest attacked me last night. After the doctor set the bone, I was taken to a room where the nurse wanted to get me changed into a hospital gown, but I refused to let her touch me. Instead I sat down on the edge of the bed, and changed out of my clothes into the gown very slowly myself, while Gus stood by the bed with his back to me, in case I needed assistance or felt faint. I tried not to let on how shocked I was when I undressed to find a myriad of bruises all along my torso. I feel certain Gus knew anyway, by how awkward and stiff I was moving. When I was done, I told Gus I never wanted to see those clothes again, and to please dispose of them for me. Once I got into the bed, the nurse came back and gave me pain medication for my wrist, and I suspect it also had some type of sedative in it, as I do not remember anything afterwards.

This morning, it is late as the sun is high in the sky, and I begin to look around the stark white room. There is a small vase of flowers on the bedside table, and a tattered mystery novel that I assume Gus was reading last night.

A nurse, old enough to have been my mother, enters the room, "Look who is awake this morning! How are you, my dear?"

I relax slightly as somehow this woman's voice is soothing to my tattered mind. "I am alright."

"Have a rough time of it, haven't you?" She comes to my bedside and checks my vitals, and pokes and prods me a bit. "The doctor is going to discharge you later today if you feel up to going home. That nice man who was here earlier, is he your husband?"

"Gus?" She nods, and I continue, "No, he is a friend. He found me last night and brought me to hospital."

She clucks her tongue in dismay. "What a friend I say, from what I hear that man stayed with you long into the night.

He rang a short time ago, and said he will be back shortly to take you home. You are not to worry." Before leaving the room, she turns one last time to look at me, "Do you need anything, dear?" I shake my head as the tears form, and she comes back to the bed, and squeezes my good hand, and says, "Oh, my dear, you are safe now. I know it seems awful, but you will get past this." She places some tissue in my hand, and shuts the door quietly behind her.

***

Gus returns for me an hour later, carrying a small bag with a change of clothes including bra and knickers. I weep at the gesture, as I had not given any thought to the fact that I told him to throw my clothes from yesterday in the rubbish bin without considering what I would wear home today. He misunderstands and begins to apologize for the intrusion on my privacy, and I hold up my good hand and manage to say, "No, Gus, that was incredibly kind and thoughtful. I am touched. Thank you." He nods, and once again, turns his back to me while I dress.

On the drive home, I am silent as I rest my head against the seat. Gus does not seem to mind, and when we arrive at the B&B, he helps me inside. Although I can walk, I feel unsteady on my feet, which I assume is due to the pain medication. I balk at the suggestion to go to bed in the middle of the day; I want to sit on the love seat, but Gus insists. I am aware he is right though, and I need to lie down, so yet again, I change from my clothes to pajamas. But this time, Gus waits in the living room. When he returns, he asks if I am ready for lunch. I make a face, but he insists.

A short time later, he comes into the room with a tray. He has warmed up chicken broth and put that and some crackers and an apple on the tray with water. No wine today. It would not mix with my pain medication. Damn.

"Thank you, Gus. There are not enough words to express my gratitude. Over everything."

He moves my reading chair and places it beside the bed. He sits down, and leans forward. He says, "I am glad to be here, Hilary, and I will do whatever I can for you. But I think you need someone female here with you for at least the next few days." I do not know where he is going with this, but I smell trouble. He continues, "I spoke to Grace this morning. She is worried and upset of course."

I interrupt, "Oh, bugger."

He hushes me gently, "Hilary. You know we are all worried about you. It does not mean you are weak. It means you are loved and cared for. You have been through a major trauma, and you are going to be in pain, both physical and emotional for quite a while. Grace says that she could come for a few days, but with the wedding soon, she really needs the time to finish up her work in the States. We are both wondering if there is anyone else you might like to ask." Alice's name is hanging in the air, daring one of us to mention it, but I refuse.

"There is no one else, but you tell Grace that she is not to come for this. She does not need to pay for an expensive last minute flight here. I will be fine. I just need a few days, and Gus, you do not need to stay and mind me. I would appreciate the occasional check-in, but no need to sit with me all day. I plan on sleeping the majority of the next few days anyway." He sighs, but nods assent. I remember something as he moves to stand, "Actually, could you do me a favor before you leave?" He nods. "Please ring the hotel in London and cancel my reservation. The number should be somewhere under the counter in reception. I will ring them later and reschedule for next week."

He starts to say something, and I feel certain it is to suggest that I not reschedule for next week, but he stops and goes to make the call, while I try to eat a little of what he brought me for lunch. It is slow eating one-handed, even though I am right-handed. I try to steady the tray with my left, but I grimace every time the tray shifts against my wrist. Gus returns shortly to tell me he found the number and canceled the reservation. He notices my distress with the tray, and hurries over to feed me the broth. I feel ridiculous, but I want another painkiller, and I know that the more I eat, the less likely I will be queasy from the medication later. After I eat as much as I can, Gus clears away the tray, and he gives me the medicine.

"Hilary, I need to head back to St. Ives for the afternoon. Will you be alright for a few hours?"

"Yes, of course. I am going to sleep all afternoon."

"By the way, Heather came this morning, and she canceled the guests for tonight and tomorrow. There was only one for each night. We felt as though you did not need the stress of having to deal with anyone in the house, or of having Heather stay to do the work. I hope you do not mind."

"No, that is probably for the best."

He looks relieved, and before leaving, assures me he will be back to bring me dinner.

***

I wake several hours later in a fog. The room is darkening, as the curtains have been drawn and the sun must be descending. The pain medication has made my brain muddled, as I try again to remember what happened over the last twenty-four hours. As I become fully awake, I sense that I dreamt of Alice, but I cannot remember the details. I turn slightly, and I groan as I move my left hand without thinking.

There is motion to my right side by the window, and I feel a moment of panic.

    Suddenly, there is a smooth hand on my right arm, and I look over to see Alice sitting in the reading chair that Gus sat in only a few hours ago. Or did he? Was that only a few hours ago? Perhaps this is the dream I thought I had, or perhaps I am in the midst of the dream now? She stands to move the curtains slightly back, so that I can see her clearly, before she walks back over to sit down. She is wearing a standard black dress that she often wears for work in her shop and she is back to wearing three-inch heels. When she sits back down, I notice her green eyes are bloodshot and her red hair is in disarray as though she has been running her hands through it repeatedly. She clasps her hands in her lap, but not before I notice they are shaking.

    I honestly wonder if she is a mirage. I know that pain medication can do strange things, and as I stare at her and she continues to stay silent, I believe I am hallucinating. But then, she breaks the silence, and timidly reaches her hand to my own once again.

The coolness of her touch breaks me out of my reverie.

"Grace rang me," she says, which is the last thing I expect to hear her say.

I start to sit up in a form of protest, but she gently pushes me back on the pillow, and says, "I am glad she did. She told me what happened, Hil." She begins to cry and reaches for a crumpled tissue she had in her pocket. She looks up, and continues through her tears, "In no uncertain terms, she told me to get over myself and come to see you."

I have not spoken a word. I am afraid if I do, it will become a dream and I will wake up.

"After she rang off, I cried for half an hour, but I knew she was right and I somehow managed to drive here. Gus let me in. Hilary, I am so sorry. I am the most stubborn woman ever. I should have given you the benefit of the doubt with Margaret, and forgiven you long ago. When I think of what could have happened to you last night," she stops to look at my wrist and amends what she says, "When I think of what *did* happen to you last night…I may never forgive myself."

I do not understand why she is talking about Margaret and offering me forgiveness, but when I glance over at her, I see what I did not before. She has found the letter I wrote. In the half-light of the darkening room, I see the heavy cream stationary laying crumpled beside her in the chair. I do not even remember where I set it after writing it the other night or if I even moved it from plain view on the table. It does not matter.

I must be dreaming. There is no other explanation to what must be an apparition; this cannot possibly be real. Yet, there is enough doubt in the far corners of my mind that before I fall back asleep, I manage to whisper, "I love you, Alice," just in case she hears.

***

I am dreaming of the man in my kitchen...he is groping me again, but this time, he will not let go of my wrist. I am in agony. I beg him. "Please, please, I will do anything. Just let go." Surely sex with him would be far less painful than him twisting my already broken wrist. Just when I think I cannot bear the pain anymore, I wake up.

The bedclothes are in bunches around my legs, and I am drenched in sweat. The room is completely dark. There is no moon tonight. But I sense someone's presence, and I feel cool hands on me. I push them away at first, panicking, while not understanding.

"Hilary, it's me. Shhh…you are safe now. You and I are the only ones here." She is still sitting in my chair by the bed in the dark. When she attempts to touch me again, she realizes my pajamas are soaked.

"Do you want a fresh pair?"

I shake my head no, but then whisper, "No." I do not want even Alice undressing me right now, and I do not have the energy to do it myself.

"Alright, let me get a flannel then, and I will wipe you down."

She leaves the room, and comes back within seconds. I feel a cool flannel on my face, neck, and hands, carefully avoiding the plaster cast on my left hand. I begin to relax, and I fall asleep once again.

***

Every time I awake over the next several days, Alice is present. I rarely stay awake for long, and we have not spoken yet about what she said the first night she came. My wrist and bruises seem to be healing, but I have also not looked at them too closely. Other than going to the loo, I have been in bed the entire time. I am not sure if it is due to the depression that I have been dealing with for months, the injury and trauma, the pain medication, or a combination of all three, but I feel lethargic, and as though I have had a close brush with death. Perhaps I brushed death with my soul.

One afternoon when I awake, Alice is not beside the bed as she normally is, but I hear her voice from the other room. I strain to hear what she is saying, and I realize she is on the telephone, as there are stretches of silence after she speaks each time.

After a few comments I cannot understand, I hear her say, "You were right, Grace. She is in a bad way, but I am here."

Then, "Charlotte is working at the store every day and has called a few of her friends in to help her. Heather has agreed to run the B&B this weekend, but we have already notified the guests staying next week that we are closed."

Later, "I promise you. I will stay until she is well, and for far longer if she will have me."

Finally, before ringing off, "I will tell her you are thinking of her. And Grace? Thank you for ringing me the other day. I may never forgive myself for holding onto my hurt for so long."

Once again, I fall under the spell of sleep.

***

One morning, I have no idea how many days later; I wake to find Alice in the chair beside the bed.

I ask her the first thought that comes into my head, "Where have you been sleeping?"

"Well, the first night I slept here in the chair, the second I tried the love seat, the third I made a pallet on the floor, and last night, my body was screaming in protest, so I curled on the edge of the bed with you. I did not want to leave you to go to a guest room; I hope you don't mind."

I stare at her. I am not sure if I am more surprised at how little she must have slept due to obvious discomfort at the expense of taking care of me, or if I am more shocked to discover that I have been in the bed for four days. But again, I say the first thing in my head, "You look as though you have not slept at all."

She chuckles, "Yes, well, I did not say I slept well, did I?"

"I'm sorry you felt the need to stay."

"Sweetheart, there is no other place I would rather be."

I stare at her, and before I can ask anything else, I sense she has made a decision.

"Now, I do not want you to panic, but I think it is high time we get you out of bed and you have a bath, while I change the sheets. You had numerous night sweats this week, and the linens need to be changed. Once you are clean, I will see about getting you to eat something more substantial than broth and a few crackers."

I do not want to have a bath or eat, but I know better than to argue with Alice once she makes her mind up. I allow her to help get me out of the bed, and walk towards the bathroom. I feel weak and unsteady on my feet. I am reminded of helping Julie to the bathroom those last few weeks of her life, and I find myself wanting to shake myself in reply. I am not dying, for pity's sake. I need to snap out of this…whatever it is.

Alice helps me sit on the edge of the bathtub, while she turns on the taps. She puts a generous helping of some type of bath salt into the water as well as some bubble bath, and the room fills with the scents of lavender and vanilla. When the tub is full with warm water, she asks, "Do you need help undressing?"

"No, I can manage," I pull my pajamas up a bit higher. I am not shy with Alice, but I do not want her to see the bruises. I do not want her pity.

"Alright, well, let me wrap something around the plaster cast. We cannot have it get wet." I gingerly hold my arm steady as she wraps a bag around it and ties a knot at the end. "Please do not stand to get into the bath. You are too weak…do you think you can undress while seated? Just throw the pajamas on the floor. I will get them."

"I think so."

"I am leaving the door open. Call me if you need help. I will go change the bed linens."

I nod, and as soon as she is gone, I begin to unbutton my top. It takes about three times as long as it should, but I manage, and then wriggle out of the bottoms, before somehow managing to swing my legs around to lower myself into the bathtub. Thank God there is a wide ledge. This little activity has already worn me out, but I cautiously move my body down into the warm water, and it feels soothing. I look down and my breasts and stomach are a horrid shade of black and blue. I shudder involuntarily as flashes of what happened cycle through my mind. I sink lower into the tub to hide the evidence under the bubbles, all while carefully keeping my left arm on the ledge. I wish I could clean my mind from these memories, as I attempt to clean my body.

I hear Alice behind me in the doorway. "Hilary, are you alright?"

I glance back. She is trying to avert her eyes, but is clearly concerned.

"Yes, I am alright."

"Do you need help washing your hair?"

I had not considered it, but suddenly nothing sounds better than having my hair clean as well. It is far too long though to manage one-handed, so I consider for a split second, and then decide that I will accept her help.

"Yes, please."

Out of the corner of my eye, I see her kneel down by the bathtub. She is wearing jeans and a black top, by far the most casual outfit I have ever seen her wear, but I am glad to see that she is choosing to be comfortable while she takes care of me. She rolls up her sleeves, and uses a glass she must have brought in from the kitchen to wet my hair. Then, she opens a bottle of shampoo I do not recognize, but I know the smell. The combination of this, with the vanilla in the bath salts is Alice's own scent that I have attached to her. The shampoo is citrusy, but most importantly, it smells clean and refreshing. As Alice begins to massage it into my oily hair that has not been brushed in days, the desire to be clean hits my core and my shoulders begin to shake as I try unsuccessfully to stave off the tears.

"Oh sweetheart, I am sorry. Let me get the shampoo washed out." I feel the warm water wash over my head, once, twice, three times. A baptism of water for my body and my soul. When the shampoo is out, my shoulders are still shaking. Alice reaches down and pulls me towards her. She carefully clasps her hands around my upper back, and does not move them. I know I am soaking her clothes, but she does not seem to mind. I feel the rise and fall of her breath, and as I begin to focus on it, I am able to slow the tears to a halt. She pulls away, and it is then she looks down and sees the bruises for the first time. She is careful not to touch, even though I see her hand shift as if she is itching to trace them with her fingertips.

Instead she lifts my face, and says, "I know it may not seem like it, but your body will heal quickly. Your mind will take far longer, but Hilary, you will get through this. And I will be here with you, for as long as you allow me."

I cannot reply, but she offers me her hand to help me get out of the bath, and I accept. She towels me off like a child and wraps my bathrobe around me, before making me sit on a chair while she dries and plaits my hair. Then, I dress in fresh pajamas without buttons this time, and I am tucked back into my freshly made bed.

After eating a hearty chicken and rice soup that Alice prepared, but had to feed me, I lie back in bed for a rest. As I start to fall under the spell of sleep again, I tell her, "I am glad you are here, Alice."

She kisses me on the forehead, and whispers, "I love you, Hil. Sweet dreams." Being wished sweet dreams never meant so much.

***

Sometime over the weekend, I wake up to find Alice knitting in the chair beside me. She does not realize I am awake at first, as I do not stir. I stare at the ceiling for a while and I listen to the rhythm of the knitting needles clacking together. For some reason, the sound moves me to tears, and Alice looks up startled.

"What's wrong?"

I shake my head. "Nothing. I just…I never thought I would hear you knit again. I have missed it." She scoots the chair closer to the bed, and reaches for my right hand.

"Are you comfortable?" She asks.

"Yes, thank you."

She must sense my desire to talk at last, as she sets her needles down with her other hand, and squeezes my right hand.

"What is wrong with me?" I finally ask.

"What do you mean?"

"Why am I so tired? Why can I not get out of bed? Surely a broken wrist cannot warrant lying in bed for almost a week."

She looks pained as if she is not sure where to begin, but she stumbles ahead, "Sweetheart…you experienced a major trauma this week. You were attacked in your home by a guest. He broke your wrist, bruised your body, assaulted your person, and would have raped you if he had more time. Gus says you were half-dressed and slumped against the door when he found you, crying from the pain. You do not recover from that in a day, a week, or even a month. It takes time. I hesitate to say anything about my experience…but Hil, it took me a long time before I could function again day-to-day. It is alright to take time to convalesce."

I swallow as I try to form the words I do not want to say but need to verbalize, "But I was not raped as you were. Surely, I should not have this type of strong reaction?"

"Do not minimize what he did. Please, do not. Nor compare what happened to either of us. That man hurt you. He had evil intent to do more. Your body has reacted this week to what your mind does not yet want to recognize."

"When will I feel normal again?"

"I do not know, sweetheart, but I believe you will one day."

"Alice?"

"Yes?"

"Will you hold me?"

She stands up and comes over to the other side of the bed, and lies down against a couple of pillows on the duvet.

At first her presence causes me to feel tension, but then I focus on relaxing against her, and I fall asleep to the sound of her heartbeat.

Chapter 27

The week after the attack, I am starting to regain mobility. It is not to the degree that I would like, and it is partly to do with Alice hovering and not allowing me to do more. Secretly, I am glad she is forcing me to take things slow, as I have no doubt if she were not here, I would overdo it, and end up passed out on the floor. I have little energy and being one-handed, simple tasks such as dressing and eating make me feel so bloody incompetent. I am frustrated beyond reason, but Alice pushes me to do one thing at a time without thinking too far into the future.

Each day usually consists of me dressing, eating, and then sitting on the love seat or bench outside for small increments of the day sometimes looking at a magazine, sometimes simply breathing, before having a lie down in the afternoon, and dinner and bath in the evening. Later in the second week, Alice lets me walk around the garden. She tells me next week she will let me venture off the property for small walks to the coastal views.

One day during this time, Alice comes into the bedroom after I awake in the afternoon, and sits down on the bed beside me. She reaches for my hand, and strokes it. I can sense she wants to ask me something but is not sure how to begin.

"Hil, I wanted to ask you about the letter you wrote me, but did not post."

I feel my body tense, even though she has a perfect right to question me about it.

"I found it on the table when I came into the flat that night. It was in plain sight, and I saw my name. At first, I thought you meant for me to see it, but I have since wondered if you ever intended me to."

I try to sit up as I feel at a disadvantage lying on my back discussing such a sensitive issue. She helps prop a couple of pillows behind me, and while I am not exactly at eye level, I can at least attempt an answer. I reach back for her hand, and I meet her eyes.

"No, I never intended to post it. The night before everything happened, I was at a low point, and needed to get my thoughts down on paper."

She nods, "I thought not."

"But…I do not regret you reading it. I meant everything I wrote."

I see her eyes fill with tears, as she whispers, "You did?"

"Yes, of course. I have loved you far longer than I first realized. I behaved terribly, but that is no real surprise. I am a selfish person."

"The ending of the letter…it sounded rather prophetic, as if you had a premonition something was going to happen."

"Yes, well…being severely depressed does not adequately explain how I have been the last two months."

She appears confused, "What do you mean?"

I cannot meet her eyes. I feel ashamed.

She sounds agitated, as she asks again, "What do you mean, Hilary?"

I think she has guessed already, but I suppose she deserves to know. At least, it will help her realize that she does not want to become involved with me again.

I continue to look down at our hands, as I say, "I was contemplating ending it."

"Ending *what*?" her voice escalates.

I cringe, as I say, "I was trying to decide if I would have the courage to end my life after Grace's wedding. I did not know how to do it, but I knew it needed to look like an accident. I have been wishing that the pain and depression would end, so I was considering what would be the easiest way. But I am a coward, and even though I had no idea how I would survive for the next three months until after the wedding, I doubt I could have done it. It would have been a terrible nuisance on my part for Grace and Gus to be newly married and…deal with me and what to do with the property. But I cannot bear to live like this anymore either."

Alice is sobbing now, but she manages to say, "Hilary, if you had taken your life, you would have taken my own as well." She becomes intense as she squeezes my good hand so hard it hurts and says, "Promise me, Hilary. Promise me, you will not hurt yourself."

I meet her eyes once again, and I realize that somehow this woman still loves me. I do not understand why, but I still feel the presence of her love. I can feel it stirring in the air around me.

"Alice...I am broken. And I am not only referring to my body. My soul is broken. I have nothing to give right now. I doubt I had much to give before. But I cannot keep going on my own. I hurt too much."

"Hilary, I know you are hurting. But you have to promise me. I cannot live if you are not living, too."

She will not let this go. I am terrified to make this promise, as I know I will do my best to honor it. I know she knows this, which is why she is forcing me into it. But I look into her green eyes, and I see the love in them. I whisper, "I promise."

I see the strain around her eyes relax, and she says, "Thank you."

I nod.

She lessens the pressure on my hand, but continues, "Sweetheart, I know it is scary. But I am here and I am not leaving you. Let me help you heal."

"How do you intend to do that?"

"By loving you and taking care of you, just as I did last year and I am doing now. But…as your girlfriend and partner again."

"You still want to be with me?" I cannot possibly be hearing her right. I have just confessed to contemplating suicide, and I have not scared her away.

"I have always wanted to be with you. Since the moment I saw you walk in my shop five years ago for the first time, and hearing you laugh at something Julie said. My love for you has never wavered, even if I let my stubbornness get in the way."

"I am sorry about Margaret. I was foolish and selfish."

"Sweetheart, I am sorry I held a grudge. Walking away from you, the woman I love was the most foolish thing I have ever done. Please forgive me…say you will take me back."

I am crying, as I say, "Darling, I am the one who needs forgiveness. Not only should I have told you about Margaret, but I should not have taken so bloody long to say how I felt about you."

"You already did, and I have forgiven you…Reading you love me in your letter and hearing you say it the first night I arrived…it was worth the wait."

"We are partners again?" I ask in disbelief.

She nods through her tears.

Right away, I feel a sudden sense of doom at what being together as partners will involve once again. "Alice?"

"Yes?"

"I want to be with you again in every way…but I am not sure I can yet."

"I know. I will not push you. You have my word. We have managed being patient before, and we will do it once more."

"I do not deserve you, Alice."

"Oh, my dearest, everyone deserves to be loved."

She helps me move the extra pillows out of the way, and I feel my body relax as I lie back down. She kisses me on the forehead, and I am asleep in moments.

***

On the second weekend after the trauma, I am sitting in the garden with Alice. I have no idea what day it is, but figure it out when Alice informs me my birthday is Tuesday.

Alice asks, "I wondered if perhaps you would be up to celebrating in some way?" She continues as I do not immediately speak, "I am afraid I have not gotten you anything yet, nor have any ideas, as we have been isolated here. But if you thought you might like to go to the pub or take a picnic on the cliffs, I am sure between Gus and myself, we could manage whatever you would like."

"I did not think you had left here. How are we getting food? How are you getting clothes?"

"Gus and Tabitha have been coming by every day or so with food, and Heather has been working on the weekends when there are guests. Charlotte came a week ago with a large suitcase of clothes and shoes for me, as well as all of my lovely knitting things you gave me at Christmas."

I nod in understanding.

Alice picks up the thread of conversation. "So, your birthday? Do you have any preference?"

"Oh, yes. I do actually."

"What would that be?"

"A picnic in the cove with Gus and you, and Tabitha if she feels up to it. And might I ask for a specific gift?"

"Of course."

I look into her green eyes, and I say, "I want you to move in with me. Permanently. Forever."

She flushes with pleasure, "I see."

"Will you?" I ask, afraid to hear the answer. I believe it will be a favorable reply, but as my whole world has been shifted on its side the last few weeks, I do not trust my head.

"I will. I thought you would never ask, sweetheart."

"You won't mind the commute, whenever you go back to work?"

"Not if it means being with you."

I watch her eyes, and I look down at her lips. So slowly I am at first unsure if I am moving towards her, I lean forward and gently press my lips to her own. I feel her mouth and even her body yield to me, as without words I sense her saying the duration and intensity are within my power. I want to pull away almost immediately, as unpleasant memories and sensations try to barge in, but I do not. I force myself to think about how much I love Alice, and I want to show her how I feel, even if it is only through a kiss.

When I allow myself to pull away, she slowly opens her eyes and smiles.

She whispers, "That was lovely."

I feel lightness in my chest, as I have a seed of hope once again.

May

Chapter 28

It is the first day of May, and I am now forty-two years old. I wake up to sunshine in my bedroom. I have been sleeping far later over the last couple of weeks than I have in years. I have lost all sense of time since the trauma or whatever the hell I am supposed to call it, so it feels good to wake up and know what day it is.

The bruises have left my body, and my wrist is not as painful as it was. It still throbs a great deal, but the sharp pain is gone. The doctor says it is healing, and to continue to recuperate. If I do, he says we can discuss taking the plaster cast off by the middle of June, and letting me work again. I need to, as I shudder to think how much it is costing me to employ Heather to do all of the work right now. I know it is better than closing completely, but it is a strain I try to bury each time it surfaces. I know Alice has the same stress on her by having Charlotte work full-time, as well as some of

Charlotte's friends on peak days. At least Heather only works when there are guests.

The bruises on my mind are still alive and well though. I have nightmares and night sweats often, and I feel sudden panic at unidentified noises or movements. Alice sleeps beside me every night now, but she leaves a wide berth between us to ensure I do not feel her in my sleep. I have often caught her in the early hours sleeping on the chair beside the bed. When I have questioned her, she tells me that I had been thrashing about so much in my sleep she had been afraid her presence was making it worse. I am not sure if that is true or if I am keeping her from being comfortable. I sometimes fear my behavior is resurfacing some of her own memories of abuse, which might be causing nightmares of her own. I am unsure though, because she is always awake before me.

I gingerly sit up in bed, and timidly move my left fingers. Yes, the pain is still present, but it will not kill me.

Alice comes into the room wearing jeans and a bright green shirt to match her eyes. She has adopted a more casual wardrobe here in my flat, and it warms my heart to see her looking comfortable and relaxed here, as though she feels at home.

"Good morning, sweetheart! Happy Birthday!" She walks around to my side of the bed and leans down to kiss my lips. After much trial and error, we have determined I am alright with either of us initiating kisses. It is other physical contact, including prolonged embraces that I still have a stumbling block to climb over. She pulls gently away, and sits down on the edge of the bed. "How are you this morning?"

"I remembered it is my birthday and that I am now forty-two."

She chuckles, "Right you are."

I am curious, "Darling, how did you manage after you were…raped?"

She becomes serious as she thinks at first before speaking, "Well, I do not remember the first week very much. I had that nasty cut on the side of my head." Even talking about it, I see her touch her hairline self-consciously. "I never went to the doctor. I had heard about what happens in hospital if a woman is raped, and I was too afraid. But now, looking back, I am quite sure I had concussion on top of my other injuries. Thankfully, the cut itself was fairly shallow, or at least shallow enough that it did heal on its own. I have a vague memory of Ruth meeting me at the train station, helping me off the train, and then I do not remember anything else until several days later. Like you, I believe I stayed in bed and slept."

I whisper, "Then what happened?"

"Well, term began. So, call it youth, immaturity, or lack of knowledge, but I did not know what to do other than to finish school so that I would never have to go back to Winchester. I do not know how I managed, but I returned to school and I never looked back."

"If you were able to return to routine after the first week, why am I not allowed to?"

"I did not say I was successful. With my studies, yes. I finished, and I never went back to Winchester. But my coping mechanism was to deny anything significant happened to me. I did not process it at first, and while I may have accomplished the goal that I believed I wanted to achieve at the time, I was not successful in the rest of my life. I pushed Ruth away, and she had been nothing but kind and patient and loving to me our entire relationship. I reached a point after university and Ruth and I split up where I ceased to function. I had already severed ties with my family, but after I broke up with Ruth, I also cut ties with our university friends. I isolated myself and I became even more depressed and for a brief time suicidal. It was at that point, I almost lost my job that I went through psychotherapy for a few years. It helped me face what had happened, but I have dealt with the scars for a long time after."

She looks down at our hands, and I want to ask more, but I sense she needs to say something more.

"Hilary, I was with Ruth for about three years. She was by far, the longest relationship I have ever had, and that was almost twenty years ago. I have struggled with intimacy, both physical and emotional my entire adult life, and I want better for you. Selfishly, since I am the one with you, I want better for myself. I am not certain, but I think if I had taken the time and received help earlier, instead of denying what happened for the first year or two, I would have been more successful in my personal life."

I struggle with this, because I know it will make me sound selfish, but I ask, "Is it wrong to say I am glad? If you had done all the right things, someone else would have you as their own right now, and then, where would I be?"

Thankfully, she laughs, "How right you are, sweetheart. I had not thought of that. Sometimes we do have to experience the bad to make room for the good."

"I love you, darling."

"And I, you."

***

Alice and I have a lovely morning in the garden after breakfast, and she has allowed me to cut a few flowers for the vases inside. She leaves me outside on the bench while she goes to put them in water.

I see a car pull into the driveway, and I wave at Gus when he comes into view. He parks and gets out while holding a haversack. With his long strides, he is in the garden beside me in seconds. He sits down on the bench, and kisses the side of my head carefully.

"Happy Birthday Hilary! Many happy returns."

"Thank you for coming, Gus."

"I would not have missed it. Tabitha sends her birthday wishes. Sophie Grace is still too small to leave for any length of time I am afraid." I nod my understanding. He adds, "Grace is cross at me. Jealous, more like. She sends her love."

"I know. I spoke to her before we came outside."

He looks at his watch. "She is up early."

"Yes, she said she set her alarm an hour earlier than usual. She wanted to talk to me before we left for the picnic. It was the first time I have talked to her since all this." I wave my hand to convey whatever all this is.

"How are you doing with all this?" He waves his hand in the same way, which causes me to smile.

I have liked Gus since the first day I met him in reception when Julie was so ill. Yet now, there is an indescribable bond we have managed to form, and he has to be the only man in my life that I feel safe and comfortable being around now.

"Each day seems to be slightly better than the last. Alice hovers, but I am not foolish at this point to think I could have done it on my own. I am frustrated at my limitations, but also grateful I have time to be limited."

"Good. How is the wrist?"

"Better, I think. Throbs a bit, but the sharp pain is gone."

He nods, and rests his arm casually behind me on the bench. I feel my body tense at first, but force myself to relax. He notices, and immediately begins to lift his arm back up, but I say, "No, Gus, please leave it there." He looks unsure, but does as I ask.

Alice comes around the side of the house carrying a picnic basket, scarves, and the cardigan she made me. I know it is not cold today, but I have been in bed so much that I swear my body temperature has lowered as I stay bundled up indoors. I know Alice will have thought of that and be concerned I may be chilled if the wind picks up.

"Hello Gus! Lovely day isn't it?" she asks.

He stands, and I notice that standing side by side, they are almost the same height. He kisses her on the cheek, and greets her.

I join them, and by unspoken consent, I lead the way, as I know they will adjust their stride to my own. Yesterday, I walked to the edge of the cliff path, and only had to stop once. I hope I can walk the same distance before resting today.

***

After far too many stops that wound my pride, we make it to the bottom. At one point, Alice carried everything including Gus' haversack, so he could all but carry me the rest of the way. It was humiliating, but I try to shake it off, as I am captivated by the beauty surrounding me. It never gets old.

Alice and Gus lay out all of the food, and I am permitted one celebratory glass of wine for my birthday. Oh, God, it is good, but I realize I have lost my tolerance over the last few weeks, as I can feel the alcohol within the first few of sips. I try to hide the effects from Alice, but I know it is pointless. She will figure it out if she has not already.

After we eat, I am surprised to see Alice pull out of the picnic basket a small cake. I have no idea how she managed to get it down the cliff path in light of our travails without crushing it, but it is beautiful. A vanilla cream cake with chocolate icing and a yellow rose in the center. I wonder if she decorated it that way on purpose to commemorate the first flower I gave her, and when I look up to meet her eyes, I know she did indeed. It tastes delicious, and I have eaten more this afternoon than I have eaten in ages.

I look over to Julie's cove, and consider going to speak to her. But I know I could barely walk down to this point. I must conserve my strength if I am to make it back to the top. Besides, I feel guilty admitting it to myself, but I do not think I need to talk to her today. I know she is with me regardless of location, as I reach to feel the medallion around my neck, and I wish her well.

I know Alice is watching me, and Gus is trying to stay neutral. But I am alright. For today, I am well. I am lucky to live in a beautiful place, and I am blessed to be loved by those here with me and those with me in spirit.

***

It is much harder to reach the top of course, but I do manage to make it back to the B&B alive and in one piece. When we arrive, we are met by an unusual sight. There is a small lorry in the car park.

A man sees us approach, and he gets out and asks, "Is one of you Alice Mills?"

Alice steps forward, "Yes, I am." She shakes his hand, and asks Gus to help him.

I find my voice. "What is going on?"

She turns to smile at me, but I sense she is nervous. "Sweetheart, you asked me for one thing for your birthday."

"For you to move in with me." The light bulb suddenly goes off, as the man raises the back of the lorry to reveal about ten boxes of various sizes.

"I probably should have discussed it with you first, but I thought you might like it as a surprise."

"Yes, of course!" I am incredibly happy, as I realize that in the back of my mind, I still worried that having her here again was only a dream I would wake up from.

She continues, "I spoke with Charlotte, and I hope she packed what I asked her to. I am leaving the flat furnished. Perhaps I can let it during the summer months to tourists. For now, I thought I would only move my clothes and a few books and personal items, if that is alright. If there is not room for everything..."

I interrupt, "We will make room."

The nervousness leaves her face, and instead I see a flash of joy. God, I love this woman. So very different from Julie, she is much more reserved and quiet, but still kind and gentle and even stubborn as Julie was.

Gus helps the man unload the boxes from the lorry, and Alice and I return indoors. The boxes are stacked against the kitchen wall for now, and Alice assures me that she will unpack everything soon. I do not mind. The boxes are a symbol of our lives finally beginning together. I had given up hope this day would ever happen.

I offer to help unpack as she is checking to make sure everything is here, when she snaps out of her thoughts, and says, "Absolutely not. In fact, you need to have a lie down."

I want to groan like a child, but I know she is right. I am exhausted. But incredibly happy.

***

By the end of the month, Alice has moved in properly, and I am only sleeping at night, with an hour or two on the love seat with my feet propped up in the afternoon. In the last week, I have started helping Heather with breakfast in the morning for the guests. There has been an influx in bookings this month with tourist season in full force. It has been odd to be cut off from the inner workings of my business; often never even meeting guests over the last six weeks, so it feels good to begin anew in small ways.

With my progress though, it means Alice can return to work. She is only working until midday right now and still takes Mondays off, but I miss her during the day. I often wonder what she is doing, and wish I could be with her.

One day, when she arrives home, she is holding a package under her arm.

"Hello, my sweetheart! Had a good day?"

"It's better now that you are here." I have been lying on the love seat reading, and when I start to sit up, she waves me back.

"I will come to you." She walks over to the love seat, and from my view, she towers over me in her black dress, stockings, and heels. I wonder idly what she is wearing underneath. She crouches down, and gives me a kiss, before placing the package in my lap.

"What is this?"

"Open it and see."

I do, only to discover the red chiffon dress for Grace's wedding.

"I had it altered right after you came in, and it arrived weeks ago when I was not working. Today, Charlotte remembered she had put it away for you. Would you like to try it on and make sure it fits?"

"Yes, please." I stand up and go into the bedroom. Alice lets me dress alone, and when I open the door, she is standing there waiting.

"You are stunning. Grace may not like you stealing attention away from her."

I laugh, "You have an overactive imagination. No one will be staring."

She arches her eyebrow at me. I amend my previous statement, "Alright, no one but you."

"Are you hoping for someone else to stare?"

"No, of course not!" I feel ridiculous, yet flattered.

She moves to stand right in front of me, and she is about eight inches taller than me with her heels on. She leans down to kiss me, and I feel desire in a way that has been absent for months. Heat radiates throughout my body, and my fingertips tingle as I cannot help but touch her. As I reach for her, she tries casually to unzip the dress behind me.

I tense, but she shushes me, and says, "I do not want to damage it. Let's take it off first." She helps me out of it, and then, I help her out of her dress and heels. Oh, she is beautiful. I had forgotten how much.

As we fall into the bed together, she whispers to me that I can be on top if I need to be. I know she is sacrificing her own desires and needs for my own, and in this moment, I sense her love as almost tangible and I am grateful. I want desperately to show her how much I love her by our lovemaking. Instead of accepting her offer though, to meet both our needs, we lie facing each other side by side, and take much longer than normal to kiss, touch, and be together once again.

When I fall asleep that night, sated but exhausted, I feel as though I have slain another demon lurking in the corner of my mind.

June

Chapter 29

Two year anniversary of Julie's death

Summer has arrived in Cornwall, and the waves of depression and sadness are lessening. Living with Alice agrees with me, and I am happy the majority of the time now. I was on my best behavior for eight weeks, and the doctor rewarded me by taking off the plaster cast a couple of weeks ago. My wrist seemed shrunk and foreign to me at first, an alien entity, but after a few days and ongoing exercises, I am starting to recognize it as my own once again. I have been cleared to take on the majority of my work, although I must be careful with heavy lifting and pushing my newfound range of motion before it fully bounces back. Heather is still working far more than I would like, but I hope once the summer winds down, I will return to full capacity.

Alice is working full-time once again, although she has decided to only work five days a week. Sunday and Monday afternoons are our special time together. Alice has given Charlotte a raise to entice her to commit to working every Monday, as well as any other time during the week that Alice deems necessary. Alice still hovers over me and cautions me from overexerting myself, but I accept it is out of love and concern and I do not complain. She has helped heal me through her love and patience as nothing else could.

However, one Wednesday at the end of June, Alice stays home from work. I have a pilgrimage I need to do alone, but she refuses to be too far away. For today marks the two year anniversary since Julie, the first love of my life, passed away. After having lunch with Alice, I put on my walking shoes and prepare to leave.

"Are you sure you want to go alone?"

"Yes, darling. I appreciate the offer, but I need to go alone."

She nods. "When should I expect you back?"

I shrug, "I don't know. A couple of hours? I will walk to the church first. Don't worry, I will be careful."

"Easier said than done. But you have your mobile?"

I nod. I kiss her softly goodbye, and I begin my sojourn.

***

As I leave out the front door and head towards the village, I have a moment of panic as I realize this is the first time I have left the B&B alone since before the trauma happened over two months ago. It is an odd feeling, as though I should look over my shoulder every few steps. I remind myself this is my home and my village. Mr. Smith is locked away far from St. Just, and I am safe here.

I straighten my posture and arrive in the village and head for the church. I did not come here on the first anniversary. My feelings were too raw and I was wallowing alone in my depression. Today, I feel happy enough with my life that I believe I can honor her memory in the church, as well as the cove.

The church has that quality of not being of earth on this Wednesday afternoon when no one is about but the birds roosting in the belfry. I enter the nave, and I follow the procedures of tradition from my childhood I had thought long forgotten, by crossing my forehead with the holy water from the baptismal font, and then genuflecting and crossing myself facing the cross above the sanctuary. I turn to the votive stand towards the front right side, and there is one lonely candle burning. I kneel down and put a pound in the box, before lighting two more. One for Julie, my wife and partner, memorializing her life on earth, and believing she has life in heaven, and one as a symbol of gratitude in my new life with Alice. I remember how the last time I was here; I told Father Ryan that I was worried about knowing if I loved Alice. I recall he told me that he believed I was a woman of conviction and once I had the realization, the worry would be a thing of the past. I am thankful for his wisdom. He was right. I watch the votive candles burn for a couple of minutes. My heavy breathing from the walk causes the flame to shudder and shake, but I focus on slowing my breath down, as I stare. I do not have words of prayer, but I do believe God knows my heart and the emotions I am feeling. Nor do I cry. Tears will come later in the cove, I am sure, but I do believe I feel the peace of the living God in a way I have not felt since before my father left home.

At the thought of my parents, I am compelled to put another pound in the box, and light two more candles, one for my mum who I miss terribly even though she has been gone half my lifetime, and as much as I do not want to, one for my father. God knows, he needs compassion and forgiveness as do I. After crossing myself once more, I stand to leave.

***

Understanding how winded I became simply walking into town, I slow my steps down even more, as I descend the cliff path. It is good to be here alone, as I can be as introspective and morose as I want.

By the time I make my slow way to the bottom, and rest for a bit before continuing on to Julie's cove and climbing up to the top rock, I am very tired. But instead of finding sadness within as well, I find myself thinking about the good memories I had with Julie.

I remember climbing down to the cove one day when we first moved to Cornwall, and the tide was starting to come in, but we wanted to continue all the way down to the rocks. I knew it was risky, but I coaxed her to climb up onto this same one. It was before we understood how quickly the tide moves in, and it became a mad dash to get back to the cliff path before the whole area was underwater. I was foolish enough to think it was amusing we had to run through almost waist deep ice water to get back in time, but Julie was furious at me. She was cold and scared, and after I calmed her down, she finally made eye contact. She said she could not believe that I did not understand how serious it was…what did she say? I think back. 'Hilary Mead, you are the most foolhardy woman sometimes. I cannot believe I let you talk me into that! But…I also love you more than I love life itself. And if you jumped off that cliff, I would do it with you. Because I don't want to know one second of life without you in it.'

    I remember another time when we came out to the cliffs late at night. It was springtime in the middle of the week. The night air was warm and strangely enough for that time of year, we did not have any guests. It was low tide and a full moon, and we decided on the spur of the moment to go down to the cove. We took a blanket and made love underneath it. I smirk as I remember how uncomfortable the rocks were, but also how much fun we had.

Then, there were the many times we walked all the way to Land's End and the Cape, countless picnics shared, gardening around the house, shopping trips in Penzance, getaways to London, a lot of laughter and tears. We worked side by side, every day for a decade. And that was just in Cornwall. There were five wonderful years in London before that; hard years with the cancer the first time, but our partnership was strong throughout. We were happy. We had a marriage full of love. A life together well lived.

Today, I can be thankful for those fifteen years of bliss with Julie. What a gift to love her, and to be loved by her. How lucky I was.

As I relax, I lean against the rock, only to pull away quickly at the sharp pain in my wrist. Now that I do not have the plaster cast, I often forget and put undue strain on it. Instead, I move to sit in a modified cross-legged position, with my heart over my pelvis. I remember Grace telling me I should do this yoga posture while breathing; she says I will feel calmer. I laughed at her as I recall. But now, I am sitting in this position, watching the waves and the birds, and I feel at peace as I begin to talk to Julie.

"Darling, I can't believe it has been two years. Some days it feels like yesterday, others as though it has been forever. I miss you very much…But, I hope you would be glad to know I am finally at peace. Alice and I are back together; she took care of me after the attack. She loves me, and I have realized I love her…she has moved in, and I am happy. Do you remember that my name means cheerful? Grace reminded me of it at Christmas when she gave me my medallion." I reach up to touch it. "She said she believed I would be cheerful once again, and that you and St. Julia are my guardian angels. I am not sure if she meant that you would help me, or simply bear witness, but I held onto that promise. For a while after Christmas, I thought I had moved past my grief. But then February happened, and we split up for two months, and the world went dark again. But now, having physically healed, and being back together with Alice, I feel as though my spirit is mending. Cheerful may be too strong a word to describe my state of being. Perhaps I am moving towards cheerful."

I know the days of me talking to Julie like this are drawing to a close. I will always love her and I will always carry a piece of her with me, but life is becoming full again. I do allow myself to shed a few tears, because I realize I have crossed a barrier today. I am finally allowing myself to be happy in the midst of the sadness and loss.

"Darling Julie, I will love you forever. You will always be in my heart. Your love for me has kept me going these last two years, and I will never ever forget you. Thank you for loving me so well. I hope you know how much I have loved you, even in heaven."

I bow my head briefly to solidify my words, and to still my heart. Now, it is time to go home to Alice.

July

Chapter 30

"Grace, Hilary and I have something for you," Alice says as Grace comes into our bedroom on the morning of her wedding. Grace has showered and dried her hair, and is wearing a bathrobe. We told her last night we wanted to help her get ready.

Laid out on our bed, Alice has placed a beautiful white lace bra and knickers set, with matching slip for underneath her wedding dress, as well as matching white lace lingerie with light pink piping for tonight.

Grace is speechless as she reaches out to touch everything.

Alice says, "I hope this is not overstepping…I have a few contacts with finding trousseau pieces…"

Grace looks at us, and says, "No, of course not. These are beautiful. I am so touched." She turns around and gives us both hugs and kisses on the cheek. She continues, "I was simply going to wear basic white underneath. I never thought about choosing something so fancy."

Alice says, "What you wear underneath comes out in how you carry yourself."

I try to hide a smile, as I know what Alice often wears underneath her clothes, and I believe she is right. Alice and I give Grace a moment to put the undergarments on in the bedroom, and then we both join her and help her into her tea-length wedding dress and assist her with her hair and makeup. Grace makes a lovely bride, and I am so happy this day has finally arrived for her and Gus. No one deserves it more than the two of them.

"Grace, you look lovely."

"Thank you, Hil."

It is my turn to change, and I know Alice remembers her innuendo from months ago when she helps me into my dress. It is a perfect fit, and I feel far sexier in this red concoction, than any forty-two year old maid of honour, as Grace persists on calling me, should ever feel. Alice puts on a new summer lime green dress, and we are ready.

***

The wedding ceremony was lovely and romantic, and I hope was exactly what Grace and Gus hoped for. They make a beautiful pair, and I know they are in shock everything finally came together.

We all walk back in procession to the B&B where the reception is to be held in the garden. The caterers have been here since early morning, and everything is set out on long trestle tables. I assess my garden with a critical eye. The calla lilies, freesias, and roses are all in bloom and spreading the most luscious scents. Everyone seems to be enjoying themselves, and even the awkward family members such as Gus' brother-in-law and Grace's brother appear to be relaxing, and enjoying the day.

Out of the corner of my eye, I see Alice speaking to Tabitha and cooing to baby Sophie Grace. She is finally beginning to put on some weight and appears healthy. The scare of her birth seems to be in the past. The fine baby hair on her head is now dark brown, and her blue eyes are bright with exploration. I take a few steps closer in time to hear

Alice ask to hold her. Tabitha agrees, and Alice reaches over and gently holds the baby close. I see her eyes grow a little sad, and I feel my heart constrict for her. For all of the cool control Alice normally exhibits, she has a great deal of love to offer. I hope I will be enough for her.

Grace comes up behind me, and breaks me out of my thoughts.

"Thank you for a beautiful day."

I smile at her, and I am reminded how good Grace is for my heart. She brings with her memories of Julie, but also somehow helps to move me into the future.

I hold her tight, as I say, "I hope it is everything you have wished for these last two years."

"Hil, this is the best day of my life."

"That is all I wanted to hear and more."

***

Later in the evening, the guests are all gone, and Grace and Gus have retired to my nicest bedroom suite. Alice and I spread rose petals on the bed earlier, and we left them a bottle of champagne. Tomorrow morning they will leave on their honeymoon along the coast of Cornwall, before moving to Bath next week. Grace has already told me that between all of Gus' family and me, they plan on coming at the weekend once every month.

Throughout my dark spring, Alice and Grace seemed to form a close relationship. While it was awkward at first, it is obvious to me that they have developed respect for one another, and as I know it is based on their mutual love for me, I am touched beyond reason. I know their bond will allow Grace and me to continue our close friendship.

Alice and I changed into comfortable clothes earlier in the evening, and I am reading on the love seat, while she knits. This is my favorite place to be right now. I feel relaxed and at peace.

"It was a lovely wedding," Alice says.

"Yes, it was."

"Are you thinking of your own?" she asks. I hear the uncertainty and sadness in her voice, and once again, I wonder if I can be enough for her.

"No, I was not. I was thinking about how happy and peaceful I am. Sitting here with you, listening to you knit. There is no other place I would rather be."

While she looks pleased, she also has a smirk on her face as she asks, "Oh, really? I rather thought you would fancy another holiday to Spain?"

That snaps me out of my thoughts in a hurry. "Spain? Really?"

She nods. "Yes, really. Paul rang yesterday. He has offered the flat to us at the end of August."

"August? I couldn't possibly. That is peak season."

My mind jumps a hundred directions, but Alice rests her hand on my left wrist which is aching tonight from so much activity. She sees me flinch, but continues first, even as she pulls her hand away, "Heather and Charlotte can call for reinforcements if they must. But we are going. I have already said yes. You, my sweetheart, need a holiday. And have one, you will."

I want to argue, but she arches her eyebrow at me, daring me to continue. Instead I relent, and she lays down her knitting, and reaches carefully for my left wrist. I inhale sharply at her touch.

"Have you done your exercises today?"

"No, of course not. There was not time."

"You can do them now."

I sigh, as I begin to manipulate my wrist in all the little ways I have been told. It is tedious and boring, and after a busy day like today, it is also painful. She watches me in silence, and I continue for what seems forever. By the time I am done, she reaches for my wrist again, and massages it gently.

When she finishes, she says, "It's been a long day. Let's go to bed."

There is no arguing from me.

Epilogue

August

Spain

The August heat in Spain is overbearing. I can barely breathe, as I stretch out on the sand by the sea. Beads of sweat have collected on my torso, and I am debating about diving back into the deep tidal pool we are lounging beside.

I feel like a lazy cat in the sun as I stretch my arms high above my head and yawn. Alice is beside me, and I glance back at the umbrella, knowing we either need to move underneath it for a bit or risk burning to a crisp. It simply feels like too much effort at the moment to stand.

When we arrived two hours ago, the sun had not quite reached its zenith. We picnicked first, and then after lounging in the sun, we were so hot that the water barely cooled us off as we swam topless for over an hour. The last half hour we have been lying here wearing our bikinis in heaps of exhaustion, and debating what to do next.

Having lived with Alice for almost four months, I feel restored. Healed by her love, kindness, and patience. There were several false starts over the summer, as I continued to process what happened in the spring, but I feel washed anew. This current state of mind is in large part due to Alice.

I know this is what I have been waiting for.

I reach into my bag, and I pull out a small handkerchief I have tied tightly together. I attempt to untie it without her noticing, but she senses my movement, and sits up.

"What are you doing?"

I cease trying to be circumspect, and sit up as well. I have it untied now, but keep it folded in my left hand. With my right hand, I reach for her own, while looking into her green eyes that I feel as though I could swim inside.

"Alice, you asked me once for some type of lasting promise that we would be together, that we would have a future together." I open the handkerchief to reveal my grandmother's wedding ring. It is a platinum band in an antique setting, with an emerald in the center and a small ring of diamonds surrounding it. I hear her gasp as I hold it up for her to see.

"Darling, this was my grandmother's wedding ring. Unlike my parents, she and my grandfather had a happy marriage, and if you would like to have it and wear her ring as a symbol of my love for you, and my promise of lasting commitment, nothing would give me more pleasure."

Alice wipes a tear away, as she whispers, "Yes." I slip the ring on her left ring finger. It is a perfect fit. "It's beautiful, Hil."

Somehow, I still feel uncertain. "Alice, is it enough? Am I enough? I want you to know how much I love you and I want to promise myself to you as your partner for the rest of our lives. I just cannot say actual wedding vows…I…"

She cuts me off with a finger across my mouth. "Hilary, *you* are all I have ever wanted or needed. Hearing you say that you love me and are committed to me is more than enough. I know you keep your promises. It is enough. *You* are enough."

"Darling, I do not know if I will ever be cheerful again, but if ever I am, I promise to be cheerfully yours forever. Your love has healed me in a way I did not believe possible."

I am crying now, but my tears are good tears. Alice's love and acceptance of me is healing me in yet another small broken place that was left in my heart until this moment. I pull her to me in an embrace as I kiss her so passionately I am afraid my body will burn from the inside out. I pull her to her feet as I do not want to wait any longer to return to the flat. We will not be taking a siesta.

Acknowledgements

Shortly after publishing *To Cornwall, with Love*, a dear friend asked, 'What happened to Hilary?' I was already writing another story that had nothing to do with my first, but this question set off a chain of events that felt as though I was on a roller coaster I could not get off of until it finished. Within about six weeks, I knew what happened to Hilary, and I felt peace knowing while grief is never truly over, love does heal. Hopefully, you will, too.

I would like to thank my friends who continue to support my writing, by reading my manuscripts and listening to me moan about my writing process: Nancy Carter, Jackie Chapman, Paige, Greg, and Tammie. Thank you from the bottom of my heart.

A special thank you to Greg for my cover art. The yellow roses are perfect, Padre.

I am fortunate to have an English friend who looked at certain phrases and kindly told me if they are used in Britain. Mark Williams, thank you for helping my characters sound English. Anything not accurate is the fault of my own.

My husband, Erik, has supported me like no other. I really do not know how he does it. He listens to my stories, helps me edit, formats my manuscripts, fixes my computer, and still loves me. My son, Levi, brings us great joy.

Finally, the Yoga with Adriene (FWFG) online Facebook community has been a tremendous support system for me. I have been practicing yoga with Adriene (Hey-o!) for several years, and she has created a Kula who has my back. They encouraged me to publish my first book, bought many copies, and even chose it one month as their book club selection. I have made so many friends all over the world, too many to mention for fear I would forget someone, but you guys know who you are. 'It's a seal, y'all.'

Like my Facebook author page at www.facebook.com/LauraWChance and follow me on Twitter @loveday0606.

Printed in Great Britain
by Amazon